CW00644612

ONE GREEK SUMMER WEDDING

MANDY BAGGOT

Boldwood

First published in Great Britain in 2024 by Boldwood Books Ltd.

Cover Design by Alexandra Allden

Cover Illustration: Shutterstock

This book is a work of fiction and, except in the case of historical fact, any resemblance to actual persons, living or dead, is purely coincidental.

Every effort has been made to obtain the necessary permissions with reference to copyright material, both illustrative and quoted. We apologise for any omissions in this respect and will be pleased to make the appropriate acknowledgements in any future edition.

A CIP catalogue record for this book is available from the British Library.

Paperback ISBN 978-1-80549-380-8

Large Print ISBN 978-1-80549-381-5

Hardback ISBN 978-1-80549-379-2

Ebook ISBN 978-1-80549-382-2

Kindle ISBN 978-1-80549-383-9

Audio CD ISBN 978-1-80549-374-7

MP3 CD ISBN 978-1-80549-375-4

Digital audio download ISBN 978-1-80549-378-5

Boldwood Books Ltd
23 Bowerdean Street
London SW6 3TN
www.boldwoodbooks.com

To my late great-aunt, Hazel, The G.A.
You are the inspiration for Margot in this book. Finally, I found the perfect way
to honour your feisty, vibrant, no holds barred approach to life!
All my love, The G.N. xx

1

N-VIZION SPA, LONDON, UK

'Bruno! That's it! That's my H-spot!'

Cara Jones squeezed her eyes tight shut at her aunt, Margot's comment. And then, Margot began to make the kind of noises you never wanted to hear from any relative, particularly when you were in such close proximity. There were only a few strategically placed, large-leafed – possibly fake – plants between their massage beds and no amount of foliage was going to aurally shield Cara from these sighs.

'What is "H-spot"?' Bruno asked. 'This sound like a good thing I should tell other clients about.'

'One step up the alphabet from my G-spot, Bruno. H stands for... *heaven*.'

As Margot sighed like she was auditioning for something on the adultiest adult channel Cara shot a hand to her left. Hopefully the face mask her masseuse, Jasmine, had offered – and she had declined – was still on the little table. She knew covering her eyes wasn't going to help but perhaps, somehow, anyhow, she could mould it into something for her ears.

'We leave you now,' Bruno declared. 'With hot stones' healing power and the chance to unwind with your thoughts or create connections with each other.'

Cara felt that the extras Bruno was adding to the salutations were made-up bollocks but as she wasn't paying for this extortionately priced afternoon she wasn't about to make a comment to her aunt. She put the face mask back down.

'Thank you, Bruno, darling.'

Cara focussed on not focussing on anything except the warmth of the hot rocks, now lined up down her back, permeating the light bamboo throws they had been draped in milliseconds before Bruno and Jasmine left the room. She let the gentle music, a cross between Gregorian monks chanting and something played by wind chimes, seep in too. Then the delicate fragrance of bergamot and lemon mixed with... *smoke*? Cara could *definitely* smell smoke. She moved her head up from the padded face cushion and opened her eyes. Margot was sitting up on her massage table now, bamboo sheet tied around her like a beach sarong, inhaling on a cigarette.

'Margot! You can't smoke in here!' Cara exclaimed.

'Ssh, Cara, raised voices are definitely not good for cosmic realignment,' Margot purred softly, before taking another deep drag.

'And your emissions aren't good for anything. Put it out.' She tried to move but very quickly realised that if she did, those stones on her back were going to go tumbling to the ground. How had her aunt got rid of hers so quickly *and* reached a packet of Pall Mall?

'I actually think that's what Bruno did to my clitoris,' Margot answered with a throaty laugh. 'But, now I have you trapped under those rocks, we need to talk.'

Cara swallowed. Margot sounded serious. Was it work? Had Cara messed up? OK, she knew she wasn't the most passionate employee of Margot's super-successful luggage business, Carried Away, but such was her gratitude for having the job at all, last month she had even tit-taped Margot's bosom before an inspirational talk at a university. Did you bring someone on a spa day to relax them before you fired them?

'God! You look terrified!' Margot exclaimed, cigarette hanging from her lips as she adjusted her sheet. 'And stop frowning because I haven't booked in for Botox this time!' She sucked on her cigarette before puffing a plume of smoke into the air. 'You and I, darling, are taking a little trip.'

Oh no. Cara's heart sank and, despite the hot stones, a cold chill invaded her pummelled muscles. The last time Margot had taken her on 'a little trip' it had been to Krakow and another suitcase magnate called Pawel had basically embalmed them with *wódka*. Cara was certain she had been able to hear her liver crying like it was being waterboarded. And then she had another thought...

'It's not... M-Moldova, is it?'

Cara hated that she had stuttered over the country's name. It proved exactly how far she *hadn't* come over these past few years. She pressed her lips together and waited for Margot's reply.

The first response was a hiss, like her aunt had rapidly extinguished her cigarette in their honeydew and basil water. She hadn't.

'I would be more than happy to never frequent that country again. Well, apart from the excellent wine, but I'm sure I could get that delivered... or buy one of the vineyards. No, I'm talking about Greece. One of the islands. Corfu. Or, as the natives say it, *Kerkyra*.'

It wasn't Moldova.

'Did you hear what I said, Cara?'

Where had Margot said? Greece? An island?

'Yes. I mean... most of it. Why are we going there?' She still hadn't 100 per cent grasped where 'there' was. 'For work?'

Margot sighed. 'You don't say "for work", you say "for business". I've told you that before. "Work" does not give off the correct entrepreneurial energy. "Work" speaks of perspiration and aching muscles. "Business" says sophistication and the interaction of sharp minds.'

Margot did always speak like she might be describing the premise of a decadent black-and-white movie from her wide selection in the cinema room of her home. Margot, and Cara's mother, Elizabeth, had been brought up around classic films as their father had worked as a projectionist at a picture house in the sixties. Margot, although only fifty-five, also rather modelled herself on Rita Hayworth – a star from the 1940s. In stark contrast, Elizabeth's vibe had always been more latter-day *Blue Peter* presenter. Dungarees in every colour and usually elbow-deep in insects. Cara didn't see herself as having inherited any of their traits. The only thing she shared with them both was their russet-coloured hair and pale blue eyes.

'So,' Cara said, squirming a little to get more comfortable on the bed. 'Whose sharp mind will we be interacting with?'

'No one's. Well, Sofia would like to think she has a sharp mind but, honestly, the moment she got married and had kids, she got static, lost her edge, you know.'

No, Cara didn't know. Because she didn't know who Sofia was nor did she know where this conversation was going. 'So, this isn't a business trip?'

Margot shook her head, cigarette back in her mouth. 'No, darling, it's pure pleasure. We're going to see my old friend from college and watch her show off all the things she thinks are important.' She blew out a ring of smoke. 'All the things I despise. Like, overrated "home-cooking". Husbands. And children.' She shuddered. 'Why don't they do allergy pills for those things?'

Cara was starting to wonder why Margot was going at all if she felt that way about the prospect of the trip.

'That's why, after this massage, we're going to nip to Liberty and get ourselves some summer essentials.'

When exactly *was* this trip and for how long?

'Then it's BA from Heathrow. Business class obviously. We leave in the morning.'

'Tomorrow!' Cara exclaimed. As much as she loved her aunt and admired her for many things, she didn't love or admire the way she lived her life on the spur of the moment.

'Well, we can't leave any later,' Margot said, finally stubbing her cigarette out in the ylang-ylang potpourri. 'Otherwise the hen party and the wedding will be happening without us.'

It was a *wedding*. And that was the reason Margot had dropped this travel bomb down at the last minute. As a multiverse of emotions rode through Cara, the last thing she heard before she vomited was the hot stones dropping to the floor.

2

HEATHROW TERMINAL 5, LONDON

Margot smacked her lips together. 'Nothing better than a champagne breakfast, is there?' She tipped up the flute, glugging the contents quicker than someone doing a drinking challenge.

'Well,' Cara began, looking at her cup of tea. 'The avocado on toast was very nice.'

Margot sucked in air through her teeth. 'Cara, we don't use the word "nice". It's a nothing word, remember? Along the same lines as "OK" or "alright". No one wants mediocrity.'

Being word-shamed at seven o'clock in the morning wasn't the best start. Perhaps she should have had the champagne... She took a sip of her tea and watched others in the lounge going about their pre-flight routines. Business people on laptops, devices plugged in to charge, small groups toasting their trips with wine, couples tucked into nooks feeding each other... It was Cara's turn to suck in air – although silently. She knew she couldn't eradicate couples from her vicinity, they were every-where after all, but she wasn't sure how she was going to cope with an actual wedding. Perhaps she needed more details...

'So, this wedding,' Cara began as Margot refilled her bubbly flute. 'Who is getting married?' Perhaps this was something she should have asked yesterday, before now, when they were practically minutes away from getting on a plane.

'One of Sofia's kids,' Margot replied. 'A boy. Probably the eldest. She has a few. Three? No, wait, is it four?'

'Do you have an invitation?' Cara asked. 'So we can at least know their names?'

'Somewhere,' Margot said. 'But I'm not unpacking the Maxi-Go prototype right now for that.'

Cara's eyes went to the rose-gold cabin case under their table. 'Margot, I didn't realise that was a Maxi-Go. There's no branding on it.'

'Because it's the prototype.'

'But I thought it wasn't ready yet. I thought it needed more testing.'

'And that is exactly what I'm doing. Testing it. Except, instead of warehouse conditions, we're going to see how it does in real life. You won't believe what I've got in there. I did a rough calculation and I think there's enough clothing to kit out the Hadids for six months.'

The Maxi-Go was planned to be Margot's golden goose. It was a suitcase of large *hold* proportions that, once packed full, you could shrink to the size of any airline's *cabin* case requirements. No one had attempted anything so ground-breaking in the industry before but Cara knew the mechanics that made the case minimise had not yet been perfected. Except Margot hardly ever listened to the experts she paid a fortune to impart advice...

'It's the first time we've been away since Krakow, isn't it?' Margot continued. 'God, what was the name of that awful—'

'Pawel,' Cara interrupted.

'I was going to say what was the name of the vodka. I have no interest in remembering the name of that man. Did you know he's started using cat fur to insulate his backpack range?'

Cara couldn't think of one thing to say in reply to that so it was time to change the conversation. 'So, whereabouts is the wedding?'

Margot slugged down most of her next glass of fizz. 'Cara, I told you this. We're going to Corfu.'

'I know, but I looked it up last night and it's not that tiny. So is the wedding in the capital or in the north or south of the island?'

'No clue,' Margot said. 'All I know is I've booked us into a sumptuous Cook's Club hotel for tonight and there's a secret hen party in Corfu Town we're expected to attend.'

Hmm. Cara was starting to doubt that her aunt knew as little as she was making out. And a hen night with a group of people she didn't know?!

Margot's phone started to buzz and she snatched it up from the table and silenced it. 'Not now.'

'Who was it?'

'No idea. But I have champagne in my hand and my gorgeous niece with me... You must promise not to drink boring drinks all day when we are going to have the aperitifs of Greece at our disposal.'

Cara smiled. 'Maybe when it's five o'clock.'

On researching Corfu a little last night she had discovered it was an island with the most beautiful vistas. From tumbling mountainsides to turquoise waters bordering tiny coves. The photos had got her excited to visit. But then there was the wedding issue...

'You know five o'clock is really a state of mind,' Margot said, closing her eyes as if she might be connecting to Buddha by Bluetooth.

That nugget of wisdom sounded a bit like something Cara's parents would say. The last time they'd spoken, a few weeks ago now, they were living amongst capuchin monkeys in Costa Rica. Her mum had always said she had been born with wanderlust. While Margot had used the black-and-white movies to style herself on the actresses, the films had just given Elizabeth Jones the urge to travel to places like Casablanca. As soon as Cara had secured her first job, Elizabeth and Daniel had upped their barely really planted roots and lived life like one long vacation. Cara had never really understood how anyone could be that blasé. There was no plan, no goal, no catch-net. They worked doing whatever gave them enough for a roof over their head, food to eat and a flight or rickety bus journey to the next destination. Cara hadn't seen them in person since that night in Moldova and, thinking about it now, that night was when she'd lost her plans, her goals and her motivation to do anything other than let Margot look after her...

'Cara,' Margot said abruptly.

She jolted in her seat, her mind crash-landing back in the present. 'Yes.'

'Did you see the news about... the dog?'

The dog. Margot hadn't really needed to put the entire weight of the sentence on those last two words for the chills to start shooting up Cara's spine. There was only one dog who got called '*the* dog' and its name was Yodi. And Yodi, well, what she couldn't blame on Moldova, she could definitely pin on the head of a rat terrier.

'I deleted the news apps from my phone, remember?' Cara replied.

'Very wise.'

It had been her therapist's suggestion and, back then, Cara was happy for someone else to make decisions for her. And the same therapist had also said she shouldn't care about what other people thought of her more than she should care about how she felt about herself. But she was better now...

'Well, the pathetic mutt is allegedly going to be the new judge on *America's Got Talent*.' Margot shook her head. 'Have you heard anything so ludicrous in your life? It's going to have something called a "woof-ometer" to gauge its approval.'

Yodi's career was going from strength to strength, whereas Cara's had dive-bombed faster than her face-plant into that Eurovision crowd in Moldova. She had gone from being the UK's big chance for European glory, with a glittering singing career to follow, to her vocal opportunities disappearing quicker than Margot's glass of champagne. Suddenly she wished she had more than tea...

'Good for him,' Cara replied, expression straight.

'Good for him? He's a ridiculous novelty act that killed your career. A *human*'s career. Someone with actual talent.'

She couldn't recall Margot being quite so blunt in the weeks and months that had followed the performance. Yes, Cara remembered her aunt being a force to be reckoned with, happy to 'no comment' to all the journalists, hiding her away in her Dorset retreat until the public finally started to forget. Until Cara started to recover a little. But Margot had never used phrases like 'killed your career'.

'Do you miss it, Cara? Touching people with your voice?'

Now she knew her expression wasn't straight because she could feel a tremble in her cheek, a pulse in her neck as she thought about what singing had meant to her. It hadn't been about null points that night. The loss of that one event had been awful, but the death of her vocation had been catastrophic. She was a singer. Music had been inside her for as long as she could remember, and she hadn't sung a note since Moldova. And then there was Seb...

She took a deep breath and picked up her cup of tea. 'I think,' she began. 'In the end people only wanted to hear that G10 note.'

The highest note audible to the human ear and Cara was one of the only people in the world to have hit it. She knew that had carried her to be picked for the Eurovision stage, but it was really just a trick, no more talent than a dog woofing who might be worthy of a golden buzzer...

'Can you still reach it?' Margot asked, leaning on the table.

She came out of her reverie, really looked at her aunt. Why were they talking about this now? One thing Margot was never very good at was hiding an agenda.

'Reaching that note requires practice and I don't sing any more.'

'No,' Margot said, raising her glass. 'No, of course not. And, where would I be without you heading up operations at the company? I would be lost without you. Right, shall we have another little drink before we head to the gate?'

Cara sipped at her tea and tried to put Yodi, Moldova and Eurovision out of her mind. All of it was definitely in the past. And the last she had seen of Seb on socials, he was halfway up a mountain with someone called Allie.

3

THE LISTON, CORFU TOWN, CORFU, GREECE

Akis Diakos sipped the froth from his coffee and sat back against the chair, looking out through his sunglasses at the other people sitting in the pavement café, pigeons at their feet. It was hot but here in the shade, underneath the large rectangular parasols, there was respite from the searing sun.

'Three o'clock,' Akis said. 'A group of six.'

His friend, Horatio, sat forward in his chair and dipped his sunglasses down a little, turning his head to the correct position. 'Never.'

'Are you kidding? It sounds like you are setting a challenge.'

'One you will not win,' Horatio replied with confidence.

'Do you put money behind it?'

'Everything I own.' Horatio dipped his fingers into the pocket of his cargo trousers and brought out money that he deposited on the table between them. 'Exactly... fourteen euro, seventy-five cents and a button from my jeans.'

'OK,' Akis said, nodding. He took another sip of his coffee but remained unmoved.

'What?' Horatio asked. 'You do not accept the challenge?'

'Patience, my friend. I am waiting for the right opportunity.'

Horatio snorted and scooped all the loose change and notes back into his hands. 'You did not even approach the group I suggested two coffees ago.'

'Because they were too young.'

'They were in their twenties at least!'

'And, if they are like us, they do not have the money to spend thirty euro each on a ticket to see our show.' Akis looked at the women he had pointed out. 'These women are more mature. They have fancy clothes and good handbags. The only thing they are missing is a great night out with us.' He grinned.

'You do not have to sell the merits of the older woman to me. I am accustomed to their attributes.' A smile hit Horatio's mouth. 'Intimately accustomed.'

'I am aware,' Akis said. 'And that is why, as it is your specialist subject, shall we say, you should be the one to invite them.'

Akis watched Horatio blush. It was craziness. He watched his friend three times a week, dancing on stage with all the confidence of a seasoned performer, yet other times he turned the colour of a radish and sucked his neck and head back in like a frightened tortoise.

'I do not have that thing you do,' Horatio said, reaching for his coffee.

'What thing?'

'The thing, with your eyes. It is like a form of hypnotism.'

Akis smiled at his friend's comment, but inside there was conflict about the statement. He was aware his eye contact could be used for gentle manipulation, but he also knew he had inherited his eyes from his mother and the way she used them was anything but gentle. The stand-off situation they were currently in wasn't ideal when there was a family wedding coming up. Right now, he didn't even know if he was going to be permitted to attend.

'See!' Horatio exclaimed, plucking the toothpick from his mouth. 'You have attracted them already!'

He had been staring into space not trying to attract anything. But, it seemed the group of older women had noticed him...

'Perhaps now is my best chance,' Akis said, getting to his feet.

But before he could move through the tables, someone else caught his attention. Was that his *yiayia*, Irini? He lifted his sunglasses up to get a better look at the grey-haired woman, squinting against the sun. Carrying two hefty-looking shopping bags, he watched her as she shooed away a pigeon with her foot. And, as the curse word rushed past her lips, loud enough for the whole of the Liston to hear, there was no doubt. Akis hurried to her aid.

'*Yiayia*, what are you doing here?'

The shopping bags thumped to the ground. 'Aki? Is that you?'

Akis was not sure if his grandmother's eyesight was really failing or if she just enjoyed getting confirmation.

'*Ne*,' he replied. 'But is it really you? Because you are a long way from Notos.'

'And I need a passport to leave the village now?'

Her eyes always spoke too, usually the language of defiance. He smiled. 'No, but if there is anything you need you can always ask me.'

'And make sure there is no reason for me to go out of the house? Shall I gaze at four walls until I die and make everyone happier?'

'That was not what I meant—'

'Yiannis brought me in his truck. He had to deliver manure; I needed things for the wedding.'

Akis swallowed then, taking a closer look at the contents of the shopping bags. There was lots of lace and items embroidered with the *mati* – the eye symbol the Greeks used to ward off evil spirits and promote good fortune. The last thing he had heard was that Irini wasn't invited to his brother, Cosmos's wedding...

'You can carry the bags to the bus stop,' Irini told him.

'You are getting the bus back to the village?'

'Do you expect me to walk?' She snorted. 'What is this? First, I cannot leave the village, now I should go back by a means that could kill me in this heat? Make up your mind!'

'I could take you,' Akis offered, picking up the bags.

'On your motorbike?'

'You have never been one to refuse a ride on my motorbike before.'

'I do not worry about me,' Irini said. 'I worry about the bags and the balance. The bus will be OK. And if I do not arrive home and I die, Pig will find his way to your mother's house for food.' Irini laughed.

Pig was his grandmother's donkey, so named because of its voracious appetite. No one knew how old Pig was, but Akis was twenty-nine and he had never known a time when Pig hadn't been around. And, by around, he really meant the donkey had his own bedroom inside the house. He also knew that his mother, Sofia, despised the donkey...

'What is that look on your face?' Irini asked, hobbling a little as she walked.

'I don't have a look on my face.'

'It is the one I see you make when your mother says the word "priest".'

A shiver ran up his spine then and he fought to not let it show on his face. Instead he created a quick smile and nudged his grandmother's elbow. '*Yiayia*, I only have smiles today.'

'*Yassas*, Irini.'

Akis felt the weight fall from one of his hands as Horatio took a bag and began to walk alongside them, skirting the paved area outside the Arcadion Hotel.

'Horatio, you have got even more handsome!' Irini declared.

'And you are all the more beautiful.'

'Shall I leave?' Akis asked.

'Yes,' Horatio agreed. 'Now, while I have 180 euro in my pocket to treat your grandmother to lunch...'

It took a second for what Horatio had said to hit home. 'You—'

'Yes,' Horatio interrupted. 'The older ladies bought tickets for tonight's show.'

Akis shook his head. 'See, Horatio, you do not need my eyes. You have charm all of your own.'

'What do you think, Irini?' Horatio asked her. 'Akis's eyes or my aura?'

Irini seemed to muse on the point for a while before making her reply. 'All I know is that Akis will need his persuasive look if he wants to encourage a dwindling congregation back to the church.'

'Irini, what did I say? You—' Akis began.

'If he lets his mother keep calling the shots on his future,' Irini finished firmly. Before anyone could say anything else, she continued. 'And in my opinion, your eyes would be a terrible clash with the colour of the priest's vestment. Therefore it cannot be. Come on, Horatio, I will let you buy me an ice cream.'

4

COOK'S CLUB CORFU, CORFU

An air-conditioned Mercedes had been waiting for them at the airport and, in less than a five-minute drive, Cara and Margot had arrived at this luxury hotel. It was the essence of cool, from the no-fuss exterior – a single olive tree at the entrance – to the relaxed, modern yet bohemian décor inside. It was all comfy couches with textured cushions, muted colours and rattan and seagrass feature lampshades. It was like the best vogue elements of the 1960s had had a baby with sleek, modern-day conveniences and swaddled it in a laid-back style. From the buzzy vibe around the pool, a DJ playing chilled tunes, to the restaurant where you could order frankly orgasmic-looking dishes from a dedicated app, it was wall-to-wall luxury, including their room, which had its own private terrace and swim-up pool. It was all *definitely* very Margot.

'Isn't this idyllic?'

Margot had taken less than ten minutes to expand her Maxi-Go case to its natural state, remove all the items and hang up those clothes that needed it. Then her aunt had slipped into a bright yellow bikini and slathered Factor Not-Adequate-Enough-For Sunrise-In-Arbroath on her skin before lying face-up on one of the woven rope loungers facing their pool. In contrast, Cara was making sure every inch of her exposed flesh was covered in Factor 50. Despite the Jones gingery genes, Margot always seemed to achieve the colour of beautiful soft tan leather while Cara was often more smoked salmon...

'It's beautiful,' Cara answered, rubbing the oil on her calves. 'Is this where the wedding is?'

'God no!' Margot exclaimed. 'Knowing Sofia she's probably rented a palace.'

Cara swallowed. She and Seb hadn't booked a palace, but they had been choosing between a windmill and a whisky vault. Her heart had felt fully committed but she'd soon discovered that Seb's heart hadn't been anywhere but wrapped up in her career. He had been there for the highs, but when Yodi happened and things unravelled, suddenly he thought they needed time to re-evaluate. Cara had thought that meant time for her to get herself together – with his help and support – but what had actually happened was they never went back to finalising that venue and Seb's 're-evaluating' took the form of actual ghosting. It had hurt. It still did. Losing her career was one thing, but losing the man she'd loved, wondering how she was ever going to trust again, that was the bitterest blow.

'Anyway, we have ages until the wedding. Plenty of time to relax, unwind and sink a few cooling cocktails before the hen party tonight,' Margot said. 'We're meeting at this delightful bar and then there's a show at a theatre.'

A show sounded very upmarket for a hen night. The one and only hen night Cara had attended – for Destiny, one of her backing vocalists –. had involved Cherry Sourz and leopard-print thongs. There had been no tickets for anything, just a free front row seat of Destiny getting up close and personal with a rapper called Jericho.

With her sun cream done, Cara got ready to lie down. And then her phone rang.

'That will be your mother,' Margot said with an irritated sigh.

Cara checked the display and, sure enough, her aunt was correct.

'Always calls when we're having alone time away from the business. Have you noticed that?'

Cara hadn't noticed that but, for some reason, it obviously ticked

Margot off. She stepped to the very edge of the pool and connected the FaceTime.

'Hi, Mum.'

'Oh... hello, angel. Actually, the whole "mum" title is one of the reasons I'm calling you.' She paused. 'Sorry, that sounded a bit much, didn't it? Ow!'

Margot tutted and Cara looked to her aunt who made a show of lying on one side and turning away from the conversation. On the call, her mum seemed to be fighting to get vegetation off her face. And what had she meant about the 'mum' title?

'Sorry,' her mum carried on. 'We're in the middle of a rainforest and Deepak likes to go a little off-piste, well, off the beaten track, not on the path most taken, you know?'

Cara didn't know. All *her* paths usually led through the warehouse of Carried Away.

'So, we've decided to change our names,' her mum continued before Cara could reply. 'Dad and I. Or should I say Nettlewood and I.'

Margot snorted and Cara edged a little further away until she was right in the corner of the terrace, toes almost in the pool.

'Mum, I don't understand.'

'We are adopting names more suited to our transcendence into the deeper realms of Mother Nature. Your dad is Nettlewood Aurora and I'm Briarbanks Wisteria.'

Cara swallowed as a side-eye to Margot meant she saw her aunt beginning to titter into her towel. 'So, what do I call you?'

'I thought you could call me Wissy.'

Margot was going to pull a muscle if she carried on trying to keep in her laughter. Cara needed to do what she always seemed to have to do with her parents – cut through the minutiae and get to the point. 'So, is everything OK? I mean, you're calling me from a rainforest so it must be important.' And there was no chance she was going to call her mother Wissy.

'Oh no, nothing planet-imploding,' her mum carried on, whipping leaves out of her path like she was Indiana Jones. 'Just wanted to touch base in case the next camp doesn't have signal. And, of course, to find out the latest plastic consumption catastrophe of the luggage industry.'

Now Margot wasn't laughing. Now her aunt looked like she was about to get up and join the conversation. Cara beat a hasty retreat back into the suite and slid the glass doors to a close, locking Margot out.

'Mum, Margot works really hard to limit the impact to the environment in her production.'

'Because people only need luggage to get on planes and planes are such captains of clean air. And, didn't you hear me? It's Wissy now.'

'Mum,' Cara said as Margot grabbed the handles of the glass doors and attempted to pull them apart. 'Is everything OK? Where's Dad?' It was unlike her dad not to appear on a FaceTime call.

'He's travelling in the wagon. He got a henna tattoo yesterday and has had some reaction. To be frank, Deepak was talking about all the different natural poisons there are in the plants round here and your dad started feeling queasy after that.'

Her dad had a tattoo. Plant poisons. New names. This was a lot. And Margot was still fighting for entry.

'Cara, where are you? Or has my sister redecorated again? It looks very spa-like.'

Cara drew the curtains across the patio doors, blocking Margot out. 'We aren't in London. We're in Corfu. It's one of the Greek islands.'

'Cara, I'm a seasoned virtually carbon-neutral traveller. I know of the existence of Greece. What poor, unsuspecting entrepreneur is my sister getting to know now?'

Cara was well aware of her mum and aunt's sibling rivalry but usually it was casually sarcastic, not laced with bitterness as it sounded now.

'It's not business,' Cara said, sitting down on the edge of the bed. 'We're going to a wedding. One of Margot's old college friends.'

'Wait, Margot is putting business to one side and making time for a friend? I didn't even know she had friends she actually communicated with.'

Her statement made, Elizabeth/Wissy sliced at a tough-looking piece of bamboo and took it off at head height. Cara wasn't going to be drawn into giving an opinion on Margot and, as her aunt had done nothing but support her in every way since life as Cara had known it had crumbled, she only had positive things to say. The mood her mum was in, that wasn't going to be what she wanted to hear.

'It's a beautiful hotel. We've just arrived and they've given us a room with a swim-up pool.'

'Oh, Cara, a few nights ago I went swimming in a water hole while baby elephants showered themselves down no more than twenty feet away.'

Cara sighed. She didn't realise this was a game of one-upmanship. 'Well, I don't think they have elephants in Greece so I suppose I'll have to make do with co-existing with cats or something.'

She'd spotted many cats on their short drive from the airport – waiting in doorways expectantly, standing on the edge of large wheelie bins.

'I expect Margot has asked for all traces of nature to be removed from her veranda. Is she still smoking?'

'Mum,' Cara said.

'It's Wissy, darling.'

'Why don't you phone Margot and speak to *her* if you want to know how she's doing?'

'Don't be ridiculous! She won't have time to speak to the likes of me. In my sister's opinion, with my "beatnik" views as she calls them, I've taken a deeper fall from grace than Huw Edwards.'

'Personally, I think you're both as bad as each other. Anyway, *I'm* fine by the way and I think I actually saw a baby elephant heading this way from the all-inclusive restaurant, so love to Dad and... bye, Wheezy.'

Cara ended the call, then closed her eyes and took a deep breath. Suddenly, she felt exhausted.

'Cara!' Margot yelled, her voice loud through the glass. 'Tell your mother to bog off back to life in Bogota, or wherever she is, and come and choose something from room service.'

Now one of those cooling cocktails did sound incredibly tempting. She got up off the bed. 'Coming.'

5

NOTOS, CORFU

Akis hadn't really had time to tail the bus to make sure his grandmother got home OK but, despite all her bravado, she was close to eighty years of age and had an arthritic hip she refused to acknowledge. He also knew that the ongoing feud between Irini and Sofia meant neither mother nor daughter seemed to be able to overlook the others' shortcomings to care for each other the way they should. Someone had to look out for Irini and he had given himself that role. Because, despite Sofia's opinion to the contrary, he *did* care about family. He just wasn't willing to sacrifice his life for the sake of some ancient curse that had to be fiction.

And then the text had arrived. He gazed out over one of the three secluded bays in this small settlement he'd grown up in. The water was all the shades of aquamarine, stretching out like a fine piece of shimmering silk cloth. The message was a few short lines from his mother, an invitation to his family home. *An invitation.* Most of his friends still had a key to their family home, could come and go as they pleased, were welcomed any time. He'd had no key since his mother had told his father they needed new doors...

He took a deep breath and tried to manifest a little solace. That was the only thing he missed living in Corfu Town. As much as he adored the hum and buzz of the vibrant capital and how different that was from this tiny village, the sheer quiet, the fact that even though you knew the island was full of tourists there were spots here where you could find tranquillity and solitude. Even if it was only temporary.

He took his phone from his jeans and checked the message again.

Wedding planning. There will be coffee. 1 p.m. Do not be late.

For all Akis knew it could have been sent to many, not just him. Perhaps Cosmos; his sister, Anastasia; his dad, Thanasis; and any number of the other people involved with creating this wedding extravaganza that seemed to be more about Sofia showing the whole island their wealth, which Akis knew was dwindling rapidly.

He checked his watch. It was a little before 12 p.m. Well, arriving early was not arriving late, was it?

* * *

Akis pulled his motorbike up alongside the palatial building that looked nothing like any of the small, terracotta-roofed homes a few winding turns below it. It had started out as a modest four-bedroom home but, over the years, it had expanded to meet Sofia's need for upgrades and improvements. Now, with the urns of flowers in full pink and orange bloom, it looked something like a Barbie's Dreamhouse. Akis's father was standing outside, examining the end of the hosepipe and looking confused.

'Ya, *Bampás*,' Akis greeted.

Now Thanasis looked as if he was verging on scared as Akis made his way up the steps to the front terrace.

'What are you doing here?' his dad asked in a hoarse whisper.

'Do not worry. I have an invitation. My presence has been requested. It is all legitimate and above board.'

'I know you have been invited,' Thanasis said. 'But the text message said one o'clock. This is not one o'clock.'

Akis smiled at his father and laid a hand on his shoulder.

Thanasis sighed. 'And you know that.'

Akis took the hosepipe from his father. 'What is wrong with this?'

Thanasis shrugged. 'Ever since your mother bought a more powerful attachment than the fire department's, it has not worked correctly.'

Akis made an adjustment to the yellow plastic device at the end and squeezed the trigger. Nothing happened.

'See!' Thanasis exclaimed. 'Everything that is made more complicated does not work.'

'Thanasi! Are my flowers watered yet?'

It was Sofia shouting from inside.

'One minute,' Thanasis called back. Then he looked at Akis with desperate eyes. 'Do I try to make it work or take the ridiculous thing off?'

'Whatever you decide,' Akis said. 'I will make you a distraction.'

Without dwelling any further, he pulled the screen door and entered the house. It was either stride in with confidence or duck for cover. Today he was choosing confidence.

'*Ya, Mama.*'

Sofia span around, the whisks from a food blender in her hands beginning to drip on the ultra-modern tiles of the kitchen.

'Argh!' Sofia shrieked. 'What are you doing here now? And look what you have done already!'

Because, in this family, he was to blame for everything, even cake mixture on the floor.

'I said one o'clock. This is nowhere near one o'clock. Are your shoes clean? Don't touch anything.'

Akis didn't know whether to check the soles of his trainers or scrunch up his fingers. Instead he grabbed a piece of paper towel and dived at the cake mixture.

'Argh! No! Do not waste it!' Sofia exclaimed, trying to snatch the kitchen roll from him.

'It has been on the floor.'

'Yes, but this floor is so clean you could eat the entire cake from it without a spoon!'

Akis retreated from the spillage, watched his mother take a spatula to the mess and put the mixture back into her bowl. She was wearing a dress he hadn't seen before, an apron tied around it, her dark hair swept back into a bun. She took care of herself, always had, in the same way she was fastidious about this house. As children, he, Cosmos and Anastasia were only allowed to sprawl when they were outside. Outside they had been able to play noisy games, swing from ropes amid the olive groves, spear fish with sticks and roll each other through the sharp bamboo. Inside, however, their toys had been corralled into designated areas, then, when play was done, they were swiftly put away in expensive rattan boxes, all trace of dolls, cars, and grasshoppers Cosmos had plucked from the garden, eradicated.

'Why are you making a cake?' Akis asked. 'You said in your message it was only coffee.'

'For you only coffee. For my other guests there will be cake.'

'Guests?' Did she mean his brother and sister? Both of them currently still lived at home as far as he was aware – hardly guests. Although it had been a few weeks since he had caught up with Anastasia. The last update he had had from her was a photo of her hanging off the back of a RIB.

'I am organising an event, Aki. There is much to do. People to ask for assistance.'

'And I have offered to help in any way I can.'

'Not in *any* way you can.'

The reply was laced with bitterness. And he knew exactly what she was referring to. It was always what she was referring to. His so-called destiny. The family duty. Just because he was the first-born male. His default was always to leave whenever this subject came up but when had that ever really worked? It might get him out of the immediate conversation, but it didn't make the problem go away with any degree of permanence. Time to make his position clear.

'I am not becoming a priest, *Mama*.'

'Argh! Why would you say that? Right here, right now? So brazen! I do not know what to touch first!'

Now Sofia had abandoned the baking bowls, snatched up a small icon of the island's saint, Spyridon, and was running around the kitchen island to take hold of a ten-inch ceramic statue of Jesus that hung out in an alcove she had made into a shrine. She was clutching both of these, holding them out towards him as if he were evil to be banished.

'Why would you say that? I ask you again! It is like you want your brother's wedding to be cursed!'

Akis shook his head. 'Now I do not know how *you* can say that. Why don't you think that I wish nothing but the best for my brother? Have I not always *always* tried to protect him?'

Sofia shook her head. 'But your intentions towards the church. They are not what they should be, Aki. That is why these things happen.'

Now anger began to bubble up fast. 'You think that Cosmos falling into that machinery was because I had not committed to the church? I was the one to save him. I am the one who lost a finger.'

Immediately he couldn't help but touch that void on his left hand where his pinkie should be. It was smooth where the amputation had been made, when it had become obvious nothing could be done to save it. But, it was what it was, his priority had been to save his brother's life. Anything else he could bear. He could even still play the piano with a little extra effort.

'And that was the work of the gods!' Sofia shook Jesus.

'*Mama*, let me be clear. I have no intentions towards the church.'

'I know! And you make this so obvious! But we are running out of time! This year you will be thirty and what then for our family? You know the stories!'

'And what are stories if they are not fiction?' he asked, gesticulating as he spoke. 'Show me the evidence that says when the Diakos's first-born son has not become a priest before they were thirty that there has been fire, flood or famine!'

Sofia shook her head, crushing the icon of St Spyridon against her chest. 'You already speak of your brother's accident. I will not speak of anything else like that in this house.'

Akis tutted and shook his head. 'Because there is no evidence. This curse does not exist!'

'Disbelievers are sons of the Devil. I have brought you up better than this.'

There was a thumping at the door and before either of them could react, it burst open and a donkey strutted into the kitchen, braying with every step.

Sofia screamed. 'See! This is what is happening to us! It begins! Now, on the very cusp of your brother's wedding.' She poked Jesus towards the animal as if it was a fencing sword. 'Thanasi! Thanasi, help me!'

Akis knew this donkey. It was Pig. Which meant one of two things. Either something had happened to his grandmother since he had seen her safely into her house, or she was only a few paces behind. Akis took Pig by the collar and stopped him from drawing nearer.

'Sofia, I am here!'

Irini's voice filled the space more than Pig had and Akis watched his mother recoil, both icons hugged close as she pressed herself up against the kitchen units, and Irini came into the room.

'Get out! This is the curse! First the hosepipe not working, next my cake mixture on the floor, then you arrive early and then you...' She was looking to Irini now. 'Why are you here?'

'You invite me to come!' Irini answered, putting a hand on one of the kitchen chairs to steady herself.

'I did not!'

'I have message on my phone. It says I need to be here at one o'clock for coffee and wedding planning.'

'That is the same message I have,' Akis replied, letting Pig nuzzle at his hand.

'Well, it is a mistake. You should not be on the list,' Sofia said harshly. 'And it is not yet one o'clock!'

'Well, I see Pappa Yiannis at the *cafeneon* on my way and he tell me he is coming here at twelve thirty so I decide to come early,' Irini said, lowering herself down into a chair.

A chill ran down Akis's spine now. 'Pappa Yiannis is coming here?'

Pig let out a high-pitched bray as if the priest's presence was unacceptable to him too.

'Pappa Yiannis is a valued friend of the Diakos family,' Sofia said, grabbing the kitchen spray and wiping down the worktops.

'But Pappa Spiros is officiating Cosmos and Wren's wedding, isn't he?' Akis asked.

'Yes, but Pappa Yiannis's main role within the church is to move things into this century. He was instrumental in setting up a messaging service for confession,' Sofia said.

Irini began to laugh. 'Pappa Yiannis thinks that his app will be more popular than the Tiks-Toks.' She mused for a second. 'Although perhaps young people will have to make a confession about the kinds of things they Tiks and Toks about.'

'I have to go,' Akis said, handing Pig's rope to his grandmother. He definitely knew what this was now. Yes, there might be vague wedding planning going on, but Pappa Yiannis was nothing but a poorly dressed-up ambush.

'You cannot go!' Sofia exclaimed.

'Why not?' Akis asked. 'A few moments ago you are telling me I am too early.'

'Everything to a schedule,' Irini said, plucking a grape from the fruit bowl on the table and popping it into her mouth. 'I expect Thanasis has to book an appointment to take a shit.'

'*Mama*! I do not have language like that in my home,' Sofia said.

'Soon you will not have anything or anyone in your home.'

'Tell Cosmos I will call him later,' Akis said, going towards the door.

'Wait! Stop!' Sofia said, rushing forward and standing as a barrier between him and the outside.

Akis stood still and met her gaze. This time he was using the power of his eyes to get to the truth. Even though he was convinced he knew the score already.

'Please, Aki, do not look at me like that.'

He didn't break eye contact. Pig let out a snort.

'Tell me why Pappa Yiannis is coming here?' Akis asked.

'To... explain.'

'Explain what?'

'How good a life inside the church is,' Sofia admitted.

'Why?'

'So that...'

'Yes?'

'So that... you can be a priest before you are thirty and we can stop worrying about this curse ruining all our lives!'

Pig wailed.

'That is the noise he makes before he shits,' Irini informed them.

'Sofia!' Thanasis's voice called from the garden. 'The hosepipe is working. But I cannot get it to stop!'

6

THE LISTON, CORFU TOWN

'This takes me right back,' Margot said, inhaling on her cigarette as she and Cara sat at a café/bar in a beautiful arched arcade. This was café culture at its finest. From the other patrons at tables around them sipping espressos or freddo cappuccinos to groups across the marble esplanade under large canopies next to a wide expanse of grass resemblant of a cricket green. It was relaxed yet it had a vibe.

'You've been here before?' Cara said. 'You didn't say.'

'I spent a long weekend here once. Years ago now. With Sofia. It was a hoot.'

'And remind me, Sofia is your college friend and the mother of the groom, whose name is?'

'I have no idea. It will be written on the wedding invitation.'

The wedding invitation that Margot still hadn't produced. For someone usually so on the ball, Margot was being very lackadaisical about things here. Although apparently her aunt knew they were meeting other people invited to the hen night at 8 p.m.

'So, when was the last time you saw Sofia?'

'Heavens, I can't remember the exact date of that weekend. I do remember a spirit called *tsipouro* though.'

'You haven't seen her since "years ago" and now she's invited you and me to her son's wedding?' It sounded a bit odd. And they were both going to the hen party too.

'Why is that shocking to you, Cara? I went to a college where all the students were from notable families around the globe. Granted, there were a few of those scholarship children but mostly they were heirs of shipping tycoons or gold miners. This is how they do things.'

Cara had never really understood how or why Margot had ended up in an illustrious finishing school in Switzerland when her mother had gone to the local college and studied geology and fashion. She had asked her mum once and Elizabeth had been surprisingly tight-lipped for someone who always loved being offered the opportunity to have a dig.

'It's not *shocking*,' Cara said. 'But, you know, the weddings I've been to, or known about, usually have a tight, close-friends guest list, not people the mother of the groom hasn't seen or had contact with for years.' That was certainly the case when she and Seb had argued over price per head for the wedding breakfast...

Margot waved her cigarette as if she was conducting away the comment into the upper echelons of this ancient walkway. 'Why do you worry about things like that, Cara? Instead of wasting time thinking about why you're worthy of this opportunity, why not simply embrace it?'

The answer was because every time she embraced an opportunity she ended up being the laughing stock, broken-hearted or both. She asked questions now. All the time. Triple-checked her decision-making. This Americano she had opted for was now making her hot and the humidity was stifling. She got to her feet.

'I'm just... going for a walk.'

'I wouldn't recommend it in those shoes,' Margot said. 'Those marble slabs are ever so slick and...'

Cara didn't hear the rest; she couldn't stay long enough to hear whatever came next. Finding solitude was her only path now or she was in danger of falling back into those negative thinking patterns.

Shop fronts spilled with baskets of tourist fodder – tea-towels with olive motifs, tiny wrapped soaps, red-painted pots – it was bustling and lively and right now that was the opposite of what Cara needed. Before she thought too much about it she was veering away from the crowds and going up a set of steps towards an arched doorway.

* * *

The irony of this. Here Akis was, sitting in the front row of wooden chairs, dressed head to toe in the black of a Greek priest. Except this ensemble wasn't quite traditional, this was his costume for the show later, complete with a *Phantom of the Opera*-style face mask to make his character 'The Deacon' even more mysterious. But, right now, he wasn't moving like he would be later, he was keeping as still as he possibly could in the hope that the tiny black kitten he had seen belly-crawling into the church looking as weak as, well, a kitten, would come out from its hiding place and let him help it. Strays were everywhere in Corfu but he had never been able to ignore something or someone needing help in his very path. Like his brother...

The door banged closed from the back of the church and Akis looked round as someone entered. It was a woman. Half-rushing, then slowing down, stopping, turning, eyes darting around her surroundings like she didn't quite know how she had got there. Now Akis was more concerned about her than he was about the kitten.

He turned back to the front, as if he was seeking guidance from the altar and the golden icons, like his mother grabbing up her gurus earlier.

'Do you take confession?'

It was the woman's voice and Akis wondered if the *papás* of this church had appeared. But, very swiftly, he realised the woman had drawn closer, was standing alongside him and had definitely addressed her question to him. She had hair the colour of the leaves in autumn, it wasn't long or short but it fell onto her shoulders like wide ribbons of shining colour...

'Sorry, you probably don't speak English. I apologise,' the woman continued.

'No,' Akis answered. 'There is... nothing to apologise for... my child.' What the hell was he saying?! He cleared his throat. 'I speak English.'

Before he could say anything more, she had settled herself on the chair next to him, held both her hands together, wringing one with the other like they were damp cloths. Instinctively, he wanted to know what had happened to her.

'I don't know if I can do this any more,' the woman whispered, eyes to the floor.

'You decide you do not want to confess?' he asked.

'No... I mean, this is the beginning of my confession.'

Here was the proof that he would be a terrible priest. He didn't even have a clue what he should do.

He should let her choose her pace.

'I'm a follower now. And I was never a follower before,' she carried on.

'Christ can come to you at any time,' Akis answered.

'What?' the woman asked, raising her head and looking at him.

'Jesus. There is no time limit with him. Or his father and the spirit. It does not matter if you are following from the very beginning or if you join the path later.'

'I didn't mean a follower of the church. I meant in my life,' the woman said sighing. 'I don't make my own decisions. I'm *scared* to make my own decisions. But I don't know how to be any other way any more.'

Her predicament pulled at him. He had this problem in reverse. But what had made her too scared to make choices? He looked at her again, took in smaller details this time. Her eyes were blue, bright blue, almost the colour of the Ionian Sea and they looked just as deep. He swallowed, suddenly feeling whatever he said next was going to be hugely important.

'What scares you about making decisions?' he asked.

'Everything,' she said, her voice wavering.

'Why?'

He felt a shift in her energy then, the air between them changing in velocity, stilling.

'I don't think this is how confession is meant to work,' she said, straightening up in her seat. 'I thought I could just tell you how I feel and then you'd offer me advice at the end.'

'Well, have you ever had confession in Greece before? Because it is known around the world that Greeks do things differently to most other nations.'

Why was he still pretending he was a real priest? And why did he feel it was essential that he provided her with something positive to take away from this? He should be calling up the real *pappás* and getting out of here.

'Is that why you're also wearing a mask?' she asked.

Shit. The mask.

'Ah,' Akis began. 'I apologise. That is because of the kitten.'

'What?'

He stood then and gestured that she should too. Gently he edged forward towards the altar. 'I was... collecting my thoughts and I saw this scared kitten run through the church. It was, I guess, looking for sanctuary.' He looked sideways to her. 'A little like you.'

'I don't understand.'

'You look for sanctuary too. Away from your problems with decisions.'

'I meant I still don't understand why you're wearing a mask.'

'Oh.' He regrouped. 'Well, the cats in Corfu, they are very fierce. And they will always go for the eyes.'

He'd tried to sound convincing, but it was all very weak. Thankfully he was saved from commenting further when he parted the altar cloth and there was the kitten looking very sorry for itself, one paw held up like it was unable to walk.

'What do we do now?' the woman asked him.

'We pick it up and we get it some water.'

'But you've made it sound like it's vicious.'

'But, remember, I have a mask.'

The woman shook her head. 'I have no idea what's going on. But perhaps I should have found a bar instead of a church.'

She turned to go and Akis found himself not wanting that.

'Wait,' he said, stepping away from the cat.

She stopped and turned back to face him. What was he going to say now?

'The way you feel, about your decision-making...' He took a breath.

'Imagine that the decision is a tiny seed planted inside your mind. You can see the seed, but it is small, and it is always small, until *you* decide to let it grow bigger. *You* decide if or when. Other people, they have their own seeds to think about. Your seeds, they are yours alone. Others might be able to see them but only you own them.'

He swallowed, watching for her reaction. Seconds ticked by until finally she gave him a small smile.

'Thank you,' she said.

'*Parakalo*. You're welcome.'

And, with that said, he watched her turn around again and head to the door.

7

REX RESTAURANT, KAPODISTRIOU STREET, CORFU TOWN

'It wouldn't surprise me if Sofia had taken over the entire restaurant,' Margot remarked as they made their way across the marble to where they were meeting the wedding party. 'Sofia always loved anything exclusive. I remember she had quite the possessive streak when it came to a millionaire we met in Monte Carlo. He was ever so good-looking, but obviously you can't be exclusive when you're that sexy. I never minded shared experiences, but sharing wasn't ever something Sofia was fond of. Still, her loss was usually my gain.'

As Margot gave more background information on the mother of the groom, all Cara could think about were tiny seeds. What sort of analogy had the strange priest given her? It didn't make sense. Because not every decision was small. What to choose from the menu for dinner – small decision. What to do with the rest of your life – big fucking decision. But, then again, when had she ever sought advice from the church before? She hadn't even wanted to get married in a church.

'Cara, is everything OK with you?' Margot asked.

'Yes, sure, of course.' That was a few too many words.

'Because when you left me in the Liston, I was a little worried you were having one of your weak moments.'

One of your weak moments. Margot had said the phrase like the crippling anxiety she suffered with was a personal choice. And her aunt never made any bones about the fact that weakness was ugly and something people took advantage of rather than sympathised with. She internally steeled herself now, imagined reeling out a roll of barbed wire and wrapping it up around her gut. A game of let's pretend...

'I'm good.' Had that sounded convincing? Before Margot could eye her with suspicion or say anything else, she followed it up with, 'Honestly, just a little tired from the flight but completely looking forward to meeting your old friend and getting into the wedding vibe.'

Perhaps that was a teensy bit over the top for someone who couldn't even come within a metre of a *Hello* magazine cover if it had a bride on the front...

'Jolly good,' Margot announced. 'Because Sofia might be a friend, of sorts, but that doesn't necessarily mean this encounter is going to be any less testing than a boardroom showdown.'

'What?'

'Just, remember your inner lioness, like we learned at that conference in Norwich, and follow my lead.'

With those words imparted, Margot made longer strides, opened her arms like she was about to embrace the entire universe and strode towards a table outside on the marble. Cara rushed to catch up then slowed her speed into that of a confident prowl.

'Sofia, darling! Don't you look wonderful? Doesn't all this look delightful? How long has it been? Don't answer, I'll tell you, it's been far *too* long.'

Cara watched as Margot embraced a perfectly put-together dark-haired woman dressed in what looked like a Dolce and Gabbana dress. She had glossy hair that was tied in a perfect chignon and her make-up was subtle except for a bright pink lipstick that suited her so well.

'Hi! Who are you?'

Cara jumped at the sound of another female voice behind her and turned around to see a woman about her age with an abundance of long dark curly hair. She was smiling and had a folder in her hand like she was about to do business.

'I'm Cara. Cara Jones. I'm here with—'

'Margot! My mother's friend who has been so helpful!'

Cara quickly did the family tree maths.

'Sorry,' the woman carried on. 'I am Anastasia. Sofia's daughter. The best-looking one of her children and the smartest, obviously.'

Cara smiled, immediately liking this woman's energy. Anastasia stuck out her hand, then seemingly thinking better of it, put her arms around Cara and squeezed her, crushing the folder against her chest. Cara barely had time to recover before Anastasia was hastening her towards the table where other women were already seated.

'Let me introduce everyone! And we are all going to speak English, yes? Because the beautiful bride and her family are English!' Anastasia boomed. 'So, when I call your name just wave. The most important one first we have—'

'I am Sofia! Mother of Cosmos, the groom,' Sofia interrupted.

There were a few titters of laughter until Anastasia carried on again. 'I was going to say the most important person is Wren, the bride.'

A very petite mousey-haired young woman waved rather meekly and then Anastasia continued with the introductions. Wren's mother, Wren's auntie, Wren's best friend and bridesmaid, Kelly, then there was a woman who had been introduced as something to do with flowers, another one owned a bakery and then there was Cara and Margot. It wasn't quite the grand taking-over-the-entire-restaurant party Margot had claimed it was going to be.

'There will be more of us for the show,' Anastasia announced as she took her seat next to Cara. 'My friends were not going to miss out on my mother paying for us to watch half-naked men for two hours.'

That was the show? Strippers? Cara had envisaged cabaret perhaps, but more jazz band and martinis than abs and *Magic Mike*.

'Plus, there's the added bonus that my mother is going to freak when she sees my brother.' Anastasia laughed and picked up a bottle of Mamos beer, swigging it back. 'Not Cosmos. He's banned from Corfu Town tonight so the women can have fun. He will get his turn in a few days or so.'

Cara was starting to have trouble remembering who was who and she noticed Margot hadn't actually sat down yet. Her aunt was working the table, making sure she introduced herself to everyone and palmed a business card into each handshake. It was as impressive as it was slightly embarrassing. But that was why Margot was so successful. When it came to coming out on top, she gave very few shits about etiquette.

'So, tell me,' Anastasia said, swivelling a little on her seat to give Cara more attention. 'Do you have a boyfriend or a girlfriend? Because you are way too pretty to be single.'

Cara smiled. 'Ah, well, that's where you're wrong.'

'I am not wrong that you are pretty,' Anastasia said. 'But I do need to know if I am wasting my time.'

'Oh!' Cara exclaimed. 'You were—'

'Hitting on you a little,' she said smiling. 'Something else my mother hates is my sexuality. Or, should I say, she hates that I tell people openly that I like men *and* women. Imagine, your parent not liking that their child is honest.'

'I like men,' Cara answered. 'Sorry.'

'Do not apologise,' Anastasia said immediately. 'But know you are doomed to a life of waiting for them to text first.'

Cara really did like this girl's vibe. She picked up a glass of wine that was in her place. 'Let's cheers to that.'

'*Yammas*,' Anastasia said, knocking her beer bottle against the glass.

8

ESCAPE THEATRE BAR, CORFU TOWN

Cara had lost track of how much she'd drunk. It seemed that after every forkful of food and accompanying sip of wine, Anastasia had topped up her glass. A dutiful hostess perhaps, but one whose aim seemed to be to get her plastered. The plentiful food had thankfully kept her a little level. Cara had opted for the pork cheeks with lemongrass, potatoes, herbs and foam from cabbage salad. It had looked decadent as well as healthy and it had tasted divine. Cara was fortunate enough to be able to access fine dining quite often when Margot entertained, but, still, this had been on another level.

Now they were inside an eclectic not-quite-a-bar, not-quite-a-theatre with round tables like that cabaret atmosphere Cara had envisaged. The tables were set out in front of a stage, the red velvet curtain lowered, its texture spotlighted by glowing lamps around the foot of the stage. It was all very speakeasy-meets-dancehall from its huge collection of spirit bottles lined up in illuminated cabinets behind the bar to the sparkling chandeliers hanging from the ceiling.

'I read the glowing reviews online, but I thought my brother had written most of them,' Anastasia announced, pulling out a chair. 'But this place is great, right? You sit down here. I will get Wren and Kelly with us and the older women can have the next table.'

'Oh, OK,' Cara agreed, about to sit down. But she started to have second thoughts when she remembered what usually happened to those people who were sat closest to the action. 'But perhaps we could sit at one of the tables further back?'

Anastasia laughed then. 'That is what Wren would want! And she is the bride! No!'

There seemed to be no other choice but to sit down. As Anastasia began directing other members of their group to settle, Cara looked for her aunt. She'd barely seen her during dinner. Margot had plumped down next to Sofia at Rex Restaurant and that's where she had remained. Not that Cara minded Margot catching up with an old friend – that was why they were here – but not knowing anyone, being in a new country, in a different situation, it was something she usually encountered with her aunt right beside her. She eyed the bottle of vodka on the table and accompanying shot glasses. No, more alcohol was not the answer right now.

* * *

Akis tore off his gloves and threw them down onto the table, fingers going to the knot at his chest that held his cape in place. 'You will have to call Panos. I cannot perform tonight.'

'What? Aki, don't be crazy! Panos cannot play the piano,' Horatio began, a stick of white face paint between his fingers. 'And Panos's moves are not yours. Plus, he does not have the eyes!'

'Use the backing track. I cannot perform. My mother is out there! My sister is out there! Wren and her relatives are out there!' He was struggling to unfasten the string.

'Is that it? Have a shot of vodka.' Horatio pushed the bottle across the sideboard he had mounted a mirror on. 'There are no glasses tonight but measurements, as we know, are not real.'

Akis stopped trying to undo his cape and looked at his friend. 'You knew they were going to be here tonight! Did *you* sell them the tickets?'

'Why are we having this conversation?' Horatio asked, checking his reflection and the stripes he was blending. 'It is a hen party. Apart from tourists looking for a good time, they are the very backbone of our summer takings. Plus, you know I can never say no to Anastasia.'

Akis sighed. 'I am beginning to think you can never say no to anyone.'

'I think this may be true,' Horatio agreed.

'Well, what am I supposed to do?'

'Do I need to walk you through the acts again? I know we have made significant changes since the last run in May but we have done many shows now and—'

'Very funny! So funny, Horatio! Because of course I meant the routine!' He grabbed at his friend's make-up palette. 'My mother has today again made it clear her plan is to make me feel so guilty I have no choice but to join the priesthood.' He put the brush to Horatio's cheek, expertly applying a highlight of blush.

'There is always a choice,' Horatio said, gently turning in the chair and letting Akis continue with the make-up. 'Except for whether you perform tonight or not. There is no choice in that. We need you, Aki. And, OK, I will admit, you are the best dancer, the favourite, the one every person here goes home to think about when they're naked.'

Akis sighed. 'So you think I put my family in jeopardy and ignore the fact that all the generations to come could be at risk if I don't become a priest.'

Horatio held up a finger. 'That only becomes a thing if you believe the curse.'

'It doesn't matter if *I* believe it. My mother believes it.'

'And you are going to live *your* life for your mother? Do you hear yourself right now?'

Akis did hear himself. And it was so contradictory to everything he believed in. The fact that you only got one life and it should be filled to the brim with every experience you could reach and those you might need to make a leap of faith for. He wanted fast and furious, seizing opportunities, trying new things, not waiting for things to happen but making them happen...

'You're right,' Akis said, nodding as he finished brushing Horatio's face.

'I am always right.'

'If this curse even exists, how bad can it be? I mean, we are all predominantly still here. The things my mother has vaguely talked about, they happened decades ago.'

'That could be because every other first-born Diakos son has become a priest in the recent past.'

'No,' Akis said, now doing the finger-pointing himself. 'No, my great-uncle, Haris, he was the second-born son because Spiros died at only a few weeks old – he did not become a priest.'

'And he is alive and well? His family do not have too many hard times?'

'No. He is dead,' Akis answered with a sigh. 'But, you know, the investigation into the accident was inconclusive.'

'Exactly!' Horatio said, getting to his feet. 'So, there is no proof. And, as we are on the subject of religion, there is no actual proof of God. Just alleged very ancient eye-witness testimony, so what does that say about the church?'

Akis sighed again. He seemed to be doing a lot of that lately. 'Do not let my grandmother hear you say that. Despite being my biggest ally in me not being ordained, she does go to church every single week.'

'Ah, about your grandmother,' Horatio said, slipping himself into a leather waistcoat. 'I might have given her a ticket for tonight too.'

'Horatio!'

'We agreed, I have never been good with "no".'

9

'Oh my God, my *yiayia* is here!'

After two vodka shots, Cara thought *yiayia* sounded like it could be a nickname for the vagina.

Before she could ask, Anastasia continued. 'My grandmother. Wren, put your bag of penis shit on that chair so she cannot sit down.'

The 'penis shit' had been produced at the dinner table and consisted of mostly useless plastic party favours shaped like the male appendage. Although Cara's particular favourites had been the nail clippers and the pen that tasted – and smelled – like seasoned pork. Just, why?

'Was she not invited?' Cara asked, watching the elderly lady having what looked like a heated conversation with Sofia. She was wearing a bright green dress and her sandals were taped together. She had bright hair clips in her grey hair that didn't really seem to be serving any purpose other than to be decorative. There were two Day-Glo yellow star-shaped ones and was the other one a peacock?

'No, she was not. She is not invited to the wedding either. What can I say?'

'But, if she is—' Cara began, seeking more of an explanation.

The lights dimmed and a low bass that made the sound system rattle interrupted her. Everyone in the audience gave an almost involuntary whimper of appreciation. It seemed like the show was about to begin.

Anastasia leaned closer to Cara, her hair touching her cheek, and whispered, 'I think that Wren will not know what is about to hit her.'

Cara swallowed. This was good. Wren, the bride, was the focus. There was zero chance of Cara having to do audience participation with a real-life wife-to-be in the mix. She cast a quick glance over at Margot's table. Her aunt was lighting up a cigarette. Could you do that inside here? And Sofia was pulling a chair away from their table, setting it down a few metres away and ushering the *yiayia* towards it.

Then the lights dropped completely and there were a few screams as ambient low-lighting turned into total darkness. Cara put her fingers to the table edge. And then the piano music began.

Suddenly there were shivers running up and down her spine at the sound. It was like nothing she'd heard before and she had heard plenty of pianists. This was *haunting*. It was giving classical, yet modern, classy yet super-sexy. And it was so slow, like the musician was teasing them. And in the pitch black, all Cara's other senses were heightened. She could feel her breath moving inside, pushing her diaphragm, reaching her throat until it escaped. Her heart was beating in her chest but also thrumming gently in her ears and at her wrists. It was a beautiful yet intense sensation. Next a spotlight came on, revealing a metal pole and, with the greatest grace, a male dancer descended so languidly wearing a tight black bodysuit with a leather waistcoat and white stripes on his face, gently rotating like a grungy jewellery box ballerina.

It was then Cara realised she knew the song. It was Beyonce's 'Crazy in Love' but the slowed-down version used in *Fifty Shades of Grey*. The piano was hot and heavy, the dancer was defying gravity, spiralling on the pole, light and elegant and there was more sexual tension in the air than she'd experienced in quite some time...

More spotlights and six other dancers were highlighted, all wearing black with white glowing make-up on their faces. And as the piano became more dramatic and the dancers began to perform harder, stomping, popping and locking, Cara felt the audience becoming a pent-up ball of hot-bloodedness.

Then, rising up from the centre of the stage, came a shiny black piano. The pianist stood, still hammering at the keys as the dancers continued to sway and steer their bodies this way and that. As good as the performers were, Cara was drawn to the music being made by this man in the shadows. He was an experienced player. That was obvious. Even with the bassline thumping out loud from a backing track, his talent was at the forefront: the riffs, the ad libs, the skill and the style.

Just as Cara was leaning forward, wanting to try to get closer to the music, the piano playing stopped. While her brain tried to compute what was happening the sound shifted and the pianist jumped up from behind the piano, his boots landing on top of it as he too began to dance. And that was when Cara realised this dancer, the one who had been playing the outstanding piano, was not completely unknown to her. She recognised his dark clothing, the robes, the cross around his neck and the mask concealing half of his face. It was the priest she'd spoken to. The priest who obviously wasn't a real priest and who she had asked to hear her confession!

As she watched him winding and grinding on top of the piano, some of the audience members now full-on screaming, she felt her cheeks reddening. How embarrassing was that?

'See that guy?' Anastasia said loudly, pointing towards the stage. 'The one on top of the piano dressed as a priest?'

Oh yeah, Cara saw him. And he was currently ripping open his robes, gyrating to 'World Class Sinner'.

'That's my brother,' Anastasia filled in. 'The other one. Not the one who's getting married.'

'That's your brother,' Cara said, eyes still on the stage.

'Yes! That's Akis. Although here they call him "The Deacon".'

Cara had no words, but what she did have in her mind was a question. It was one thing for her to be embarrassed about confessing to a fake priest, but why on Earth had Anastasia's brother gone along with the pretence? Or perhaps it was simply just role play for this job and she'd been an unwitting volunteer. Whatever it was, she needed to get some air and control of her pulse rate.

She got to her feet.

'Shit! Don't stand up!' Anastasia said.

'What?'

'Don't stand up now! I told Horatio it's the signal! But it was meant to be *Kelly* and Wren.'

'Signal?'

Cara didn't understand... until the moment one of the dancers leapt from the stage and started walking towards her.

10

This was Cara's worst nightmare. She avoided being on stages at all costs these days, had even hidden in the toilets when Margot's business had won an entrepreneurial award so she didn't have to be up there in the spotlight. Yet, here she was, sat on a chair on one side of the stage while Wren was on the other, the priest-who-wasn't-a-priest performing slow body rolls in front of her like his six-pack was the product and this was a soon-to-be-interactive advertisement. And as much as she would be signing up to a subscription for her viewing pleasure, the whole being watched by an audience of flesh-hungry women was about as appealing as swimming with sharks.

'You could smile,' Akis said as his crotch rocked and writhed mere centimetres from her face.

'Is that a joke? Why would I smile when I don't want to be here?' She had to raise her voice above the pumping bassline of the music.

'You not smiling might affect my tips. I need the tips.'

This time he ducked right into her personal space, priest robes discarded, bare chest rippling up her torso. *Seeds*. No, not seeds of any kind. He had impersonated a member of the clergy. That was law-breaking.

'Well, you should have thought about that before you hoodwinked me into believing you were a member of God's family.'

He was smiling now and it wasn't so much sexy but smug. 'I do not know whether to laugh at whatever the word "hoodwink" means or remind you that each one of us is a member of God's family. If you believe.'

Cara was about to counter him quickly until he spun around and suddenly there was rope around her and she was being bound to the chair. What the hell was this? A quick look to the left and she could see Wren and another dancer getting into a similar situation across the stage. And far from looking nervous or embarrassed, Wren seemed to be putting her hands all over the dancer's torso.

'Greek olive oil,' Akis said. 'Cup your hands.'

'No.'

'Come on, extra virgin. There are other women down there who would give their husband's Amex for this chance.'

'I would give you my own Amex to get off this chair if I didn't think my aunt would be disappointed in me.' She paused. 'Did you call me "extra virgin"?'

Before Cara could say anything else, he had taken control of her hands and poured oil in them. And unless she did something it was going to start dripping all over the rather lovely skirt Margot had stumped up for in Liberty. She stood up and the chair came with her. But, instead of rubbing the oil over Akis's contorting abdominals, Cara went for his face. Slapping her hands on his cheeks, she massaged the oil into his skin, teasing fingers around his firm jawline, tracing a finger under the edge of his mask...

'*Ochi.* No,' Akis said firmly. 'Not the mask.'

A statement rather than a warning.

Then, somehow, the rope around her and the chair fell away and Akis picked her up.

'We have approximately two minutes and thirty seconds until this song is over and you are meant to be left quivering with need with every single person in this audience wishing they were you.'

His breath was hot in her ear and with his almost carrying-over-the-threshold cradling, there was no space between them.

'So, you have two choices. We can do sexual things with food like Wren and Horatio. Or I can just put you on the floor right now, and ride all over you until the song climaxes.'

Cara hated that somewhere down in the depths of her uterus there was a definite vibration. Out of the corner of her eye she spied the tell-tale shape and colour of a cucumber. There was only one option.

'The floor,' she told him. 'And I am not going to move a centimetre.'

It was definitely a sexy smile crossing his lips now. 'We will see about that.'

11

SWAY BAR AND KITCHEN, THE LISTON

Horatio took a drag of his cigarette and blew the smoke into the air. 'Tonight was a *really* good show.'

They were sitting outside this vibey bar enjoying the slight drop in temperature.

Akis threw back what little was left from his vodka and shook his head. 'You say that after every show.'

'No, after every show I say it was a good show. Tonight was a *really* good show.'

'Yeah,' Akis said, never having loaded one word with as much sarcasm. 'Really good to have my mother and sister in the audience, not to mention my future sister-in-law and my grandmother.'

'There was no doubt that they all enjoyed it. Your grandmother gave me one of her hair clips.' Horatio tapped the shining accessory he had clipped to the lapel of his jacket.

Akis knew his mother hadn't enjoyed it. She might have smiled and clapped her hands at the appropriate times but he could see right through her. Just like she could see through his half-mask. Him dressed as a priest, the very thing she wanted, and he was ridiculing it. He had given his character 'The Deacon' that mask for many reasons. To hide a little in plain sight. To pretend he was someone else. The someone else he had been before Cosmos's accident. Though Akis was the one who got injured, even he still called it 'Cosmos's accident'.

Horatio slapped a hand down on his shoulder. 'I made over two hundred euros in tips.'

'Because you will do anything for them.'

'Why would you not, if you enjoy doing anything?' Horatio grinned. 'Do not tell me you did not enjoy your one-on-one time with the girl with the amazing hair colour.'

Akis swallowed. His face still had a sheen from the olive oil she had massaged into it. And, no matter what move he'd made astride her on the floor, she had not shifted at all until the song had ended and all the lights had gone out. Then she had whispered to him in the dark:

There will be fifty euro in it for you if you don't come near me again.

It wasn't something he had ever been asked before – quite the opposite in fact. And it only made him want to know more about her. Who was she? How did she know Wren and Cosmos to be invited to the wedding? Why had she told him in the church about her inability to make decisions?

'What is wrong?' Horatio asked him. 'Did she not fall for the eyes? Because, I have to say, Wren was becoming quite invested in our cucumber for someone who is getting married soon.'

'Aki!'

Akis didn't have time to respond before the sound of his grandmother's voice cut through the patrons' chatter around him. Then he saw her heading their way with a tray in her hands.

'Please tell me the whole hen party aren't all coming back here,' Akis said. He took Horatio's cigarette from him, inhaled on it and then gave it back.

'I have vodka!' Irini announced.

'Shit!' Horatio said, moving the ashtray and their drinks to make way for the tray holding a large bottle and small shot glasses. 'Irini, you are partying tonight! Are you coming to 54 with us?'

Akis shook his head. 54 Dreamy Nights was the biggest nightclub in Corfu Town and somewhere he had been a bit too often in the past.

'54?' Irini said. 'Sometimes I dream of 1954.'

She was struggling to get up on the high stool, shoes slipping a little.

'Come on, *Yiayia*. Let Horatio and me help,' Akis said.

Without waiting for a reply, he and Horatio got off their stools, boosted her up onto the seat and made sure she was stable before going back to their own.

'Open the bottle, Aki.' She patted Horatio's arm, eyes bright. 'What a show tonight!'

'You liked it?' Horatio asked.

'You looked like a ballet dancer. So elegant and handsome,' she said, snatching up one of the shot glasses Akis had just poured.

'I do not think I have been called "elegant" before. Let me think for a moment... no, I definitely have not.'

Akis hissed and shook his head.

'And you,' Irini said, slapping a hand on Akis's forearm. 'Dressing as a priest. I nearly fell off my chair and I thought your mother was going to explode like a volcano.' She laughed. 'And then, I remembered, to explode like a volcano would be to show emotion in public and she would never allow that to happen. Anastasia tells me that she has scheduled two episodes of crying for Cosmos's wedding. One at the end of his vows and another when they cut the cake.'

Everything stage-managed. No allowance for spontaneity. His mother had been like that his whole life.

'But what about the girl you danced with?' Irini said, pouring herself another vodka. 'Cara.'

'You know her name. Well done, Irini,' Horatio said, nudging Akis's arm.

'I am not sure I danced *with* her,' Akis answered. 'The fact that she did not say no is certainly the only reason I have not been arrested.' He downed a vodka shot. 'Who exactly is she?'

'She is the niece of your mother's friend from college. I did not know they were still in touch. Well, I am not permitted to know things from your mother's life, am I? Ah, here they come. No reserved seating here; perhaps your mother will have to sit on a bench.'

As Irini laughed, Akis's gaze went to the hen party who were arriving from down the street, his mother leading the way like a tourist guide.

Wren was between her mother and her crazy friend, Kelly, looking close to incapable of walking at all, then last of all was Cara.

Akis watched her. She wasn't rushing to catch everyone up, instead she was slowing her pace, as if she was trying to *not* be part of the group. Finally, as most of the ladies stopped by the tables at Sway, she peeled away, heading on.

Akis slipped down off his stool. 'Give me a second.'

12

Cara was so tired. From the early start this morning, to the phone call with her mother, to being part of a sexy stage act, drinking dirty-named cocktails, to now. What she wanted to do was crawl into that lavish bed at Cook's Club and let the high thread count sheets ease her towards a long deep sleep. Except Margot never left anywhere before 2 a.m. unless it was under a police escort. Yes, she could leave her aunt and get a taxi back alone but, well, she never did that. Not since Moldova.

She walked up the rise, past a rather grand-looking arched entrance to a Starbucks and crossed the street. Motorbikes and cars were lined up, parked in every available space, taxis waited next to blue and green bins, then ahead was a pedestrianised area, trees lining the avenue, all colours of flowers blooming around marble statues, and further away was the imposing rock of the old fortress.

She sat down on a bench, closed her eyes and took in a long slow breath.

'*Signomi*. Do you take confession?'

She snapped her eyes open and there was Akis standing right in front of her. There was no mask covering any of his face now but those eyes – a little bit blue, part green with a hint of amber were still the standout. He was also no longer wearing anything connected with the priesthood. But the jeans and white T-shirt combo was a good look. So good it was hard not to remember his body in super-close proximity to hers only a couple of hours ago.

'Apparently everyone around here has some kind of right to offer that,' she snapped.

He smiled. 'You're still mad at me.'

'Oh, you think?'

She *was* mad. And she didn't really get mad these days. She didn't really get emotional about anything. It had been part of her recovery. Shutting off the kind of sensors that destroyed your equilibrium.

He sat down next to her and suddenly the bench felt small. His knee touched hers and then he quickly adjusted, drew it back.

'So, what are you more mad about?' he asked. 'Your assumption that just because I was in a church I was a priest? Or the fact my sister managed to make you part of the show?'

'Oh, please tell me I wasn't part of the show when I was trying so hard to make myself part of the stage floor.'

He laughed then and the sound hit the air like the sweetest birdsong. That was weird...

'I'm Akis,' he introduced, holding out his hand.

'Wow, your hand,' Cara said. 'It just feels a little off as you've already offered other more intimate parts of your body in my direction.'

'And you very much turned them down, so I thought we'd go back to basics.'

She took his hand and he held tight.

'I'm Cara,' she said. Suddenly, with his hand in hers, the humidity was rising. And she needed to get a grip. What was it Margot always said about winning the war of conversation? Straight out of the bunker and charge!

'Actually,' Cara began. 'You did impress me. With the way you played the piano.'

'Seriously?' he asked, shaking his head.

'What? You don't want people to compliment your musical skills?'

'No. It's just... no one has.' He shrugged. 'The piano isn't really what the people come for.'

'Well, it should be.'

'And, if I am honest, tonight wasn't the best I have played. But, perhaps it was the best I have played since my brother's accident.'

He held out his left hand and waggled three fingers and a thumb. He was missing a pinkie.

'Sorry,' Cara said immediately. 'I mean, not sorry that you lost your finger, well, I am sorry about that, obviously, but I'm just trying to work out how someone plays that incredibly with something quite vital missing.'

'Perhaps a few of those notes were hit with a more inappropriate part of my body.'

Irritatingly, she could do nothing to stop the full-on body flush that was now cocooning her like the very best sleeping bag Mountain Warehouse had to offer.

'I am joking with you,' he said, nudging her leg with his. 'It takes practice and I am meant to do lots of different exercises that I should take time to do but, you know, I am a busy man and, as I said, most people do not come to see what I can do with my hands.' He winked then. 'Although Horatio always thinks we should sell tickets for after-show exclusive access for that.'

She was still blushing. Why did this guy simply say whatever was on his mind with no filter?

'I don't think that sounds like very priestlike behaviour,' she told him.

He lowered his head into her space. 'And you would be right.'

Her phone vibrated in her bag and she took a second to enforce a break in the tension and take it out.

'My aunt,' she said. 'Asking where I am.'

'Are you on parole?' Akis asked, an eyebrow raised.

'No. She just, you know, worries about me.'

He nodded. 'Like you are ten years old.'

'Not at all like that.'

Except there were taps of movement in her gut like a fiesta of grasshoppers were parading, suggesting Akis may be right. And she hated that.

'So, you want to go somewhere?' he asked.

'With you?'

'I promise I won't get on top of you again.' He grinned. 'Without your permission, at least.'

This was crazy. She wanted to go back to the hotel and sleep. She should go back to Margot and the others. But there was a flicker of something inside her that was calling her to question these options and pick something else.

'I don't usually go anywhere with strangers.' She was taking her time.

'Please, you have met my mother, my sister, my soon-to-be sister-in-law and my grandmother. No one I have dated has even met so much of my family.'

It was 'she shouldn't' versus 'she wanted to'.

'Come on,' Akis said, nudging her knee again. 'This is a small seed. It doesn't even need planting.'

She stood up. 'Well, where are we going?'

'Not to church,' he answered. 'Come on.'

13

ROULA FISH TAVERNA, KONTOKALI

Cara had ridden with him again. This time on the back of a motorbike, a slightly too big helmet on her head, holding Akis's waist as they had whizzed through the narrow alleyways of the town, scaring sleeping cats, almost snaring lines of washing until they were out on the main road. And within ten minutes or so they had arrived here. Here was a gorgeous taverna right on the water's edge and, seeing as it was well after midnight, they were, unsurprisingly, the only people here. The lights were low, the water was so still and you could see the masts of many yachts moored in a marina. She turned her attention away from the scene to Akis who was talking with the owner. How was she at a restaurant with a man she barely knew? Who was this I've-only-been-in-Greece-for-a-few-hours version of herself? Perhaps she should send Margot a text to let her know she was OK...

'I've ordered everything.'

Akis was back, sliding into the seat opposite and putting a large bottle of beer in front of her.

'Oh, I don't really drink beer and I had quite a lot of—'

'You don't *really* drink beer? Or you don't drink beer?'

'Isn't that the same thing?'

'Have you tried *Greek* beer?'

'No, I—'

'Try it. You don't like it and I will let you off from paying me the fifty euro you promised me.'

Cara smiled and lifted the bottle to her lips. She took a swig and the bubbles hit her tongue. 'Ooo, no, this is terrible.'

'You lie to me!'

She laughed. 'OK, I admit, it's not bad.'

'You like fish?' Akis asked.

'To look at?'

He laughed. 'To eat!'

'Yes, I like fish but we ate, before your show.'

He checked his watch. 'That was hours ago. And have you ever had *Greek* fish?'

'I have not.'

'Well, this is one of the best places for it. Straight from this water to the plate.'

And within twenty minutes or so, that was exactly what happened. Piles of steaming seafood arrived. Dozens of tiny fish coated in bread-crumbs, larger flatter silver fish opened up and cleaned of bones, pieces of octopus tentacle, squids, giant prawns, and a vat of mussels. All along-side hunks of bread and a canister of olive oil.

Whilst Cara speared a sardine with her fork, Akis went in with his hands. He picked up speedily then ate slowly, closing his eyes and looking like he was savouring every morsel.

He opened his eyes and caught her looking. 'I have no manners when it comes to good food. I would apologise, but I am not sorry.' He picked up a serviette and wiped around his mouth.

'It is delicious,' Cara admitted.

'I come here as often as I can. After a show I am always hungry.'

'I'm not surprised,' she said. 'I mean, it's quite the workout.'

He smiled. 'You noticed.'

'It's hard not to when bits of you were flying everywhere.'

'Oh, Cara, I do not think so. One thing I am certain of is that I am fully in control of my bits.'

And now she was blushing again. Seriously, how did this guy manage to do this to her? She picked up a mussel and opened its shell. 'So, how long ago did you lose your finger?' she asked.

'You think that's why I don't use cutlery?'

'No, I—'

'I'm joking,' he said and took a swig of his beer. 'It was almost nine years ago now.'

'What happened?' She swallowed. That was a really stupid question to ask someone who had been through trauma. How many times had people tried to ask her similar things and made her feel like she was in the midst of it all over again? 'Sorry,' she said quickly. 'That was really rude of me.'

He shook his head. '*Ochi.* No. It's OK. My brother fell into some machinery. I pulled him out. All of him made it back out again, the machine took my finger. But, you know, I was not destined to be a heart surgeon so it is OK.' He sighed. 'Although I felt I could not continue with the orchestra so—'

'You were part of an orchestra?'

She didn't know why she was so surprised. She had heard the way he played tonight, knew it was something exceptional.

'Try this,' Akis said, putting some fish onto a fork and holding it out to her.

'Honestly, I am so full. I've been here less than a day and I already know that the rumours of Greeks feeding you up like the witch in *Hansel and Gretel* are true.'

He laughed. 'I know of this story and, as a Greek, I think the witch was light on those portions.' He offered the fork closer. 'Please, just a taste.'

It was easier to give in than refuse because it looked so white and light and delicious. She took the fork from him and put the morsel in her mouth. It tasted divine. Like nothing else she'd tried before.

'Good, right?' he said, knowing the answer already.

'So good.'

'Goes well with the Greek beer?'

'Maybe.' She put down the fork. 'And you avoided talking any more about the orchestra.'

He shook his head. 'Not avoided. Moved on. To new subjects. Like... why you were in a church tonight looking to confess.'

It was suddenly like being under those stage lights again. She put her mouth to her beer bottle and took a drink.

'OK, we don't have to divulge all our secrets tonight,' Akis said, breaking the silence. 'I am assuming that you are going to be at all the pre-wedding events my mother has planned.'

'I don't actually know anything much about the wedding at all,' Cara admitted. 'I didn't know it was even happening until the night before I got on the plane.'

'I see,' Akis answered, nodding, a smile on his face.

'What?' Cara asked.

He picked up a piece of squid with his fingers and popped it in his mouth, eyes dancing with hers.

'What?' she asked again.

'You made a decision to come here,' he said. 'A small seed perhaps but—'

'No, I am just a plus one to my aunt who was actually invited so it was pretty much her decision that we—'

'*You* got on the plane,' Akis said.

And all at once she knew that he didn't understand her anxiety at all.

She nodded, picking up her beer bottle and knocking it against his. 'You're right,' she said. 'Go me.'

14

COOK'S CLUB CORFU

Akis knew he had said the wrong thing back at the restaurant, about getting on the plane being her decision. He had known it the second he saw her expression flicker. It was almost unnoticeable, but he had caught it. A drop of eye contact, reaching for a prop – the beer bottle – a reinstallation of a smile, immediate affirmation regarding his statement, all happening within seconds. And she had moved on fast, asked about Cosmos and Wren, asked for details of the wedding he didn't have. He had answered, but his mind was wandering and wondering – what was her story? She had talked mainly about her aunt and her aunt's business, there was nothing personal, no anecdotes relating directly to her. Was she simply a private person? Or someone who had to be rather than wanted to be?

She tapped his shoulder and he stopped the motorbike. She had taken off the helmet and slid off the back before he could even silence the engine.

'You can drop me here. There's a security guard and, well, I've almost been up for twenty-four hours so...'

'Well,' Akis said, getting off the bike and taking the helmet from her. 'Thank you for staying awake.'

'Oh, I didn't mean that I didn't have a good time. I *did* have a good time. You know, once I got off the stage.'

Akis smiled. 'I think you enjoyed the mussels on the plate more than the muscles in the show.'

'I think both kinds were equally impressive.'

He nodded, still smiling. 'It was nice to meet you, Cara.'

'It was nice to meet you too.'

And now what? Taking a girl to dinner hadn't been his style for a good five years now. And if this was a casual hook-up he wouldn't have left Corfu Town, would have suggested a club and then going back to his apartment. So, what was it? Nothing? Something?

Before his brain could put anything into a specific box, he had put a hand in her hair, leaned in and kissed her cheek. Quickly, he followed it up with a second quicker peck on the other side – as was the Greek way.

'*Kalinichta*,' he said, getting astride the bike again. 'Goodnight.'

'Goodnight,' Cara replied.

He started the engine, needing the noise, wanting something to distract him from this strange feeling inside himself. The sensation was dangerously like he wanted to know more about her and that didn't sit well. He put on the helmet, snapped down the visor and spinning the bike around, he roared back towards the main road.

* * *

Cara put a fingertip to her cheek. The space was still gently tingling where his lips had met skin. Despite having his crotch centimetres from her earlier, this was strangely more intimate. And it was an intimacy she hadn't experienced – hadn't allowed – since Seb. She had lost count of the number of times Margot had tried to set her up with a son/colleague of one of her business contacts and she could only count on one hand the people she had reluctantly agreed to have coffee with so there would be some respite before the next forced meeting. But, she guessed, this was an enclosed situation too. A wedding she was a bit-part at, in a foreign country, another Margot arranged event. Except it had been her choice to get on the back of Akis's motorbike. And, somehow, despite food and conversation, she still didn't know why he had been in that church in costume...

She moved then, towards the gate and the security guard, passing through and making her way towards the hotel entrance. Tiredness was definitely overwhelming her now and she couldn't wait to sink into those fresh sheets and enjoy the air-conditioning. But the second she pressed the key card to open the door someone grabbed the handle and prevented her progress.

'Cara, is that you?'

Margot.

'Yes,' Cara whispered. 'Of course it's me. I'm the only other person with a key for the room... right?'

'Did you not get my message?'

'Can't I just come in? I don't want to wake everyone else up.' She gave the door a push but was met with more resistance.

'Room 115.'

'What?'

The door was partially opened, a mere crack, but there was Margot's face.

'All your things. They've been moved to Room 115. I mean, what was I thinking sharing a room anyway? You deserve your own space to relax... Stop it!'

Cara frowned. What was going on? Was someone in their room with Margot?

'Room 115, darling. I will see you for breakfast.'

With that said, the door was slammed shut and Cara swore she could hear giggling.

15

IRINI'S HOME, NOTOS

'Is she dead? Please tell me she is not dead, because if she is then that is another sign that my marriage will be unlucky.'

'Shut up, Cosmo. I cannot hear a thing.'

Akis knew that his grandmother wasn't dead, could see the shallow rise and fall of her chest, but her breathing *was* a little noisy. Either it was a very deep sleep or she had another chest infection. He leaned in closer.

'Wren has made good luck chickens and voodoo dolls. What am I supposed to think about that? One thing to wish for good things to happen, the other to make bad things happen to anyone or anything that even thinks about bad things happening.'

'Cosmo, please!'

Pig brayed and nudged Akis's hip. Then his tail hit a stack of magazines and they all tumbled to the floor like a toppled Jenga mountain.

Suddenly, Irini opened her eyes and sat bolt upright. 'Am I dead?'

'Thank you, God! Thank you!' Cosmos said, eyes to the ceiling, hands together in prayer.

'*Yiayia*, you are OK. Would you like a drink?' Akis asked, supporting her back and using one hand to plump up pillows, cushions and apparently several more magazines in the bed.

'Yes,' Irini answered. 'I would very much like another vodka.'

'What did she say?' Cosmos asked.

'She said she would very much like a coffee,' Akis said. 'And I would like some too. Could you make it? And take Pig out of here.'

'What should I do first? Take Pig or make coffee?'

Akis looked at his brother. Turmoil was written in his expression, as if instead of asking for a few manageable tasks, he had demanded that Cosmos compete in *Survivor* – whilst running for prime minister at the same time.

'Leave Pig alone,' Irini ordered.

'Make the coffee,' Akis said.

'I will make the coffee,' Cosmos repeated, heading out of the bedroom and into the kitchen.

Akis sat down on the edge of his grandmother's bed. 'What time did you get home?'

'I do not know. Ask Pig.' She pulled a sparkly hair clip from her hair.

'Did you come home with Anastasia and my mother?'

Irini laughed then. 'Your mother? Have someone like me in her precious black Mercedes that looks like it belongs to a member of a drug trafficking family? Or squeezing up beside me in a taxi? Sharing the same air. I do what I always do. I call Yiannis. He come. I do not know what time.'

'I think I need to thank Yiannis. Offer him some cash for fuel.'

Irini snorted. 'I pay Yiannis with my cooking. He does not eat well since his wife died.'

'But, *Yiayia*, you do not cook.'

'I do not cook for one person! What is the point of that! When I make something for Yiannis and his sister I make something from scratch. And it is none of your business! What are you doing here anyway?'

'Pig came to the house again. Cosmos thought you were dying. He called me.'

Irini shook her head, pulling the bedcovers off and trying to swing her nightdress-covered legs out of the space. 'I am surprised I did not wake up to a priest... but then again. That is exactly how you were dressed last night.' She smiled. 'I found it very entertaining. It took me right back to when you were five years old, singing Elvis songs in my garden, dressed only in your underpants.'

'Please do not tell that story in public.'

'OK, leave now, help your brother with coffee, I want to get dressed.'

Akis stood up and took hold of Pig's collar.

'Leave Pig. He likes it when I use him for balance.'

Akis patted the donkey on the neck and made his way out of the bedroom.

'This place, it is a mess,' Cosmos complained when Akis had joined him. He had a cloth in one hand and the coffee pot in the other and seemed to have not started making anything at all.

'You sound like our mother,' Akis said, taking the coffee pot from Cosmos's hands.

'In this case she is not wrong.'

'She *is* wrong,' Akis snapped. '*Yiayia* has a lot of things. Things she loves. That's what she wants to be surrounded by. It is an untidy host of memories, that's all.'

'Why are you shouting at me?' Cosmos asked, eyes tearing up. 'You know I don't like it when you shout at me.'

'Cosmo, come on. What's wrong?'

And then his brother burst into tears. Loud sobs like the world was about to be destroyed. Cosmos was the youngest sibling, had always been the most emotional, babied by their mother, almost terrified of life itself from the second he arrived. Akis always remembered sending his army cars flying over ravines and Cosmos worrying for the plastic doll passengers.

He put a hand on his brother's shoulder and guided him from the space to outside. There was a slight breeze this morning, moving the eucalyptus and olive trees on his grandmother's land.

'Tell me, what is going on with you?'

'A wedding! You know that!' Cosmos exclaimed, hands almost tearing at his curls.

'Yes, I do know that but, Cosmo, it is meant to be the happiest day of your life. You get to commit to Wren who you have loved for the longest time now.'

'I know... I know... but what will I do when Wren becomes bored with me and has an affair with Milo? I see how he looks at her. The way he passes over the bread each morning. There is something behind his eyes, you know. Or what if one day Wren dies? What do I do then? I mean—'

'Cosmo, Cosmo, take a breath,' Akis said, taking his brother's hands out of his hair. 'And stop pulling like that or you will have no hair left for the wedding.'

'And Wren will not love me without hair. Milo has strong hair.'

'Cosmo, you are catastrophising without any reason for it. And I expect Milo just has a stye or something. I have never seen anyone more in love than you and Wren. She only has her eyes on you.'

Akis swallowed. Well, Wren did have her hands on Horatio last night, but he also knew Anastasia would have pumped her full of alcohol to loosen her up and what woman didn't have her hands full of something on her hen night? This was something his brother did not need to know.

'And then there is you refusing to become a priest. *Mama* says that if you do not do this, the wedding will be doomed from the outset and we may not be able to have children.'

For fuck's sake. This was getting out of control.

'Cosmo,' Akis said, his tone laced with anger. 'That is a wicked thing for *Mama* to say. Nothing is going to happen to you and Wren if I don't become a priest.'

If? He needed to be clearer about this. He went to make that statement but Cosmos beat him to the next word.

'That is not what the scriptures say. And I have done online research. Where there is this history of the first-born son becoming a priest, if the tradition is not followed, the families have experienced all kinds of trauma. One family had to leave their village because frogs moved in. Not just into their home, the entire village was besieged by a plague.'

Akis shook his head. He didn't believe this shit. 'So, what happened?'

'What do you mean?' Cosmos asked. 'You want frogs to swallow up Notos? I hate frogs.'

Right now, Akis wouldn't mind a giant toad opening its mouth for their mother.

'What happened to the village?' he asked. 'When the disobedient first-born son didn't become a priest and they all had to leave, what happened next? Did the frogs follow them from place to place? Wherever they settled more frogs would come? Or did they have bad luck in other ways? Did any of the frogs become lethal and hop into the first-born son's ear, poison him and then eat his brain while he slept?'

'Aki!' Cosmos exclaimed, putting his hands over his ears like he used to when he was a child and was uncomfortable with loud noises. 'Don't say that!'

'You don't know what happened. Because even if the first part of the story is true in some tiny way, no one followed it through. I expect everyone was fine. I don't even believe the frogs were brought by anything but the rain. If this was Skripero they would have given thanks and eaten them all.'

'Please, Aki. Please become a priest. You do not have to do it forever. You can even get married. Well, you can marry before you are ordained so there wouldn't be much time but—'

'Are you hearing yourself, Cosmo? You are asking me to give up my life for a fable with no substance, become a priest, not marry unless I find someone in what – a week? It's insanity!'

'So that Wren and I can have children,' Cosmos reminded him.

'This is *Mama* in your head, Cosmo! Like she tries to be in all our heads! Like she tells Anastasia not to bring a girlfriend home! Like she tells our father what to think and feel! Like she doesn't care at all for *Yiayia*!'

'But I want to have children. I have always wanted to have children. And Wren would be a wonderful mother.'

Akis couldn't stay here any longer. This was a nightmare. His family was a nightmare. And it was exactly this kind of drama that had had him moving out of the village and making a home in Corfu Town. How could he possibly have thought he could be any part of this? Be Cosmos's best man. He turned on his heel and strode towards his motorbike.

'Aki! Where are you going? You know we have the cake and wine tasting this afternoon! Aki! Please!'

Akis put his helmet on, started the engine and hoped that the sound would drown out his brother's pleas.

16

SOFIA DIAKOS'S HOME, NOTOS

'Looks like she went to town with the rustic stone,' Margot announced. 'Very *Grand Designs*.'

They had left their taxi and started to approach the driveway, towards a very impressive villa that could have come straight out of the pages of an overseas home magazine. Cara was still damp from the pool at Cook's Club. When Margot had eventually surfaced for breakfast, it was close to any normal person's lunchtime and there had been little explanation as to why Cara had had to have a new room in the middle of the night. Although she wasn't stupid. She knew Margot had taken a man back to the hotel, but why hadn't she simply booked another room for herself instead of making Cara swap?

Having glided their way through a sumptuous brunch they'd headed to the pool and it was only when Cara decided to dry off and sunbathe that Margot had announced they were leaving for another wedding-related activity...

'Is this where the wedding is going to be?' Cara asked.

'No! Don't be silly, darling! It will be much grander than this. Likely a beautiful hotel with sea views, Sofia's son and that Wren person dangling off the edge of an infinity pool with ships passing by in the background.'

'But doesn't it say where it's going to be on the invitation?'

'Why do you keep focussing on this invitation?' Margot snapped, narrowly avoiding the edge of a blooming cactus plant.

'Because I haven't seen it, I don't know when the wedding is, or *where* it is and I didn't know the bride and groom's names until last night.'

'Well, you're only the plus one, Cara. Let me worry about the details,' Margot said, forging on.

Only the plus one. Well, that had certainly put her in her place. She took a second to look some more at the house and its impressive garden as Margot went, all arms outstretched, greeting the group of people up by the front entrance. It was the kind of place she had always admired online or on TV, the type of home that she might have been able to buy with one royalty cheque if her singing career had been what she had been led to believe it would be. Instead, Yodi the dog was most probably sleeping on a Simba mattress in a pet house modelled exactly like this. He probably even had his own car...

'*Yassas*.'

Cara jumped, almost as much as she had when Yodi had invaded the stage. It was Akis wearing another pair of jeans – black this time – and a grey slim-fit T-shirt that skimmed over every contour.

'Do not worry, I am not going to get you under a spotlight again,' he told her.

'Well, I'm hoping, as it's a cake and wine tasting, there won't *be* any kind of stage.'

'And you do not know my mother at all.'

'How many people are coming to taste the cake and wine?' Cara asked as they walked up the driveway together, grasshoppers leaping from the concrete back to the well-tended plants as they passed. 'I thought it was usually something only the bride and groom did.'

'As I said, you do not know my mother. Wren and Cosmos had a private tasting to *shortlist* the tasting for today. And that was after my mother and her friends had curated the longlist.'

'Wow,' Cara said. 'That is dedication to wine and cake.'

'You like wine and cake?' Akis asked her. 'Perhaps more than Greek beer and seafood?'

'I guess we're about to find out.'

'You go ahead,' he said, stopping short of the steps that led to the front porch. 'I only have an invitation from my brother, not my mother so...'

'So?'

'So I will wait until Cosmos plucks up the courage to tell my mother that he wants my opinion on wine and cake and—'

'Aki! *Ela! Ela! Parakalo!*'

'OK. I will take that as my invitation.'

'Who is that?' Cara asked, looking at the man waving his hands as if he was in a crowd at a football match.

'That is my father, Thanasis. Otherwise known as my mother's slave. As children we thought there was something wrong with his neck because he could only nod, never shake to say no. Then we realised.'

'Oh.' Cara didn't really know what to say to that.

'Am I selling this afternoon with my family to you? Can you not wait to be involved?'

'Well, let's hope the shortlist of wine and cake is good,' she said, heading on.

* * *

'Do you prefer this one, Cosmo? Drink.' Sofia put a glass to Cosmos's lips and tipped it a little as if he was incapable of doing so himself. 'Or this one?' The first glass was taken back and another planted in its place.

'I like the first one,' Wren told her.

'I know,' Sofia said. 'You have said this already. Many many times. I am asking Cosmo.'

Cosmos mis-swallowed and wine dribbled down his chin.

'Cosmo! You are wasting it!' Sofia exclaimed, standing up and taking the glass away.

Akis shook his head and swigged from the bottle of beer his father had given him. This whole banqueting table in the garden was like a setting for a wedding itself. Pristine white tablecloths, crystalware, ice buckets, flowers around the pergola, even the stray cats were sat in an orderly pile barely in view.

'This one here is particularly divine,' Margot said, hoisting the bottle out of a cooler and holding it aloft.

'See! My friend, Margot, knows an excellent wine,' Sofia announced. 'Anastasia! Get off your phone and pay attention.'

Akis didn't really know why he was here. His mother didn't want him here, his father was using him only to hide behind or occasionally send a knowing look to, Anastasia was glued to Instagram, his brother was doing his usual weak routine and Wren was never going to make his mother listen to her. The others were like confetti to this event, there to add colour, yet superficial and ultimately unnecessary except to praise his mother's organisational skills. But then there was Cara. The only member of this gathering he didn't yet have a read on. She had tasted each cake but made no comment. She had sipped a few of the wines... and then she had discreetly plucked a white rose from the vine and picked every single petal apart, crushing each one in her palm.

'I want Akis to taste this one,' Cosmos moaned, wiping his mouth with a napkin.

'I am not a connoisseur of wine,' Akis answered immediately.

'Nonsense!' Sofia replied. 'And you will definitely need the practice. Everyone knows that priests know good wine.'

Akis's blood chilled. It was one thing for his mother to make these declarations to him, or in front of the immediate family, but now she was saying this to a large party, making it public knowledge. He fixed his expression to neutral and rubbed his fingers up the stem of his wine glass. If he reacted he was only going to add credence to this priest ambition his family had for him.

'Sofia, I need you to check something in the kitchen.'

It was his father.

'Nothing needs looking at in the kitchen, Thanasi.' She poured a very small amount of wine into Akis's glass.

'No, please, I think something... is on fire.'

Sofia dropped the wine bottle to the table and went rushing off, Thanasis at her back.

'What do you think of this wine?' Cosmos asked. 'Is it not like the one that *Yiayia* used to make?'

Akis took a sip of the cherry-coloured liquid and immediately he was taken back to Irini's kitchen, cutting up figs, kumquats, oranges and all kinds of berries to make a concoction that would keep the villagers inebriated for another year. His brother was right.

'I agree,' Akis said quietly. 'But I know how expensive this wine is. If you tell *Mama* it tastes like the wine *Yiayia* used to make there is no way you will be allowed to have it at your wedding.'

* * *

'This is a performance, isn't it?' Margot said, a wry smile on her lips as she lit another cigarette.

'I thought you liked this kind of thing,' Cara replied. 'Isn't it why we're here?'

'It is,' Margot agreed. 'To remember how the other half do things.'

'What do you mean?'

'Well, how hard people try to, you know, be something they're not.'

'Margot, I think that's a bit—'

'At college, Sofia always needed to be one tier higher than anyone else. Or at least think she was. The rest of us just existed as we were. And all these extra wedding events that aren't really needed, it's just extravagance for extravagance's sake. Amusing, really.'

This was the side of Margot that Cara didn't like very much. It was a cruel side, a side that wanted others to feel inferior. Sometimes she wondered if that was how Margot might have made her mother feel when they were growing up. Perhaps that treatment might have made someone want to spend their time travelling the world, having no fixed abode, being very much in charge of their own path, bucking some of society's norms.

Cara knew exactly what she was going to say next.

'Who did you bring back to the hotel room last night?'

'What?' Margot gasped.

'Well, was it a one-night thing or do you think it will be a whole-Corfu-stay thing like the week in Milan with Giovanni?'

Margot frowned as if Cara had spoken the question in a language she didn't understand. 'Who's Giovanni?'

Cara sighed. This was Margot in full-on childish confusion mode. She played that card a lot in the boardroom. It always seemed to lull people into a false sense of security, made them drop their guard and think that Margot was a lesser opponent when it came to brokering deals. Then her aunt capitalised on their poor decision-making and struck the killer business blow.

'You actually never said where you disappeared to last night,' Margot said, turning the tables.

Cara smiled. 'No, I didn't.'

'Not that I disapprove. I was delighted you absconded really. So nicely out of character.'

Cara plucked another rose head from the bush and pulled off the first petal.

'Would you like a cigarette?' Margot asked, offering the packet. 'Save the nature. Your mother would be starting a fundraiser if she could see you doing that.'

'Cara! Anastasia says she forgot to ask you last night! What colour is your dress for the wedding?'

Cara baulked as all eyes landed on her. She crushed the rest of the rose head in her hand, hiding it in her palm. 'I... am not sure.' And why did the mother of the groom need to know what a plus one of an old college friend was going to be wearing?

'It is peach,' Margot piped up, stubbing her cigarette out into a bowl of what looked like potpourri. She was making a habit of that.

Cara turned a little in her chair, looking at Margot. Why was her aunt deciding what dress she was going to wear? Yes, the peach-coloured one was really nice, but she did have other ones with her, and she was someone who looked out of the window or on a weather app before making a final outfit choice.

'Peach?' Sofia said, coming closer. 'What is "peach"?'

'Like the fruit,' Margot continued, getting to her feet. 'You Greeks probably call it something else. Something with lots more letters. Let's go inside and I will find you something in your beautiful house that is close to the colour.'

Cara watched Margot slip her arm through Sofia's and attempt to draw her away from the table and her guests. Cara recognised this Margot move. This was the separation technique. You went in and removed someone from the pack either to continue negotiations on a one-to-one level, or to detach an aggressor, someone who had the ability to turn the group's thinking in opposition to your goals.

'We do not need to go anywhere,' Sofia said, unlinking herself from Margot and looking confused. 'You will find this peach on your phone and I can see the colour.'

A hand went on Cara's shoulder then and she looked up to see Anastasia standing by her seat.

'My mother takes colour coordination to a whole new level. The bridesmaids are having a spectrum of blue and each one of them has to remember to stand in the correct order throughout the event.'

'Wow,' Cara answered. 'But, I'm not really part of the event in that way. No one is going to be looking at my dress.'

'I am sure they will look as well as listen,' Anastasia said, sweeping a wine glass from the table and drinking the dregs of the contents.

Cara momentarily froze. 'I don't understand.'

'Cara, there will be plinths with balloons on the stage,' Sofia called. 'Will that be an issue for you? I was not sure how much room you needed, if you, you know, were one of those people who walked up and down and around or whether there was some kind of dance routine.'

I am sure they will look as well as listen. Dance routine. She was starting to be deeply concerned at these comments.

All the guests seemed to have paused their cake-eating and were looking at her, waiting for a response, small forks suspended.

'Balloons are... fine?' She didn't know what else to say because she didn't know what was going on. But Margot seemed a little flustered, like she might know exactly what was going on.

'We are all so excited you agreed to be the wedding singer at such short notice! It is going to be an incredible day!'

Wedding singer.

As an icy shard stabbed at her stomach, Margot caught her eye and then joined in with the other guests as they applauded.

The applause. The lights. The cameras. Yodi. Seb.

Cara got to her feet. She needed to escape.

17

The heat was stifling, here in the grounds of Sofia and Thanasis's home where there wasn't even any shade amid the olive trees. Cara took a long, slow breath and held it tight inside as she found something else to focus on. She strode on. This area of the garden didn't look as tightly managed as the area of patio where the cake and wine tasting was taking place. Here, nature was the CEO and the branches of the trees didn't look curated, instead growing out at all angles, wildflowers scattered at the foot of their trunks. The cicadas were loud, like an almost comforting white noise, but with each tree Cara got close to, the chirping would get quieter, then if she touched her fingers to the bark, it would stop completely. Could they see her? Sense her? Did they know how terrified she currently was?

'Like magic, isn't it?'

Cara jumped at the sound of the voice, exhaled loudly and drew her hand away from the tree. It was Akis. Again.

'Are you following me?' she asked him.

'Always? Or on this occasion?'

'Maybe an answer for both?'

'Always. No. Right now, totally yes.' He smiled. 'I thought you could use a friend.'

'I'm fine.' She wasn't. Her chest hurt, as though something heavy was pressing down on it.

'I think not. You performed a manoeuvre I have performed many times over. Exiting the formal outside dining space, jumping over the wall into this wilder space.'

'I didn't jump over the wall. I went down the path.'

'Crazy,' Akis said, shaking his head. 'Jumping over is much quicker.'

She didn't know what to say.

'Listen, Cara, my mother, she can get – what is the word? – too enthusiastic and it can become overwhelming. I get it.'

'Well, she's organising a wedding. I believe that's meant to be more stressful than moving house or childbirth.'

'I do not know of childbirth but moving house... it is OK as long as you do not have too many things. Like a piano.' He took hold of her hand then and placed it back on the tree trunk. He rested his hand on hers, pressing it gently in place. 'Let us keep still and focus.'

'Is this a game?'

'Ssh.'

It was hard to keep still and focussed when her hand was being held to the bark by a guy with eyes that could win a beautiful eye contest, whose touch was currently making her insides prickle with heat. And she didn't know what she was being still or focussed for. The *cicadas* on this tree were silent now as if, in a tribute to her, *they* were holding their breath.

'Do you feel it?' Akis whispered.

'I'm not sure what I'm supposed to be—'

'Look,' Akis whispered again. 'There it is. Hiding in that hole in the trunk.'

He motioned with his head to a hollow in the tree and all Cara could see at first was darkness, a small net of cobwebs covering over it like a veil. But then something popped up its head. Large round-tipped ears, big beady eyes and a small pointy face.

'It's a mouse,' Cara exclaimed quietly.

'It makes a perfect house, no? Quiet, calm, insulated, no one around.'

It did sound perfect. A haven. No one knew you were there, but you were safe, invisible, going about your life your way without any preconceptions, without anyone interfering. Except she had given Margot free rein on interfering when she'd given up being able to make her own decisions. She wished she was stronger.

'But it's small,' Cara answered him. 'Where would you put your piano?'

He smiled. 'That is a very good point.'

It was then Cara really realised that even though she was looking into the eyes of a mouse, she was a tiny bit calmer...

'You cannot be a mouse though,' he continued. 'Or, rather, you cannot be what people perceive a mouse to be.'

'Cute and furry? Likes cheese? I feel a little called out.'

'I simply meant, unlike the small seeds when it comes to decisions, you should want your life to be the opposite. Big! Huge! Like as big as the Earth.'

He had raised his voice and the mouse ducked down and disappeared back into the hole out of sight.

'I heard this saying once. It was, "Life isn't short, it is wide." It stuck with me because, well, we all worry about making our lives as long as possible. We want to live until we are over one hundred years old, yet even if we all *did* live that long, think of the time that would get wasted. Is it not better to know that however long we have, we have the opportunity to make it as wide and as full as we can?'

Cara turned her attention away from the mousehole and looked at Akis. Who was this guy with these life philosophies and the most amazing eyes? It was only then she realised he still had his hand over hers.

As if he had just realised it too, he broke the connection and put both his hands into the pockets of his jeans.

'So, do you want to talk about it?' he asked, scuffing the dry grass with his trainers.

'Talk about what?'

'Well, I'm guessing you didn't have any idea that you had been booked to sing at the wedding.'

Cara sighed, bubbles of nervousness peppering her insides again.
'No.'

'So, do you want to talk about it?'

She shook her head.

'Well, I might have something to change your mind. Something I do
not like talking about but would be willing to share with you if you want
to trade?'

Was she intrigued enough to ask? Could she really tell him anything
about singing? She didn't know.

'Come on,' he said, a cajoling energy to his tone. 'I promise what I am
going to tell you will be worth the exchange.'

'You play piano, you dance for money, you love seafood. I'm
wondering what else you can fit in.'

'I told you,' he said, grinning. 'Life is wide.'

She shook her head, smiling. 'OK, you can tell me. But I only promise
to tell you something if I think what you've told me warrants it. If it's
good enough.'

'You are going to judge it? Maybe give it points?'

'Well, I didn't mean it quite like that.' And now she felt bad.

He smiled. 'It is OK. I am confident it will score high.'

She watched him take a deep breath and, for the first time, she
noticed a change in his demeanour, a kind of nervousness invade his
shoulders.

'OK, so, are you ready?' He paused before carrying on. 'So, according
to the tradition of my family, I am expected to join the church by
becoming a Greek Orthodox priest before I am thirty years old.'

This wasn't real. It couldn't be. And he had form for pretending he
was a priest – taking her confession, dancing dressed as one. She wasn't
going to be falling for this.

'Well,' she said. 'That would score good points if it was actually true,
but when we met you were pretending to be a priest so—'

He sighed. 'If the first-born son of a Diakos does not become a priest
before he is thirty, the legend is that something terrible will happen to
the whole family. Death. Destruction. Famine. Poverty. Or things that
could be worse than that. My mother, she would have me ordained today

if she could, because she thinks my not being part of the clergy will curse the wedding and cause Wren and Cosmos the inability to have children. And, believe me, neither Wren nor Cosmos are characters to feed that kind of worrying information to. So, what do I do? Do I believe these stories from the past? Let them and other people decide what my life is, to protect the people I love or, do I not?'

His tone was deadly serious and Cara could see it in his eyes. This was something he was really, really battling with. This wasn't a story, this was his truth. There was only one question she needed to ask first.

'Akis?'

'Yeah.'

'How old are you?'

He looked straight at her and paused for just a second before he gave a knowing nod. 'I'm twenty-nine.'

18

DIAKOS FAMILY CHAPEL, NOTOS

When Akis veered his motorbike off the road and down onto hay-like grass, zipping between olive trees, Cara did worry for a second that he had either lost control of the vehicle or lost control of his mind. However, only a few minutes later they were pulling up alongside a tiny white building, paint peeling from its domed roof. It was the only thing around apart from the trees, grass the colour of straw that was up to Cara's knees and a rather random piece of farming machinery thick with rust.

'Here it is,' Akis said, spreading his arms out wide as they approached the building. 'My potential place of work.'

'This is a church?' Cara asked. 'It's so small.'

'Which is why Cosmos and Wren are not getting married here. It is not big enough or grand enough for my mother.'

'It is beautiful though,' Cara said, stepping closer and wondering about the history soaked in the stone.

'I used to think so too,' Akis said. 'When I was around six years old and I didn't know my fate was wrapped up here. We used to light candles and try to cook corn over them. Pig was born here.'

'A pig gave birth inside the church?'

He laughed then. 'Sorry, Pig, it is the name of my grandmother's donkey.'

'So, a donkey gave birth in the church?'

'Yes,' Akis said. 'Now you want to see inside even more, yes?'

The key was in the lock and he turned it, then pushed at the old metal door. It creaked open and Cara followed Akis inside. It was dark, small arched windows, one either side, not really letting in any light. But then he flicked on a switch and Cara gasped. The room lit up and right away, the first thing that struck her were the frescos painted on the wall. Some were worn away with age, their edges bleeding from the plaster, but others, including those on the ceiling, were beautifully intact. All colours had been used – reds, golds, blues – and they were mainly figures – saints she presumed – holding scriptures or other religious artefacts.

'Say hello to my ancestors,' Akis said, indicating the murals. 'The good ones at least. The ones who did become priests.'

'Will they paint you on the wall?' Cara asked.

'Only if I become a priest.' He moved one of the dozen or so chairs squeezed into the space. 'Shall we sit?'

She joined him, plumping herself down onto a quite small wooden chair with fraying ropes bound together to form the seat.

'So,' Akis said, looking at her. 'Now it is your turn. To tell me why you needed to run from the cake and the wine. What concerns you about singing? Unless you are a very bad singer. But I cannot believe my mother would not have asked for audition tapes even if this was a late arrangement. We had Placido Domingo booked, you know.'

Cara smiled but already her heart was palpitating. This was on Margot. She'd known there was something off, something more about this flying to Corfu for a wedding.

'I wish Placido had been able to make it.'

'Really?' Akis asked. 'Because I think the guy knows he's good, you know?'

She swallowed. She could tell him something. It didn't have to be everything. She could make a start. After all, he had told her about this awful priest dilemma. She owed him.

'I... do sing. *Did* sing. I haven't, for a while.' That was enough.

'Why? What happened?'

Of course he would ask.

She shook her head and looked into the soulful eyes of one of the paintings – a sad-looking man holding a baby. 'What happened' was only two words but somehow it was one of the biggest sentences of all. *So much had happened.*

'Did anyone die?' Akis asked her. 'I mean, if someone did die then I apologise for bringing it up but—'

'No one died,' Cara answered.

'Then everything else can be resolved.'

'Says the guy who might have to become a priest.'

'Ouch.'

She took a deep breath; somehow his vibe gave energy *and* calm. It was a good mix. 'I had a bad performance.'

'One?'

'Yes.'

'Wow, OK, well, I do not want to ruin how special our show was for you last night, but there have been times I have fallen on my face and at least three times in the course of this summer run alone I have fallen on someone *else's* face.'

'I had a bad performance in front of over one hundred and fifty million people.'

She watched his eyes bulge and then he said one word. 'Fuck.'

'Almost the whole world was watching. That's pretty hard to come back from.'

She sighed, watching the dust motes dance in the small rays of sunlight coming through the bars of the windows.

'Not impossible though,' came Akis's reply.

'What?'

'Well, the way I look at things, it is only impossible if you lead your life worrying about what others think of you. If you do not care what others think of you then nothing is impossible. You might succeed. You might fail. But only your own opinion matters.'

She had never met anyone who looked at things the way he did. It was like he'd taken the rulebook of society and shredded all the pages. Except...

'But if only *your own* opinion matters, why don't you just tell your mother you don't want to be a priest?'

'I have,' Akis said. 'I tell her every time she brings the subject up.'

'So, you have made your decision not to be one.'

'No.'

'Why not?'

'Because I love my family and whether I believe these tales of doom and gloom or not, there is a part of me that wonders if I lost my finger for a reason.' He stood up, putting his hands to the back of his head, elbows at right angles, and started to pace.

'What? I don't understand.'

'And if I believe that maybe I wasn't destined to play for a world-famous orchestra because of Cosmos's accident, then maybe being a priest *is* what I'm meant to do. Maybe it wasn't even an accident. Perhaps it was this curse starting early, paving the way.'

'What, like, divine intervention?'

'I don't know. I sound like a mad man right now.'

'Well, you've proved you can still play and it's powerful and beautiful and—'

He stopped pacing and turned back around to face her. 'It will never be good enough... in my own opinion.'

'Is that what it is?' Cara asked. 'You're going to be a priest to *punish* yourself? Because you lost a finger in what I'm sure was an accident? Because you don't think you're good enough to be whatever you want to be? What happened to life being wide?'

'My life has already been wide, Cara.'

'Right, so, that's it?' she asked, getting to her feet, feeling incensed by this turn of events. 'You're going to stop dancing? Stop playing the piano? Stop eating fish with your fingers and live in this chapel?'

She was close to him now and she was feeling *impassioned* about something. That never happened any more. Because she had lost her passion. Not just from her music. From her life.

'I do not have to live here in the chapel,' Akis told her.

'OK.'

'And I am pretty sure I can still play the piano a little.'

'Right.'

'And I can definitely eat fish with my fingers.'

She shrugged. 'I don't know what you want me to say.'

'I say that we make another pact.'

She shook her head. 'OK, I see where this is going.' She went to take a step backwards.

Akis took her hand and laced their fingers together. 'I think we put a little faith in each other. I will stop throwing myself a pity party and remember that even though I love my family and wouldn't want anything bad to happen to them, there are also many reasons why I live in Corfu Town.'

'And what do I have to do in this "pact"?'

'Oh, well, that is very simple,' Akis said, his smile returning. 'You will let me hear you sing.'

She shook her head and detached their hands. 'No.'

'But what if I promised it would only be me and maybe one other person?'

'Akis, I told you, I don't sing any more and now I find that my aunt has booked me to sing at a wedding, your *brother's* wedding, and the thought of that just makes me want to... makes me—' She was starting to feel the panic build, her chest tightening, and her words not coming.

The next thing she knew, Akis's lips were on hers and suddenly her head was spinning in an entirely new direction. It was fierce, yet not harsh, it was hot and passionate, yet also reassuring and comforting. And she was apparently indulging in it. What was she doing?!

She detached herself. 'Excuse me, but what was that?' She couldn't look him in the eye.

'That,' Akis said, 'was, of course, nothing but a technique often used in times of anxiety. A shock tactic. For you to realise that there are... worse things than letting me hear you sing.'

All she had heard was the word 'nothing'.

'So,' he carried on. 'Come, what is there to lose?' He smiled. 'And the other person I tell you about to listen? I would like you to meet Pig.'

Not a pig. His grandmother's donkey. Why was she hesitating about saying no? She didn't want to sing. She never sang any more. But, then again, she had never kissed a virtual stranger in a church by an olive grove before...

She took a deep breath and didn't think any more.

'OK.'

19

IRINI'S HOME, NOTOS

Akis sighed. He had kissed her. What had been going through his mind when he had done that? It hadn't been about her panic, well, not entirely, it had been a little about wanting to make her feel like her world wasn't imploding in that moment, but it had also been about how beautiful she was and how, for some unknown reason, she was everywhere right now and he was finding himself wanting to open up to her about pretty much everything. It was uncomfortable. He should be running in the opposite direction, but instead, he was stepping closer. And now he was stepping closer with a donkey's tether in one hand and an old keyboard under his arm.

Cara was standing in the garden, between the washing line drying his grandmother's large pants and aprons, and a collection of roof tiles his grandfather had always kept in case they might one day be needed. She was stroking a grey tabby kitten.

He shouldn't have taken advantage of her, that's what it felt like. He had stolen that kiss, with no warning, no prelude, it had been selfish.

She turned around.

'What is that?' she asked.

'I tell you, this is Pig,' Akis introduced. 'Pig, say *yassas* to my friend, Cara.'

Pig doffed his large head but made no sound.

'Hello, Pig,' Cara said. 'But, I was actually asking about that very ancient-looking keyboard under your arm.'

Akis let go of Pig and the donkey sauntered a few steps away and began to chew on the grass. 'Are you making a criticism of my first musical instrument?'

'I thought you said you were only twenty-nine. This thing looks too old to even accompany Placido Domingo.'

He laughed. 'It has a little dust, but everything still works. I have put in new batteries.'

'So what are you going to play for me?'

'Well,' Akis said, hands going into the grass and pulling out one of his *yiayia's* old fold-up chairs. 'I thought you could tell me a song and I could accompany you.'

'Well, I... you... aren't going to know what songs I can sing. I mean, no disrespect to your playing abilities but—'

'You doubt me. And here I was thinking we were friends.'

Friends. He had to stop emphasising that point. He had said the word twice in quick succession and he didn't go around kissing people he was friends with.

'I don't doubt your playing,' Cara answered, arms stiff by her sides. 'I'm just not really a Beyonce "Crazy in Love" kind of girl.'

'You think that I have a very small brain of songs?' He raised an eyebrow and turned on the keyboard. It made a terrible hiss that had Cara jumping as if she had stood on a snake. 'Sorry.'

He watched her recover from the scare.

'Well, what songs do you know?' she asked.

'What song do you want me to play?' he countered. He began to play a little fanfare and moved it into Frank Sinatra's 'My Way'.

She laughed. 'Not that.'

'OK, how about this one?'

He began to play something he thought she might know a little, Adele's 'Set Fire to the Rain'. He got through the intro without her saying it wasn't something she wanted to sing, but despite the audience being him and a donkey who had wandered off far enough not to be able to hear, she seemed to be terrified. And then she shut her eyes and as he played the introduction for a second time she finally came in.

Her voice was nervous to begin with, but as she managed to progress through the song and move towards the first chorus, that was when her tone gave him goosebumps. It sounded like it came from the depths of her, each breath producing soulful, perfect notes. Now it was him who was nervous, trying to make these cumbersome keys do what a piano could do but what a keyboard circa 1990 certainly didn't appear to be able to. But then suddenly she stopped, wide-eyed, her expression scared.

'Was that a dog I heard?' she asked.

'Sorry, I do not know,' he replied. 'I was focussed on listening to you and—'

'It was a dog, wasn't it?'

She was standing super still now, looking like she was trying to concentrate.

He got up, putting the keyboard on his chair and moved towards her. 'You do not like dogs?'

'Oh, well, they're OK, I just, you know, when they get too close.'

She was lying. He knew enough about body language to pick up that dogs were not only not her favourite animal, but that she was scared of them.

'The way some of them slobber,' he said, trying to lighten the atmosphere. 'Like they want to give you a bath. It is disgusting.'

'*Did* you hear it?' Cara asked him again.

'I am not certain. With the piano and—'

She put her hands to her head and sighed. 'Sorry, I shouldn't be here. I should be reminding my aunt that she should not be accepting bookings on my behalf or getting me on a plane under false pretences or basically any of the things she's done since we left London.'

'Or,' Akis began, 'you could actually sing at the wedding. I'm sure my mother will be paying much more than any sane person would. Not that you wouldn't be worth whatever she was paying and more. I didn't mean—'

'This was a mistake,' Cara said, turning away and looking like she was going to head back through the garden.

'No, Cara, wait, this wasn't a mistake.' He took hold of her arm, just enough to make her stop, and then he let go again. Because touching her was going to have to be off limits now he knew it made him a little crazy. She stopped.

'Your voice is incredible. I mean, it's next level. You don't sound... like anyone else.'

'No, because most singers wouldn't suddenly stop if they thought they heard a dog, would they?'

'Cara—'

'I have to go. Thank you, for trying, but if the only reason my aunt and I were even invited to the wedding was because your mother thought I was going to sing then I'm sorry I'm going to disappoint everyone.'

'Cara—'

'Goodbye, Akis.'

And with that final farewell, she was walking away from him.

20

COOK'S CLUB CORFU

'How long are you going to keep this silence up? Because it's very droll, Cara. Rather like the behaviour of a child. Your mother used to do something similar when she was young. She got this beady-eyed stare, would look at me like she was looking right through me and just brush the hair of one of her awful second-hand dolls.' Margot sniffed. 'They call it preloved these days, don't they? Making old, grubby things sound like people actually cared for them. I don't understand it at all.'

In her head, as she was ignoring her aunt in the air-conditioned comfort of their room while she got dry from her shower, Cara was actually running through all the things she was going to do *alone* tonight. She was going to walk out of the hotel and see what nearby Gouvia had to offer. There was a marina apparently and a beach and even a little church in the bay. She would spend some time regrouping and reflecting on her short but packed-to-the-brim-like-a-Maxi-Go time here. She didn't even want to be in this room with Margot but apparently the room she had slept in last night was no longer hers to have. Cara wouldn't put it past her aunt to have paid up for the one night just so she had to come back to the shared one.

'You have to start somewhere, Cara, you know that, don't you? Whether it's at this wedding or it's not. This can't be you forever. You're a singer. You sing. That's just how it is. I know I've kept you away from that for a while now and I thought I was doing the right thing, giving you time to heal, but I didn't honestly think it was going to take this long. So—'

'Stop it!' Cara hissed. 'Stop talking now.' She rubbed at her hair with the towel.

'Good,' Margot said, smiling. 'Good, getting that anger out is an excellent starting point. I can work with that.'

'This is not a negotiation!' Cara exclaimed. 'I am not some deal you're desperately trying to land. I'm your niece. Who you have lied to. About this wedding. About the whole reason we're here.'

'Not exactly,' Margot said. 'There are many reasons why we've ended up here, it's not all to do with a little wedding gig Sofia's trying to get on the pages of *Hello! Greece*.'

'Well, what other reason is there? Other than to set me up for more humiliation, that is.'

'That's negative thinking, Cara. One of your therapists was bound to have mentioned that. I have, instead, presented you with an opportunity. A fantastic, yet small-scale opportunity in a country where probably the least amount of people know about your past. And on one of its islands too, not centre stage at the Parthenon.'

Negative thinking. People used that phrase too often. It made *you* the problem, not the anxiety. As if *you* were in charge of what was happening to you. It wasn't as simple as that.

'I wouldn't care if it was the tiniest stage at the back of a pub,' she shot back, 'I can't sing in front of an audience. I can't even sing the whole of an Adele song in front of one man and a donkey apparently!'

When silence cloaked the room Cara knew she had made a mistake and there was no point in trying to backtrack. Margot was off the chair she'd been sitting in and prowling closer.

'You sang!' Margot announced. 'You said "the whole of an Adele song" which means you sang *something*.'

Margot's voice was full of praise as if Cara was a toddler who had eaten two carrots so could now leave the rest of her dinner. She shook her head.

'Did you sing in front of Sofia's son? The hot one who makes his money taking his clothes off? The one who was getting rather energetic with you at the hen night? I saw him leave the table after you. Well, what did he think?'

'Currently he thinks I'm hearing things in my head.'

'I was asking about your voice.'

'It doesn't matter what he thinks about my voice, this wedding singer thing is not going to happen! And not only that, why the hell did you not say anything about this before we came here?'

'Why do you think? Because if I had said something you wouldn't have got on the plane!'

'You got that right!'

'For God's sake, Cara, stop towelling your hair like that, you're going to ruin it!'

Margot snatched the towel from her hands and threw it onto the bed.

'It's my hair and I will ruin it if I want to! See! My small seed, my decision!'

'What are you talking about? Honestly, it's sounding more mumbo jumbo by the minute.'

There was no easy way to make this stop and have an outcome that was healthy for both of them. Cara had two choices: she either gave Margot more of the silent treatment now she had made it clear she wasn't going to be singing at the wedding, or she steered the conversation. She picked up her hair brush and began to comb.

'Is there something going on with the business that you haven't told me about?'

'What?' Margot asked. 'Why would you ask that? And what has it got to do with you singing at Sofia's wedding?'

She wanted to say it wasn't Sofia's wedding, it was Cosmos and Wren's wedding, but it was a pointless battle and she needed to adjust the focus.

'Well, I know the last time you were really worried about the business, when Go-Bag were making their foldable rucksacks, you put your head in the sand about it and found something else to focus on.'

'I came up with the Maxi-Go concept. It was hardly putting my head in the sand! I am not a head going into the sand kind of person, Cara. You should know that.'

'No, OK, but you are the kind of person who portrays outward calm when you're internally raging like a Spanish bull.'

There was just a flicker of change in her expression, which told Cara there *was* something else going on.

'I don't internally rage either, Cara,' Margot said in a soft, managed tone. 'If I need to vent some frustrations – and note I said "frustrations" rather than "rage" – then I will organise a game of squash followed by a deliciously no-strings-attached vigorous night with someone I will never see again.'

Cara smiled. 'And wasn't that exactly what you did last night?'

'I told you I do not wish to discuss last night. In fact, I'm quite bored of this whole conversation now, so I am going to go to the bar and should you wish to join me that is where I will be.'

Before Cara could say anything more, Margot had whisked herself out of their room and closed the door behind her.

Cara couldn't quite believe what had just happened. Now it seemed that the tables had been turned and she was somehow the one in the wrong. But what she *did* know, from Margot's behaviour, was that this was not just about the wedding, there was definitely something else going on.

21

THEATRE BAR, CORFU TOWN

'It was another wild night, no?'

Horatio was wiping oil and shaving foam from his body as he talked. The night's dance show had just finished and they were getting cleaned up and changed.

'I have scratches along my shoulders,' Akis answered, checking out his wounds in the mirror.

Horatio laughed. 'Everyone wants a piece of The Deacon.'

Akis shook his head and rushed to get out of his costume.

'How was the wine and cake tasting today?' Horatio asked, beginning to take off his make-up.

'As organised and scheduled as the wedding will be. I was surprised my mother did not pay for a sommelier just to pour for her.'

'And Cara, was she there?'

Akis picked up his T-shirt and pulled it over his head, saying nothing.

'Oh my God,' Horatio remarked. 'You are ignoring me. This is bad. Or should I say, this is actually good. This is someone you are into.'

Akis shook his head again. 'No.'

And he offered his friend nothing more. Because how things had been with Cara when she had rushed from his grandmother's garden had been the very opposite of good. He had pushed her and she had retreated. Didn't he know exactly how that felt? You didn't back someone into a corner, even if you thought it was for their own good, because the second you did that you lost them. It was like taking away their decision-making, something she had confessed to him that she struggled with as it was.

'What, the eyes are not working for you?' Horatio asked.

'I am not playing, Horatio. And she is a guest at Cosmos's wedding, a wedding I still don't know if I'm going to be present at.'

'But you are the best man,' Horatio reminded him. 'The organiser of the bachelor party.'

'When it is something my mother is at the heart of, things could change by the hour. Actually, I take that back, they could change by the minute.'

'OK, so, we drink to forget tonight, yes? A little something to eat and then 54 Dreamy Nights?'

'Not tonight,' Akis said, doing up his jeans. 'I am going to find Cara.'

'Wait, what?' Horatio remarked, stopping mid eye-liner removal. 'But you said—'

'I didn't say anything,' Akis said. 'But things ended a little awkwardly and I want to smooth it over if we are to be wedding guests together.'

He wasn't going to mention to Horatio about the wedding singer issue.

'If your mother lets you join in.'

'Exactly.'

'So, you are? Going to call her, I mean?'

'I don't have her number,' Akis admitted.

'OK, so you are, what? Going to Cook's Club? To stand outside and hope she comes by?'

Akis thought about that sentence and then frowned. 'How do you know she is staying in Cook's Club?'

Horatio palmed his hands to the sky. 'Anastasia told me. She loves the DJ nights there. It is all she speaks about in the winter time, remember?'

'Right,' Akis said.

'OK, your plan is terrible. Give me one second and I will make a few calls. I will find out where she is.'

This was turning into something more than he had anticipated.

'Aki, go and get us both a drink and I will be two minutes.'

'Maybe this is a bad idea,' Akis said, having second thoughts. Couldn't he just wait until the next wedding event? Besides the bachelor night, there was the blessing of the snakes.

'No, this is a good idea. I have not seen you this full of anticipation since you auditioned for the orchestra.'

'And look how that turned out,' Akis said, waving his three-fingered hand.

22

GOUVIA MARINA

She had done it. Cara had left the hotel and she had followed simple road signs and now she was sitting at a bar/restaurant right next to the water in this upmarket marina, Margot left behind at the hotel. Tall masts made the skyline; boats and yachts that all had to be worth vast sums of money sat parked next to each other on the virtually motionless water. And within a minute she was thinking about Seb. He had loved the water – not to swim in, he hated that – but it was his dream to take after his father and own something you could power up the River Thames on or have sitting on its own mooring in the South of France. Cara had always thought that boats were trapping. Once you were on one, that was it until you got to the next piece of dry land. And the same went for the people you were travelling with – there was no escape for a walk or the ability to slip into another room. But looking at them now, she could see the beauty, the tranquillity their gentle movements provided. And, with a glass of Metaxa brandy in front of her, cubes of ice gently bobbing, there was no pressure to jump on board. It was like looking at a piece of art in a gallery and not feeling you needed to buy it for your home.

Breaking the peace a little, came the sound of a motorbike, which pulled to a stop by the edge of the water just ahead of her. She took a better look at the rider. Jeans, a T-shirt, and when he had removed his helmet, she saw the dark hair.

Akis. How did he know she was here? She swallowed, watching him put a hand through his hair. And why had she made the assumption he was here for *her*? He might simply have an interest in luxury yachts. Although he hadn't given her the impression it was something he might be into. From the way he talked about the expensive wedding, she got a 'disinterested in wealth' vibe from him. Maybe he was meeting a girlfriend. But, he had kissed *her*. And she hadn't really emotionally acknowledged that yet.

She turned a little on her seat, feeling suddenly as if someone had swung a spotlight on her.

'Can I sit?'

He wasn't here to see the luxury boats it seemed.

'I don't work here,' Cara answered. 'But I'm sure not all the tables are reserved.'

He smiled, pulling out the seat opposite her and sitting down. 'You are mad with me.'

'No,' she answered with a sigh. 'I am still angry with my aunt. Other than that I am only angry with one other person.'

'Pig?' Akis queried. 'Because I should have remembered that he is not a fan of Adele.'

She smiled. 'I'm not sure he stuck around long enough to really hear me murdering her.'

'Oh, come now, Cara, I think we both know that it was me who was murdering my relic from the Nineties.'

She couldn't help but laugh. He seemed to have a habit of breaking her down. It was like only this moment mattered; anything else was gone and forgotten about. If only all of life was that simple.

He put his hand in the air and a waiter arrived to take his order before disappearing again.

'How did you know I was here?' Cara asked, before sipping her drink.

'Would you believe me if I said divine intervention again?'

'You play the priest card a lot for someone who doesn't want to be one.'

'Wow, that is low,' he said, shaking his head. 'I tell you my secrets and you come back at me with them?'

'You came at me with an ancient old Yamaha in a field earlier.'

Now it was his turn to laugh. 'You are right.'

'And you still haven't told me how you really knew I was here.'

'I sense people,' Akis answered.

'I'm not buying it.'

'OK,' he said as his bottle of beer arrived. 'Well, let us just say that Corfu is a small island and my friend, Horatio, pretty much knows everyone.'

'And everyone knows who *I* am?' Cara asked, confused. 'I've been here two days.'

'What can I say? Before the world made CCTV, there were the Greek *yiayias*.'

It didn't sound as if that was an explanation she could argue with.

'So, I wanted to find you,' Akis began. 'To apologise. It was not my place to make you sing.'

'Well,' Cara said. 'You didn't force me to sing. It was my choice. And I got my answer that I'm not ready to do it in front of an audience.' She sighed. 'And if I know anything about my aunt, she won't want me to sing if I'm going to fail like the last time. Her reputation is everything to her.'

'No wonder she and my mother are friends. It sounds like their values are aligned. But, you know, again, reputation is nothing more than other people's opinions.'

And she already knew that he was a firm believer that other people's opinions didn't matter.

'What do *you* want to do with your future, Cara?'

The sincerity of his tone hit her hard. It was such a big question. She needed a minute.

'What do you mean?' she asked, buying time.

He smiled. 'What do you *think* I mean?'

'Well, maybe I shouldn't care how you mean it,' she said. 'Maybe I'll make whatever interpretation I like and answer it my way.'

He knocked his beer bottle against her glass and nodded. 'Now you are getting it.'

But what was her answer? Did she even have one? She swallowed. 'I don't know. Yet.'

'OK,' Akis responded.

She leaned forward in her seat, picking up her brandy glass and cradling it in her palm. 'I mean, singing was always what I loved to do. I never thought about doing anything else but then...'

'Then?'

'Well, naively I didn't realise how tough it would be and, to be honest, if I hadn't had something that stood out from the crowd, I probably wouldn't have made it as far as I did.'

She shivered. Now she had revealed more about herself than she had ever intended to. And she could see from his expression that he knew it.

'I am not going to ask,' Akis said, before she could carry on. 'But, you know, if you did decide to tell me more, it would be as secret as confessing to a priest.'

She smiled. Was there any point in backtracking now? Would it instead do her some good to simply be honest?

'I could... sing a note called a G10. It's the highest note ever to have been sung. In fact, it's not even really a note, it's referred to as a frequency.'

She swallowed and watched for his reaction. But his expression remained unchanged. He looked like he was listening intently and giving her space to add more.

'It's, you know, just a trick really. Like that one show-stopping moment everyone waits for at the end of a performance. A magician making someone levitate and turning them into dust. Or at the end of your show when all the dancers dropped through the floor. A split-second thing that makes people wow for a breath and then they move on.'

'And does everyone always ask you if you can break glass?' Akis asked.

'Usually they ask if I can summon dolphins.'

He laughed and then straight away put on a serious expression. 'And can you?'

'Well,' she said, keeping her own expression straight. 'I've never done it close to the water before.'

He got to his feet. 'You know what? We should do that.'

'What?' Cara asked.

'We should get on the water,' he said, beckoning. 'Bring your drink.'

'But... I haven't paid for it yet. I can't just leave.'

'Mario!' Akis called.

Cara watched the waiter turn around. A quick exchange in Greek and Akis was offering out his hand to her.

'So, all you have to tell me is that you can swim.'

'Well, I can swim but—'

'Let us find some dolphins.'

23

'Please tell me we haven't stolen our drinks,' Cara said as she tried to keep pace with Akis alongside the edge of the marina, water lapping softly at the floating pontoon they had dropped down onto.

'I will pay Mario when we get back. Do not worry. Ah, here we are. This one.'

Before Cara could say anything else, Akis had sprung on board a motorboat that looked like it could star in a commercial for any exclusive high-end brand. It was white and blue, all sleek lines and glossy paint-work, exactly like something Margot had once turned up on at the docks in Bristol.

'Please tell me we aren't stealing a boat,' she said, watching Akis do something clever with knots on ropes.

'Come on, Cara, where is your sense of adventure? That thick, width of life you speak of?'

'I don't remember saying anything about grand larceny!'

'I do not know those English words. It is a shame.'

'Akis!'

'Relax, Cara, your future maybe begins right here!'

She folded her arms across her chest. 'My future is not going to begin with getting arrested in a foreign country.'

He turned and faced her then, holding the rope in his hands. 'How sexy and dangerous does that sound, no?'

She swallowed. It *did* sound sexy and dangerous. It sounded like it belonged in someone else's life. Someone without anxiety. Someone who dived at life, not hid in the corner of a warehouse behind suitcases checking Seb's Instagram.

'It doesn't sound like the behaviour of a priest,' she replied.

'Then it is a good thing that there are no priests here.' He held out his hand.

'I'm not getting on this boat until you assure me we aren't stealing it.'

'I promise we are not stealing it,' he answered a little too quickly.

'Akis!'

'I am being honest with you, I swear. Now, give me your hand.'

She didn't know if she had offered her hand out but suddenly she was being pulled on board and she landed first on the padded seating and then stepped down onto the deck, the vessel swaying a little.

'OK, let me just find the key and we can get out of here,' Akis said, opening small doors in the panelling. 'Ah! Here it is!'

Cara gazed out over the other boats and realised how crazy this was. She was on a speedboat – possibly about to be a *stolen* speedboat – in Greece, looking at yachts that probably cost more than a substantial-sized home *and,* for the first time in a long time, Margot had no idea where she was. As the engine of the boat roared into life, she was struck with a pang of guilt. Perhaps she ought to check her phone. Margot might be worrying and she wouldn't want her to worry. She put her hand to the zip on the small bag that was over her shoulder, but then she had second thoughts. Margot had done something unforgiveable by saying she would sing at this wedding. Maybe an hour or so of wondering would pave the way to resetting some boundaries...

'Are you ready?' Akis called to her.

'You're making it sound like we're about to take off!' Cara said over the engine noise.

'Ah, well, there is a speed limit in the harbour but after that...'

'Akis!'

'Sit, relax, we do not need a high note to bring out the dolphins in Corfu.'

* * *

Akis hadn't driven a boat in so long. Why was he even doing it now? It was as if, with this priest curse hanging over him and ever since he had met Cara, suddenly he needed to grasp at everything he loved doing, like if he didn't it would all be lost to him. And then there was how Cara felt about life. That mind overworking all the time, the fear that took hold when she dared to place a toe over the line of her comfort zone. For some reason he wanted to show her everything he loved doing too.

He looked at her now, leaning up at the front, the humid breeze blowing through her hair as they rode through the water. This was both luxury and simplicity. It wouldn't matter to him what kind of boat they were on – this high-powered, expensive one or the smallest vessel with oars – being on the sea was pure escapism.

'Cara!' he called to her.

She turned her head, hands still gripping the rail.

'Do you want to take a turn at driving?'

'What?'

'I said, do you want to take a turn at driving the boat?'

'Oh no, that's OK. I don't have a licence to drive boats.'

'Neither do I,' he answered, slowing the engine.

'Are you joking?'

He laughed. 'Cara, come here. Drive the boat.'

He watched her carefully shift herself backwards until she could stand and then slowly she made her way towards him, until she was standing by the wheel.

'OK, so, all you have to remember is it is nothing like driving a car,' he said.

'I don't actually have a licence to drive a car either,' Cara replied.

'Wow, OK, well, maybe, in this case, it is an advantage for you.' He drew her forward, positioning her in front of the controls. 'So, all you have to do is very small movements, like tiny corrections. You keep your eyes in front of you and maintain your course and you make little adjustments with the wheel.'

'It's so dark,' Cara said. 'The sea and the sky.'

'But adjust your eyes. Everything else is brighter. The lights from the land, the stars above.'

'I can't look at the stars if I have to keep my eyes on our course,' Cara said, hands gripping the wheel.

'OK, I will look at the way. You look up at the stars.'

He watched her tilt back her head and look up.

'Oh, wow,' she gasped. 'I haven't seen anything like that before. It's like you can see every single star in the universe. It looks like... a map of diamonds.'

He held his breath, remembering he had said something so similar the first night his father had taken him and Cosmos out on his fishing boat. Cosmos was afraid they would catch a shark in the nets and refused to look at anything. Akis, on the other hand, had wanted to look at *everything*.

Suddenly, Akis realised he'd looked up too and that he hadn't been watching their direction. Adaptation was needed. He put his hands over Cara's and gently rotated the wheel a quarter turn and waited for the boat to settle.

'*Signomi*,' he said. 'Sorry, I was...'

'Looking at the stars,' she answered.

And there it was again, that tension beginning in his gut and quickly sliding south. Sexual definitely. But it was more than that. It was something inside him, recognising something inside her. He couldn't hold her hands any more and as he let go, so did she. He grabbed the wheel and she took a step back.

'Sorry,' Cara said. 'I was a poor co-pilot.'

'Mate,' he corrected.

'Mate,' she repeated.

The 'friends' terminology wasn't lost on him and he knew it wasn't the humidity that was making him perspire a little. What he needed was a cold shower. Or...

'We should go swimming,' he announced like he was in charge of a tour itinerary. 'I know a place.'

He didn't wait for Cara to respond, he simply increased the speed a little and hoped the noise of the engines would drown out his thoughts.

24

CHURCH OF THE HYPAPANTE, GOUVIA

Akis had dropped the anchor in a bay opposite a beautiful little white church stuck out on a promontory all on its own. It had arched windows, a tiled roof and a bell tower, like every idyllic chapel depicted in a Greek wedding. It was bigger than the church in the olive grove that belonged to Akis's family, but from here on the boat in the sea, it felt just as secluded.

'Are you coming?'

Cara looked away from the view of the church to Akis and saw he was stripped down to his rather moulded-to-his-attributes underwear, the shirt and jeans discarded on the seating.

'You were serious about swimming?' Cara asked.

He laughed. 'You cannot be "serious" about swimming. Swimming has nothing serious about it. It is getting in water and moving your arms and legs.'

'You know what I meant.'

'Do I not look like I am meaning it?' he asked, arms outstretched.

All his pose did was highlight his lithe and subtly muscular physique. It wasn't the torso of someone who focussed on heavy weights, more someone who toned every single individual muscle... and Cara was still gazing.

'Is it hot? No... I mean... is it cold? The water.'

And now she was close to blushing.

'Why not find out for yourself?'

With that said, he jumped from the edge of the boat and splashed into the sea.

Watching him resurface, she quickly gave herself a whispered pep talk. 'It's swimming not singing. It will be fun. You can tell your mum you communed with nature at night. Margot wouldn't hesitate.'

She shook her head. Why was she still making comparisons to others or seeking approval? It was her decision! If she wanted to swim, she should. If she didn't, that was fine too.

'There is a ladder,' Akis called from the water. 'If you do not want to jump?'

Done with thinking, she stripped herself down to her not-too-conservative-but-not-transparent underwear and, casting an eye at the rather tiny metal ladder that looked like it needed to be folded down, she got up onto the seating. There was only one thing for it. She jumped.

When the water hit her it was a shock at how cold it was. She came up for air and could hardly get the words out.

'It's... freezing,' she said, moving her arms and legs to tread water.

Akis laughed. 'It is actually around twenty-five degrees but, you know, it is close to being thirty-four degrees in the air. Keep moving. You will adjust.'

That sounded like a mantra for life more than just for warding off the chill in this moment. But it really didn't take long for Cara to appreciate the coolness rather than feel overwhelmed by it. She followed Akis's lead, swimming around the boat then heading in a gentle direction towards the church.

'For someone who says they don't want to be a priest, you seem to be taking me to a lot of churches,' Cara remarked when they had stopped close enough to be able to touch their feet to the rocky seabed.

'You think that is a little crazy? To like these buildings and be grateful my grandmother has her faith to cling to, but to not want to commit my whole life to it?'

'Well...'

'Can I ask you a question, Cara?'

His gaze was pretty intense and she wondered what was coming next. She nodded. 'OK.'

'Do you still *want* to sing?'

'I don't know what you mean,' she said as her pulse rate quickened. It wasn't a simple question at all.

'I mean, beneath everything, forgetting the bad performance you said you had, putting to one side what your aunt has done here...' He paused before carrying on. 'Would you still want to sing if there was nothing riding on it? If it was only for fun. Only for you.'

Singing had been everything. Her whole life. For as long as she could remember. Always with the aim of it being her career, her future. Now he was trying to make her think differently about it. What it had been once. What it was now. How it could be again?

There was only one true answer she could give. 'Yes, of course.'

He nodded. 'I thought so.'

She ran a hand through her wet hair and took a deep breath. 'What do you mean?'

'I mean, like with the churches, just because one element of something scares you, it doesn't mean you have to turn your back on the whole thing.'

She let his statement sink into her consciousness. In fact, it felt like such a big declaration, it was almost like she could feel it across her shoulders, evaporating the sea water and chilling her skin.

'When I see a church now, or when I go into the family chapel, it is like I *want* to be challenged.' He swept a hand through his hair. 'I want to look right into the eyes of the icons and question the validity of this curse. But I also want to feel that whatever decision I make, it won't change what I think or who I am. I think, even if I joined the church, I would hope to be able to separate things, you know? That it wouldn't have to be everything.'

'You're really thinking about it? Going through with becoming a priest?' Cara asked.

'It would make it all stop,' he admitted. 'Cosmos would have one thing less to worry about. My mother's craziness would subside for a time. And if I could separate the different parts then...' He stopped talking, brushed some water droplets from his shoulders. 'I don't know.'

'But, don't you want children?' Cara asked. 'Or to get married one day? Priests can't do that, can they?'

'Well, in fact, it is possible to marry. But only *before* ordination, so if I have to be ordained before I am thirty, I would need to find a wife by October and, well, you know, I am not in any kind of relationship now so...'

The sentence hung in the air between them and Cara felt goosebumps break out on her arms. It was obviously the water temperature. Because marriage was never going to be on *her* agenda again. She didn't even know why she had brought it up now.

'Cosmos worries. All the time. That has always been what Cosmos does. He worries and he hides from life. It is only with Wren, that I see little pieces of something different from him. He smiles now. He laughs. He still overthinks but there is less misery, you know?'

She swirled her fingers in the water. 'Less misery is good. I did notice he was heavily invested in the icing to cake ratio. I mean, I know it's his wedding but—'

Akis smiled. 'He has always been an unimportant details person. I think it stops him thinking about what others might class as more important details.'

'Like how his brother is thinking of giving up his whole life as he knows it so he doesn't have to worry.'

Akis nodded. 'Maybe.'

She took him in anew. This guy who loved life and thought it could be the brightest, burning, most vibrant experience if you put your heart and soul into it and worried a little less about public opinion, was also someone who was thinking about giving all that up just so his younger brother could have less to fret about.

'So,' Cara said softly. 'If I were to, maybe think about trying singing again, do you have something better than that ancient relic of a keyboard you could accompany me on?'

'You are serious?' Akis asked, obviously unable to keep the surprise from his expression.

'Well,' Cara said, smiling. 'Singing doesn't have to be serious, you know. It's really just getting your vocal cords to wave around a bit.'

'Hey! You make fun of what I said about swimming!' He splashed her.

Cara screamed and ducked her body back down into the water. 'Last one back to the boat has to drive it.'

She set off swimming at pace but in not too long a time he was alongside her and he was first to the ladder at the back of the boat. Meanwhile, she arrived breathless, wondering why the hell she would make such a bet.

'I have a piano,' Akis told her. 'At my apartment. It is not the best these days, not like the one at the theatre, but it belonged to my grandfather.' He paused before continuing. 'If you wanted, after the blessing of the snakes tomorrow, we could, you know, make music together.'

Cara swallowed. Him using that term had her mind travelling not back to singing but to his dance moves at the hen party. But the thought of having fun with singing, no pressure or expectation, it was as exhilarating as this late-night swim in this secluded bay was.

'OK,' she agreed with a nod.

'OK?'

'Why not? It doesn't have to be serious, like you said.'

'And it does not have to be Adele either. You can challenge me.'

'You might regret that,' Cara said.

'I will let you know later,' he replied. 'When you have driven us back to the marina. Hopefully before the port authority has notified the police of the larceny.'

'What?' Cara exclaimed. 'But you said—'

'I am kidding with you, Cara. It is my friend's boat. I promise.' He smiled. 'Come on, before the dolphins have all gone to sleep.'

25

COOK'S CLUB CORFU

Cara's hair still smelled a little of the sea when she woke the next morning. She'd been too tired to take a shower last night and she had slipped into the sheets, her limbs aching from the swimming, her left leg a little bruised from climbing the tiny inadequate ladder back into the boat and her eyes a bit sore from lack of sleep. But there was no doubt, somehow today she felt different. She couldn't put her finger on exactly *how* she felt different but there was definitely a lightness flowing through her thoughts when usually her head felt clogged. And then she looked to her left. No Margot. And that side of the bed was virtually pristine.

Checking her watch, she saw it was almost eight o'clock. She hadn't thought much about Margot not being in the room when she'd got back. She'd presumed Margot would have been many cocktails down regaling the barmen with stories, but now, with the sheets undisturbed and it being later than her aunt's usual 7 a.m. cigarette, it was a bit disconcerting.

She reached for the phone on the nightstand. Five missed calls. All around 6 a.m. From an unknown number. Now Cara was worried. What if it was the police? Or the hospital?

As her mind started to perform an anxiety dance, she pulled back the covers, wondering what to do first. Phone Margot was the obvious first answer. She hit the call icon, phone nestled against her ear, as she searched for something easy to dress in.

She froze when the automated message she received was in Greek. What did that mean? Why hadn't it just clicked through to voicemail? If it was the case of a flat battery that's what would happen. What other explanation could there be? That Margot might have lost her phone? Or it had been stolen?

Find My Phone. Yes, Cara would check the app and it would provide a location for the phone.

She pulled her sundress on over her head as the app pinwheeled along. If this didn't work she was going to have to phone back the number that had called her five times. She didn't want to do that. There would be a sensible, logical, typical Margot explanation and all this panic would be for nothing.

Cara jumped as the phone next to Margot's side of the bed rang. *Reception.* She camo-crawled across the duvet and dived for the receiver.

'Hello.'

'Cara?'

Cara frowned. 'Akis?'

'Yes, listen, I—'

'Akis, I can't talk right now. I'm trying to get hold of my aunt and—'

'I know,' he interrupted. 'That is why I am calling.'

'What?' Cara sat up and paid better attention.

'Listen, I am coming to pick you up.'

'What? Why?'

'Margot is OK, OK? But she is at the hospital.'

Cara's heart dropped like someone had tossed it off the top of the Shard. 'The hospital.'

She stood, looking around for things you might need to visit a hospital. What did you need for that? Why was she having to do that? She had only been gone for one evening. And what did 'OK' mean? Did it mean bruises and scratches or did it mean serious but stable?

'Listen to me,' Akis said, firmly but gently. 'She is fine. I have been told she is conscious. She is talking. She hates it at the hospital, which is good, because she is right, so nothing mental is impaired. I am getting on the bike now, I will be as fast as the traffic lights let me, OK? Do not worry. Meet me out front.'

Do not worry. That was the biggest impossibility in this situation. She had been selfish. She had been so obsessed with herself and the surprise wedding performance situation, so angry that Margot had made another decision for her without asking and now this! This was the universe calling her out for being ungrateful for everything her aunt had done for her since Moldova, since her parents vanished to be nomads, since forever really.

'Cara,' Akis said forcefully. 'I can hear you are worrying. Please don't. Everything will be OK.'

Cara's mind was racing but she needed to end this call, put on some shoes and get ready to face whatever had happened to Margot. *Travel insurance documents.* Margot had dealt with all that. Where would she have put that stuff? Her handbag? Her case?

'Cara, I'm leaving right now. Meet me outside,' Akis said.

'OK,' she answered. 'OK.'

26

CORFU HOSPITAL

Cara braced herself for whatever she was going to be faced with as she paused at the entrance to the ward. Just a few minutes ago, Akis had sped into the hospital car park on his motorbike and they had both rushed into the building, him leading the way. He had offered to come into the ward with her, but she had shaken herself, tried to switch into organisational mode and internally told herself if Margot was awake and talking then how bad could it really be?

'Nurse! I want to speak to your manager! I told you that an hour ago! An English hour, not a Greek one! Why is no one listening to me?'

Cara felt herself relax. That was Margot, the complaining and rude version. This was good.

Cara headed towards the source of irritation. However, when she got to the bed, she gasped at the sight of her aunt. Her head was wrapped up in bandages like a mummy, her upper chest showed signs of trauma – bloody indents that had been stitched together – and her hands had marks that looked like shrapnel wounds. What on Earth could have caused that?

'Margot,' Cara said, scared to sound too concerned, scared to not sound concerned enough. 'What happened?'

'It's nothing really. Why are you even here?' Margot asked, accusing. 'I was hoping they'd take off this stupid unfashionable headwear and let me go back to civilisation before you woke up.'

'Well,' Cara said, stepping closer to the bed. 'You didn't come back to the hotel last night and I couldn't reach you on your phone so—'

'I'll need a new phone,' Margot stated. 'Mine is irreparably damaged.'

'Margot,' Cara said. 'Please tell me what happened. It looks so painful.'

Margot sat forward, eyed the other patients. 'Come closer,' she whispered. 'Greek walls have more ears than English ones I've already discovered.'

Cara got as close to her aunt as she could and leaned in like the world's secrets were about to be divulged.

'There was an explosion,' Margot whispered.

'What?!'

'Cara! Be quiet! Or I will say no more about it.'

'But an explosion! Are you sure you don't mean earthquake?' Margot had obviously had a knock on the head judging by the elaborate bandage work.

'I think I know the difference between the earth moving and something blowing up.'

'Well,' Cara said quietly. 'What blew up? And where were you when whatever it was blew up? Are there any more casualties?'

'Where I was is irrelevant. What isn't irrelevant is *what* blew up.' Margot paused briefly before saying, in even quieter tones, 'It was... the Maxi-Go.'

Cara gasped and put her hands to her cheeks in pure hot shock. 'What?'

'Dial it down, Cara! No one can know! I mean, *no* one! It would ruin me! Literally.'

Cara paused before replying. 'I know they said there was an issue in production and that's why it was taking longer than we had hoped but I didn't realise it had the potential to explode.'

'Please stop saying the word "explode",' Margot ordered.

'OK, but can you imagine what would have happened if this had happened on the plane?'

'Don't you think I've been imagining that? It's all I've been imagining from the second I pulled the first shard of the triple layer comfort handle out of my knuckles!'

'Well, what are we going to do?' Cara asked.

'The very first thing we are not going to do is panic,' Margot stated, beginning to unpeel the first layer of bandage from her forehead. 'Panic might be in your nature, sadly, obviously, but it's never been in mine and I'm not about to give it a seat at the table now.'

'You have an idea? To fix it?'

'I don't have an idea,' Margot said, a slight smile returning. 'I have a plan. I have actually *always* had a plan. It's the main reason why we're here.'

Cara was confused. 'But I thought the main reason we were here was because you were invited to Sofia's son's wedding.'

Margot shook her head, a more conniving expression on her face now. 'I would never have been invited to Sofia's son's wedding. Sofia hates me. She hated me all through college and that's never going to change. And, to be really honest, the feeling is mutual. However, we are both too wise to let those kinds of insipid feelings get in the way of passing up opportunities to move upwards.'

'Now I'm really confused. So, we were only invited because somehow she contacted you when Placido Domingo pulled out and you said I would sing instead?'

'Ha! Is that what she was telling people? That Placido Domingo was singing?'

'Margot! Get to the point!'

'The original wedding singer was someone called Simeon Barkastra and so sadly, so unfortunately, he had to cancel.' Margot unwound more of her bandage, leaving it trailing like a towelling snake on the hospital bed.

Now Cara was getting it. 'You *paid* him to cancel! So you could provide Sofia with a last-minute alternative. Me.'

'And you and I were added to the guest list,' Margot said triumphantly. 'Did you really think I'd want to spend my days tasting wine that could take the varnish off my nails?' She sniffed. 'Although I did enjoy the hen night.'

'But what's so important about you being here at Sofia's son's wedding that you would go to these lengths to get on the guest list?'

Margot sighed. 'Someone I haven't seen for a long time. Someone I need to see now.'

Cara waited with bated breath.

'The maharaja. Or, as I called him, Raj.' Margot sighed and it was a sound loaded with regret. Cara took a minute to gather her thoughts. She had never heard Margot sound quite this way before. But she still didn't fully get it.

'He's coming here,' Margot carried on. 'To the wedding. Obviously he's far too busy to take part in this elaborate pre-ceremony malarky but he and Sofia, although never romantically aligned, were in this rather weird best-friendsy situation once he realised how sexually boring she was.'

Cara didn't know how to respond to that.

'Anyway, Raj can help me, help us. I need the Maxi-Go to succeed in the biggest arena. I know I've pretty much captured the whole of Europe but I want Asia, America, Australia. Raj has contacts all over the world, people who deal in gold and cryptocurrencies like they're playing with Monopoly bills. He can make the difference between moderate success and world domination.'

Cara didn't know whether to be in awe of her aunt right now or appalled at this entire set-up. But there was a much more important factor in her mind.

'But, Margot, didn't the Maxi-Go just blow up?'

'Ssh!' Margot hissed, finally finishing with her unwrapping.

'Sorry,' Cara said, lowering her voice. 'But how is anyone going to invest all their bullion or Bitcoin into something that has the potential to bring down an aircraft?'

'That's why I need the investment more than ever. To straighten out these little teething problems. I know it's a set-back that I didn't envisage when I was putting my pitch together but, you know, think of all the great inventions in the world; most of them ended up in pieces before the final successful result.'

Now Cara really didn't know what to say. She was astounded that all this plotting and scheming had gone on right under her nose. Using Sofia as a way to get to someone who might make a big investment in the Maxi-Go that had just exploded and injured her aunt. Then she had another thought.

'Margot, was anyone else injured by the Maxi-Go?'

'What?' Margot asked, shifting on the hospital bed and looking like she might be about to attempt to get off it.

'The explosion,' Cara shout-whispered. 'Was anyone else hurt?'

'I have no idea,' Margot said. 'I was too busy being unconscious and ripped apart by flying zippers. Help me get off of this bed. I need a gin and tonic!'

27

MARRON CAFE, KONTOKALI

'Horatio, you are being crazy! You should be in the hospital to get that looked at not in a café.'

'Stop staring at it, Aki. It will be fine,' Horatio answered, a wad of napkins pressed to his injured arm. 'My grandmother always said that the only time to call a doctor is if you cannot lift a cup of coffee to your lips.' Horatio balanced the napkins on his arm, reached for his cup, held it out in a cheers and swigged some liquid down.

'You are using your other arm,' Akis told him.

'For now,' Horatio replied. 'But it will be fine in a few days. Lucky we do not have a show for a few days, right?'

'Well, I think you need stitches and you don't know if there is something embedded in there,' Akis said, still focussed on his friend's wound.

'There is nothing embedded in there any more. I pulled out the spiked heel of the shoe that did the damage.'

Akis shook his head. 'I still do not understand what happened.'

'Really?' Horatio asked, keeping pressure on his injury again. 'Because I told you everything. I was walking past the hotel, I see the woman from the hen party struggling with the suitcase, I go to help and suddenly "bang".'

Horatio's rather enthusiastic 'bang' had one of the customers jumping to attention.

'Sorry,' Horatio said, waving apologetically.

'But, I still don't—' Akis began.

'Is the woman OK, do you know?' Horatio asked, mouth to his coffee again.

'Her name is Margot,' Akis said. 'And you know that because you told me her name when you phoned me to call Cara at Cook's Club. Like you also knew that she was here with Cara.'

'Did I?' Horatio asked, shaking his head. 'I don't remember. Maybe I got a knock to the head too. It all happened so fast.' He put down his coffee cup. 'So, was she OK?'

'Well, from what I was told, which I then helped translate to Cara before she went in to see her aunt, she is OK. A possible concussion, lacerations to her chest, grazes on her hands, but nothing that rest and time will not heal.'

'Good,' Horatio said, nodding. 'Because, you know, we would not want anything messing up your mother's seating plan for the wedding, would we?'

Akis sighed. 'I wish everyone would stop calling it my mother's seating plan, my mother's wedding. It is not my mother's anything. It is Cosmos and Wren's day.'

'Anastasia asked me to come to the blessing of the snakes this afternoon,' Horatio said.

'Shit, really?' Akis asked.

'I think she is trying to invite everyone she knows who is *not* scared of snakes and the list is very small.'

'It is a crazy tradition anyway. How is having snakes slither across the wedding venue going to make the union a success?'

'How is you being a priest going to save the whole Diakos family for generations to come?' Horatio countered. 'It is all scripture, yes. But who is to say that in ancient times, all the philosophers and storytellers didn't just get together, get completely wasted and write a lot of mad shit?'

'They probably did,' Akis agreed, sipping his frappe.

'Then what is the deal?'

'The deal is my mother believes it all! My grandmother believes some of it and the rest of the village believes enough to think that my decisions could be a risk to them and their families.' He sighed. 'It is one thing to have a curse hanging over the Diakos name, but it is another to have the possibility of plagues arriving and affecting more than just us.'

'So that is the latest tactic, is it?' Horatio said, shaking his head. 'What is next? Another old fable saying if you don't become a priest it will be Armageddon? The end of the world for the whole of humanity?'

Akis nodded. 'That is a possibility.'

'Well, you know *my* philosophy,' Horatio stated. 'Live life so fast that consequence will never catch up with you.'

'Life is wide,' Akis said quietly, his mind back on Cara.

'What?'

'It was something someone said to me and... I like it.' He swallowed, took another drink of his coffee.

'Aki,' Horatio said, a serious note to his voice that wasn't used very often. 'You know what this is like, right? This is like when everyone gathered around Cosmos when it was *your* finger lying on the floor.'

Akis shook his head.

'Except it wasn't just your finger that was taken, it was all your plans and your career. And you knew, in that split second when your brother was about to be hurt, what you could end up sacrificing.'

'Because that is what you do for the people you care about,' Akis answered, without hesitation.

'I agree,' Horatio replied, sitting forward in his seat. 'But does it not go both ways? You have done this huge thing before. So you are to keep doing these things? *Giving up* these things? If your family loves you, why are they not understanding that you do not want this? Why is their first thought to follow some insane story instead of protecting *you*?'

Akis had never thought about it that way before. There was a lot of truth in what Horatio was saying. Cosmos was incapable of doing anything for anyone, just his existence exhausted him. Anastasia was always there for him, his father and grandmother too. But none of them were bold enough to stand up to Sofia.

His phone buzzed in the pocket of his jeans and he put down his coffee cup and took it out.

'Ask the barista if they have a First Aid box,' he told Horatio. 'Or I am taking you to the pharmacy.'

'Nice change of subject, Diakos.'

Akis looked at the message on his screen. It was Cara. He had made sure they had swapped mobile numbers so she could call him if she needed transport.

Margot insisting on leaving the hospital. Will call a cab to get back to the hotel. Thank you for the ride. See you at the snakes.

She had added two snake emojis at the end.

'Things are going well with Cara, I see,' Horatio remarked.

'What?'

'Well, by the way your face lit up at that message, I would say you have more going on in your life than just this clerical business.'

'First Aid box,' Akis repeated. 'Or maybe I will take you to my grandmother.'

'Please,' Horatio called to the barista, raising his hand. 'Do you have a bandage?'

28

COSMOS AND WREN'S WEDDING VENUE, NOTOS

'Oh my God!' Margot exclaimed. 'It's a building site!'

The taxi hadn't really known whereabouts in Notos they wanted to go until suddenly, when they mentioned whose wedding they were attending, the penny dropped. The taxi driver had smiled, nodded and said, 'Like the sleeping beauty.' Now Cara could kind of see why. Right ahead of them, towering up over everything in the vicinity except the tall, lean cypress trees, was a castle straight out of Disney. However, it looked very much still under construction. There were workmen in jeans and vests, some actually working, others on a smoke break, and most of the façade was covered in tarpaulin. It didn't look like something ready to be blessed today and, unless all stops were pulled out, not something ready for an impending wedding.

'I wonder if Sofia knows it looks like this,' Margot continued, with a good degree of pleasure in her tone.

'Margot, are you sure about being here?' Cara said. 'Don't you think it's better that you rest? Considering you were in hospital first thing this morning.'

Margot was a little unsteady on her feet, despite all this 'carrying on as normal' bravado.

'Stop asking me that. I said I'm fine. Even more fine now I've seen this. Where's my phone? I want to take photos.'

It did look very incomplete. From plants that had obviously been brought for the occasion, drooping in their pots, to the unfinished turrets at the top. It wasn't so much a feast for the eyes as a poorly packed and insufficient shoddy picnic.

'Oh, Cara, thank God, you're here!'

It was Anastasia, sweeping down the half-built pathway.

'Hi,' Cara greeted. 'Wow, this looks so... substantial.'

Anastasia scoffed. 'It's a fucking mess is what it is. My mother is splitting her personality between screaming at Stavros, the project manager, and crying with Pappa Spiros.' She then did a double take, looking at Margot. 'What happened to you? You look worse than this castle.'

'Believe me,' Margot replied. 'If you had seen me at 8 a.m. you would think the way I am now is nothing short of miraculous. Now, take me to your mother, I know exactly what to do.'

'I am not sure that is a good idea,' Anastasia said. 'She is trying to stop Wren arriving and that involves telling Cosmos about how this place looks and he will start to cry and of course my mother is already saying that it is the Diakos curse and—'

'There's a curse?' Margot said, her demeanour now suggesting that despite looking like she'd been target practice at a shooting range, she had never felt better.

'Erm,' Cara said, linking her arm through Margot's. 'Why don't we take a little walk.' She addressed Anastasia. 'Is there somewhere nearby we could get a coffee maybe? Or a glass of wine? Until this is all sorted out.'

'I think we'd need to drink a whole vineyard to have enough time for anyone to sort this out,' Margot remarked.

'Well, perhaps there is no need for us to be here anyway,' Cara continued. 'This blessing event sounds much more like a family occasion.'

'Oh no,' Anastasia said quickly. 'You *have* to be here. All the main guests of the wedding have to be here, or the blessing won't work.'

Cara frowned. They were 'main' guests? Was this a title Margot had managed to get them because Cara was booked as the wedding singer? Something she still hadn't told anyone apart from Margot that she couldn't do.

'Let me see your mother. I can talk to whoever is in charge of this shambles and get things moving. I am an expert at getting people to do what's needed, aren't I, Cara?'

Was the maharajah not a 'main' guest? Surely royalty would be one seat below the immediate family...

'Cara!' Margot barked.

'Sorry, yes, yes you most certainly will be able to make a difference in this situation.' She hoped she had heard enough to get a grasp of what she needed to say.

'Sofia!'

'Oh, no, it's my grandmother,' Anastasia said. 'She wasn't supposed to be here! But she seems to find out about everything she is not supposed to.'

Cara turned to see Irini, making her way along the road, leading Pig.

'I thought it was a blessing of snakes not donkeys,' Margot said, sounding confused.

'Listen,' Cara said, taking charge. 'Why don't you two go into the... erm... castle and I will make sure Irini and Pig are OK until everything's decided.'

'I don't see a pig,' Margot remarked, putting a hand to her head as if she was concerned this was as a result of concussion.

'Come, Margot, perhaps my mother does need someone to make decisions for her right now,' Anastasia said. 'And who better than an old friend.'

Cara watched them go, making sure Margot was steady walking on the rather rough ground and then she turned her attention to Irini and Pig.

'*Yassas*,' Irini greeted. 'Is Akis here?'

Pig rubbed his face on Cara's shoulder and almost made her topple over.

'Oh, no, he isn't. Not yet. We arrived a bit early and—'

'Look at this!' Irini said, arms up in the air as if she was beckoning the heavens. 'I have never seen something look so ugly. I mean, look at it, all thick boulders of grey blocks. What is it supposed to be? A prison?'

'I think it is actually meant to be a castle,' Cara said. 'I am sure it will look a lot more... fairy-tale wedding venue when it's finished.'

'The only way this could look better is if it was flattened by a wrecking ball and all the trees they tore up were replaced!'

Cara swallowed. They'd cut down trees to build this? Her mum would be chaining herself to the building and protesting if she were here. And it didn't sit well with Cara either. Corfu was so green and beautiful, an abundance of olives, figs and almonds. This 'castle' couldn't have been more out of place.

'Sofia, she thinks this is all my fault,' Irini continued, leaning a little on Pig. 'When she was young we did not have much of anything and Sofia, she craved everything we did not have.' She shook her head. 'But this... this is out of control.'

'*Yiayia, perpátises?*'

It was Akis arriving.

'*Ne, epeidi boró,*' Irini replied.

'*Signomi*, Cara,' Akis said, turning to her. 'I asked my grandmother if she had walked here.'

'And I said "yes, while I can".'

'OK,' Cara said. 'Well, I'm getting quite hot here in the sun and I don't think we're really allowed near the—'

'Holy shit!' Akis exclaimed, as if he had only just noticed the building ahead of them. Pig brayed as if in total agreement.

'Yes! All the shit from the heavens has landed at this place where your grandfather and I once danced,' Irini said, shaking her head. 'It always used to feel so magical to me.'

There was sadness in the old woman's voice and Cara watched her eyes going back and forth to the building work and then to the trees, their branches being tickled by the light humid breeze.

'Come, move into the shade,' Akis seemed to tell them both. 'I will go and find out what is going on.'

'What is going on,' Irini said, 'is that some people here pick and choose when to support the gods. Sofia is so fixated on the Diakos curse but does not care that she stamp all over Phaunos, the god of forests.'

Cara put a hand on the old woman's arm.

'I will be back,' Akis said, striding off.

29

'You! What are you doing eating whatever you're eating when you should be... I don't know... doing something with that thingamajig?' Margot was berating the workmen and pointing towards tools that had been discarded on the ground.

Akis took everything in. The inside of this fortification was worse than the outside. There was nothing but bare floors and bare walls, a carcass of a building and no matter how hard anyone worked now, there was no way this was going to be fit for anything for the wedding day.

'Is lunch,' the workman replied. 'Then soon it will be siesta.'

'Siesta!' Margot hissed. 'You don't get a fucking siesta when this castle looks like Bang Kwang prison! Tell them, Sofia!'

Akis looked at his mother. She was wearing a white trouser suit that was far from pristine now. There were dark dust marks down one side of the jacket, paint spatters on her trousers and her usual elegant pinned hairstyle was coming loose, tendrils of her hair escaping. But it was the expression on her face that hit Akis the most. She looked lost, desolate, not in control...

'*Mama*, what is going on here?' Akis asked.

Sofia turned to him and tears were falling from her eyes. He watched her rapidly wipe at them with the sleeve of her suit jacket, adding mascara stains to the mix. 'We need to... prioritise, I think. I am prioritising and Margot is helping.'

'*Mama*,' Akis said. 'This place, it cannot be ready for Wren and Cosmos's wedding.'

'It has to be ready! They said it would be ready! I came to see it two weeks ago and it was *better* than it is now and I spoke to the foreman yesterday and he told me that everything was in hand!'

'*Mama*, what will have been in hand is a chicken *souvlaki* in each fist while he was talking to you.'

'Please, I am right here!' a man with a yellow hard hat called.

'And you should be working! Not listening to other people's conversations! Shoo!' Margot ordered, flapping her hand and ushering the man away from their gathering towards some very flimsy stairs that seemed to lead to the upper floor.

'I was so busy! I was seeing to the flowers, the cake and the wine, Wren's dress – which I am still not entirely happy with – the chocolate fountains, the vows – they are still not finalised either – the bridesmaids, who have all changed shape by the way.' She heaved a giant breath as she ran out of air. 'And then I do not sleep because all I can think about is the curse! And when I get here I see this and I think, the gods, they know. They know that you are not going to be a priest before you are thirty and they are ready to rain down their might on this occasion as a taste of what is to come.'

And then Sofia let out a scream so loud it had Akis reaching for his ears, while the *tiropita* – cheese pie – in one of the workmen's hands fell to the ground.

'For God's sake!' Margot bellowed, clamping a hand over Sofia's mouth and stopping the noise. 'Get a grip of yourself! You've lost all sense of decency and decorum and you were always quite good at that, I'll admit.' Margot looked to Akis. 'Does she do this often?'

'Never,' Akis replied.

'Right, well,' Margot said, turning back to Sofia. 'No more of this silly nonsense. No one has died, have they? Although, if the staff don't start pulling their weight I can't promise that will hold true for long. I'm looking particularly at you.' She eyed the man who had dropped his food. 'Now, I'm going to take my hand away and you're going to take some nice deep breaths. OK?'

Akis watched as his mother drew in some very shaky breaths, tears still bubbling away.

'OK, Margot, could you give us a minute?'

'Absolutely,' she replied. 'I will find someone in this place who actually knows how any of these tools work and get some action.'

As soon as she was gone, Akis put a hand on his mother's shoulder. '*Mama*, Wren and Cosmos, they can't get married here.'

'They *have* to get married here! The whole event has been planned around this castle and—'

'*Mama*, look at this place. The time it will take to achieve the effect you want...'

'I am going to cry again,' Sofia said.

'No one is going to cry again today. OK?' He placed his other hand on her shoulder.

'Aki, your finger,' Sofia gasped. 'I mean, where it was...'

'It's fine,' Akis answered, knowing she was talking about the reddened skin. 'It gets like that sometimes when I ride the motorbike too long.'

Sofia shook her head. 'Why does Cosmos have to get married *now*? I mean this year, this time, when we have the curse hanging over us.'

'Because he is in love. Because he wants to be the best husband to Wren. Because he wants to start a family. Because the idea of this curse should not dictate what the family does and when. There are many reasons.'

'But,' Sofia began, walking to one of the arched windows that was dripping with some kind of solvent. 'I need to make it perfect. And I can't make it perfect now.'

'*Mama*, it will be perfect because, wherever the wedding is, it will be about Wren and Cosmos becoming married,' Akis said. 'Do you not remember that at the beginning Wren wanted to be married on the beach?'

Sofia scoffed. 'I remember she also wanted to get married surrounded by birds, but I was not having everyone in their finery trudging around the perimeter of Lake Korission.'

'But,' Akis said, standing next to her and looking out at the view of the woodland. 'Does it have to be about a statement castle?'

'I have a reputation to uphold,' Sofia bleated. 'I have the best. Of everything. Always.'

'But, *Mama*, it isn't your wedding. It's Wren and Cosmos's.' He steadied her shoulders again, looking into her eyes. 'I think you are focussing on the things that matter the least.'

He waited a beat for what he had said to sink in and hoped it would make a difference.

'OK,' Sofia said in a barely audible whisper.

'OK?'

'I guess I will have to find a compromise. I will talk to Stavros. I will see what he can commit to finish and, if we get the photographer to take from certain angles then—'

'*Mama*, no. What you need to do is decommission this place. Forget it. Talk to Cosmos and Wren about what they want.'

'I can't do that,' Sofia said, eyes widening in terror. 'Because the wedding is not far away! Where else are we going to get that's of a standard that—'

'It is not *my* wedding, *Mama*,' Akis said. 'You need to speak to Wren and Cosmos.'

She took a deep breath, as if she was still contemplating whether he was right or not. Finally, she gave a nod.

'Good,' Akis said, taking a step back.

'But, if I speak to Wren and Cosmos,' Sofia said. 'Will you do something for me? Will you speak to Pappa Spiros? Just to let him tell you a little about the life of a priest. I am sure it is not like you think and—'

There was only one answer that Akis could give. He took a deep breath. 'If you speak to Wren and Cosmos about what they *really* want for their wedding, then yes, I will speak to Pappa Spiros.'

'Oh, Aki!' she exclaimed, throwing her arms around him and hugging tight.

And as he took a second to remember what it felt like to have his mother proud of him again, he also wondered how long he could carry on at the centre of this curse dilemma.

30

AKIS'S APARTMENT, CORFU TOWN

It was so hot in the town today, everyone was seeking the shade of the large canopies around the Liston where Cara and Margot had sat on their very first day on the island. Even the pigeons had looked hot as she and Akis had ridden through on his motorbike, zipping up the narrow alleyways that appeared like they were part of some magic maze game. A game that also involved ducking for hanging laundry and swerving past cats. And then they had stopped, at the end of one of the alleyways, outside a terracotta-coloured building with green shutters. Once they were off the bike, Akis had pushed at a partially opened old thick wooden door and they entered a marble-covered entrance hall.

'I am on the top floor and I am afraid the lift is broken,' Akis announced, heading towards a flight of marble steps.

'How many floors are there?' Cara asked him, already feeling perspiration trickling down her back.

'Five,' he said. 'But we can go slow.'

They started to climb.

'I meant to ask you, back at Notos, if your grandmother is OK,' Cara said. 'She's got a bad cough.'

He sighed. 'She is the type of person to not admit when things are wrong. She suffers with her chest but, you know, she will not do anything but drink honey tea, and if I suggest the doctor she will hit me with her slipper.'

'I thought your mother was going to hit the foreman with more than a slipper at one point,' she said as they got to the first landing.

'My mother is actually going to talk to Cosmos and Wren about where they want their wedding. Perhaps it is something she should have done from the very beginning of wedding preparations but, with my mother it is like a bullet train rushing towards a destination.'

'It is the same with my aunt,' Cara agreed.

'What happened with your aunt? I mean, do you know what caused the accident?'

'Oh,' Cara said. 'I... don't really know. She wasn't really able to give me any specifics.'

She swallowed an immense feeling of guilt for not telling the truth. Here Akis was, about to take her to his apartment and help her try to unlock her voice and she was lying to him. But she knew she couldn't let *anyone* know about the Maxi-Go. It was potentially a business-destroying situation.

She took a deep breath as the stairs began to take their toll. 'Are there many more stairs?'

He laughed. 'We are almost there. And, just so you know, the lift is never working.'

It took a few more minutes to get to the top but, finally, they stopped outside a rather unassuming door. There was a label in the doorbell that said the name 'Spyridoula'.

'That was the previous occupant,' Akis said, putting his finger to the name. 'I have tried everything to get it out, even taken the whole thing apart but still it will not come.'

Cara laughed. And when he put a key in the lock and opened the door, what lay inside took her breath away.

Light flooded in from four sets of large windows across the breadth of the space and old wooden floorboards held the minimal furniture – a sofa and a large armchair, a coffee table – with a neat, compact kitchen at one end. At the opposite end of the room was a black upright piano, paint peeling a little.

'Damn it! I forgot to close the shutters this morning. It is like an oven in here.' He moved towards them.

'No, don't close the shutters,' Cara said, striding into the space. 'Can we open the windows instead? Oh, this one is a door and... oh, there's a balcony.'

'We can open the doors and windows,' Akis agreed. 'But, the way the weather is out there, it is likely to be hotter than it already is.'

'I don't mind,' Cara answered. 'I want to see everything.'

Akis unlocked the patio door and as soon as it was open, Cara pushed out onto the balcony. The humidity hit her, but the view made more of an impact. It was a high-rise snapshot of what they had ridden through, this beautiful town in all its glory. She could see rooftops and church bell towers, people going about their day carrying take-out frappes, teenagers in groups around benches, backpacks swinging, colour everywhere from the vibrant green of the trees, the orange and pink flowers in displays, to the cloudless blue sky. She breathed deeply and simply admired it all.

'So many tourists,' Akis remarked, standing next to her and leaning against the iron railing.

'It's beautiful here,' Cara said. 'It's nothing like London. Here you can see it's busy, hear it's busy, yet it still feels so calm.'

'Ah,' Akis said. 'That is because you do not live here. Everyone feels calmer when they are somewhere temporarily.'

'No,' Cara said. 'I don't think it's that. I think it's the vibe of a place. The vibe here is just chill.'

'You know,' Akis began. 'If we have all the doors and windows open it will be easier for others to hear our music.'

'I know,' Cara replied. 'But, here, no one can see us.'

* * *

He watched her looking down at the town he knew so well, the place he had decided to move to to get away from how claustrophobic Notos and life in the family home had started to be. It was only a few kilometres but it felt like another planet.

And what Cara had just said about no one seeing resonated. That was exactly how it had been for him after the accident. Once he realised that playing the piano wasn't completely out of the question, he didn't want people to see, he only wanted people to hear. If they only heard then they couldn't know he was different or make assumptions, it would only be about the music.

'Is that what worries you the most about singing again?' he asked, looking at her.

She nodded. 'You think that's silly, right?'

'No,' he said immediately. 'I think it makes perfect sense.' He nudged her arm with his. 'You want a frappe?'

'I would love a frappe, but not too much milk, it doesn't help with singing.'

He smiled. 'Ah, but we are making music for fun, not following the rules.'

'OK,' she replied.

It didn't take long to make the drinks and then he opened up the lid of the old piano, its keys a little yellow with age. It still smelled of two things: olive wood where it had ended up being stored in Irini's wood-shed next to the winter logs for many years, and peppermints. His strongest memory was his grandfather's sweet of choice, always on hand, drawn from pockets or cupboards and generously shared.

'It's gorgeous,' Cara said, stepping up to the piano and running her hand over the body of it.

He played some chords. 'And it still sounds so good.'

'Oh my God, it does. That tone.'

'So,' he said. 'Where do you want to start?'

She took a sip of her frappe as if she were in deep contemplation. 'Maybe at the beginning. There was this song my mum used to sing to me when I was little. It was something my nanna taught to her and one of the first songs I ever learned all the words to.'

'Hit me with it,' Akis said, pulling out the stool and sitting down.

'It's "Son of a Preacher Man" by Dusty Springfield.'

'Ha!' Akis exclaimed. 'You are messing with me now! You want the fake Deacon, the person my family wants to become a priest, to play a song about a preacher man.'

He watched Cara put her hands to her face, her expression one of horror. 'Oh my God! I didn't think! I am so so sorry.'

He laughed then and shook his head. 'It is OK, really. But I do not know this. Give me one moment.' He took out his phone, unlocked it and handed it to her. 'I have Spotify.'

'And then you can learn it?' she asked, sounding surprised.

'What can I say? I have a gift for this.'

Two listens through and he had it nailed.

He looked to her. 'So, whenever you are ready?'

'Yes,' Cara said with a sigh. 'That's the problem. I don't know if I ever will be ready.'

'OK, this is not a problem,' Akis said. 'I will sing with you.'

'Really? You can sing too?'

'Not like you,' he answered. 'Nothing like you. But, you know, it will be fun. Not so much fun for my neighbours, but Stamatis has stopped doing night shifts so he won't be sleeping and...' He checked his watch. 'Siesta is almost over.'

'O-K,' Cara said.

'Just for fun, no?' He grinned. 'And much more fun than what we would have been doing right now with snakes if the castle wasn't falling down.'

She smiled at him. 'OK.'

'OK, let's go.'

31

Cara closed her eyes and held the last note, feeling the vibration running through every single fibre of her body. The sensation was as natural as it was alien, like it was a beautiful routine she had forgotten about and needed to re-engage anew with. She opened her eyes... and it was then she heard the applause.

Akis got up off the stool and went out onto the balcony.

'There are many people, Cara,' he announced. 'At other balconies and down on the street, looking up.'

She swallowed. *Her worst fear.* People wanting to watch her. She tried to stop the swell in her stomach, waves of fear threatening to arrive. But, she was safe here. No one could see her. And people had enjoyed her voice. That was enough.

'Hey,' Akis said, coming back into the room. 'You know, no one can see you, even if they can *see* you.'

'What?' Cara said. 'That's not true.'

'It is exactly true. You think, when I dance on stage that I am on stage, thinking about the audience?'

'Aren't you?'

He shook his head. 'No, of course not. And I do not believe you always are when you sing. Because the music moves you, does it not?

That's the main thing that music does. It takes you away from where you are and it puts you in another time, another place, when you were happier, when you were sadder, when you were feeling a little sexy.'

She swallowed. The more time she was spending with this ridiculously good-looking guy with these alternative views of living, the sexier she was finding him.

'OK,' Akis said. 'I think I need to show you what I mean.' He took his phone from the top of the piano, put it in the pocket of his jeans and then he grabbed what looked like a speaker from a shelf. 'Come on.'

* * *

'OK, I need a bench,' Akis said, once they were outside in the town, near Spianada Square. 'A moped, yes, this one is good. A lamp post. OK, here.'

'I have no idea what you're doing,' Cara said.

'Letting people see me but not see me,' he announced. 'But we need people.' Suddenly he was jumping on top of the bench, hands either side of his mouth, yelling something in Greek and then English.

'Come! See a taster of a new dance for the hot show at the Escape Theatre Bar on Friday! Completely free! Right now!'

If he had done this somewhere in London, Cara knew the kinds of looks he would be getting, but here people seemed to be interested, were slowing their pace, stopping and waiting.

'OK,' Akis said. 'I have only run through this half a dozen times and it has never gone completely right before but this is not the point of the exercise. Now, you sit here and... let's see if you or anyone else can see me.'

A few moments later and the music started, pulsing bass coming from the speaker he had positioned at the foot of a tree. Cara recognised it instantly. It was 'Under the Influence' by Chris Brown and the second Akis began to move she was completely spellbound. And the crowd started to grow as he span and stretched and prowled across the ground, moving effortlessly from the ground and into a handstand then back down again. She couldn't take her eyes away from him, he was mesmerising in every single way and it was obvious every other person in this makeshift audience felt exactly the same.

Using a bench to propel himself off, Akis did a turn in the air before flipping over the moped and grabbing the lamp post like it was a pole from the stage and twirling around it with so much power. Then his feet were back to the ground, sliding this way and that, hips winding, with all the finesse he had shown at the hen night show. But, somehow this was different. It was more organic, felt less like a formulated routine, and now, as she continued to watch, she noticed that no matter how enthralled the audience were, his eyes were only on her. She shivered despite the heat of the day, the heartbeat in her throat thrumming.

And with a final pop and lock, the routine was over.

The way Cara felt could only be described as having the immediate after-glow of the greatest sex. She sat up a little straighter, trying to stabilise herself. She swallowed as she watched Akis accept the applause and then he was tearing off his T-shirt, wiping his body down with it and coming over to her.

'So, that's how you're seen, but not really seen,' he said, a little out of breath.

'I don't think I understand any better,' she admitted. 'I mean, it was incredible, obviously, and there were people right there, watching you, not able to think about anything else but what they were seeing.'

'Yeah,' he told her. 'But... I wasn't really there.'

She frowned. 'I don't get it.'

He smiled. 'In my head,' he said, touching his brow. 'I was back in my apartment thinking about how it felt to hear you sing.' He took a deep breath. 'The only person who could have been able to see me was you.'

A tidal wave of passion slapped Cara hard and her insides coiled as if a snake blessing was imminent. She *had* seen him. And despite everyone else circled around, she was the only one he'd let in.

He put his hand on hers and it felt so hot and intense she half-expected to see sparks in the air.

'People can only really see you if you let them,' Akis whispered.

She swallowed as she drowned in those eyes and then *her* eyes dropped to his lips. Those lips that had almost scorched hers once already. What was it between them? Circumstances, or perhaps the universe, putting them together and their connection keeping them there. She hadn't actually ever felt anything like this before.

He stood up, letting her hand go.

'So, I should go get that speaker before someone takes it,' he said, taking a step back from the bench.

'Oh, yes, yes, you should.'

And she watched him retreat, and it felt like it was in more ways than one.

32

COOK'S CLUB CORFU

'She's late,' Margot said, checking her watch.

Cara and Margot were sat on the veranda outside the main hotel building, a carafe of white wine between them. They were waiting for Sofia, for something Cara had only found out her aunt had organised when Akis had dropped her back at the hotel. Apparently, this tête a tête was to get more info about the maharajah now that the Maxi-Go situation was more 'incendiary'.

'Well,' Cara said. 'She is planning a wedding and the castle fiasco is a lot.'

Margot tittered. 'It was awful, wasn't it? What was she thinking?'

Cara didn't like Margot's obvious glee at the situation. At the end of the day this was Wren and Cosmos's special day and no one should be finding problems amusing.

'Did they decide what they're going to do instead?' Cara asked, then took a sip of her wine, leaning back in her chair.

'Yes, you left again, didn't you? With the dancer,' Margot said, a knowing look on her face.

'He's a pianist, actually,' she corrected.

'I bet he is.' A smutty laugh ensued. 'Well, they don't know what they're going to do but apparently the bride and groom are going to get some input now. My guess, from having met them both, is *she* will want to get married in a field of wildflowers and *he* will do whatever she wants as long as it doesn't involve him having to think.'

'Margot!' Cara exclaimed.

'Honestly, when Raj sees this countryside backwater she lives in he's going to be booking a room here at Cook's Club.'

'She's here,' Cara said, sitting up in her seat and sweeping her hair behind her ears. She could see Sofia moving from inside the foyer towards the doors that led out to the terrace.

'OK,' Margot said. 'So, like any of the negotiations we've handled together, you be the quieter, friendlier one and I'll be—'

'Cruella,' Cara replied.

'Sofia!' Margot said, getting to her feet.

'Margot,' Sofia greeted. 'My God! What happened to you? Were you like this earlier when I saw you?'

'Yes, actually, a small accident involving an air-conditioning unit, not here I hasten to add, as this hotel is divine. Anyway, earlier on you had so much on your mind.'

'Yes,' Sofia said with a sigh, sinking into the spare chair. 'Hello, Cara.'

'Hello, Sofia. Let me pour you a glass of wine.'

'*Efharisto poli*,' Sofia said in thanks.

'So,' Margot said. 'Have you been able to find an alternative venue for the wedding?'

Sofia shook her head. 'Not quite yet. I tried to talk to Wren but her mother is here, as you saw, and she wants to have involvement as if it is not my son's country and my son's wedding.'

'I understand completely,' Margot stated, nodding as if she were the wisest sage.

'At this late stage we are going to be unable to secure any of the best hotels although I have tried to get people I know to talk to people they know and get other secure bookings, you know, not so secured.'

'Hmm,' Margot said. 'Euro talks if you have enough of it to splash around.'

'Well, sadly,' Sofia began, cradling her wine glass. 'My husband says no more spending. If only he knew how much I had *actually* spent.'

Margot laughed. Sofia laughed. And Cara wondered how her life had got to this point.

She thought about Akis then. When they'd gone back to the apartment after his dance, they had sung again. He had started with her like he had before, but then she had taken the lead and he had just played. With every song they had performed together, she had grown in confidence. And it hadn't felt like it had before when she'd been fighting for a recording contract, when she knew she'd wake at night concerned she hadn't done enough vocal exercises, praying she was good enough to make it. It had felt warm and wonderful, playful and fun, like no matter what she sang, the joy that each note gave her was the only important thing.

'Can't Raj help?' Margot asked, her fingers gripping the edge of the table. 'The Raj I remember was dripping in everything from sheer testosterone to Gucci. Surely he'd be able to help out with a few...' Margot lowered her voice a notch. 'Backhanders so to speak.'

'I'm not sure it would be appropriate,' Sofia answered.

'You could call it a pre-wedding present.'

'Oh, well, Raj has already sent a very generous gift. It's a golden monkey.'

Cara had to quickly swallow her mouthful of wine before she choked.

'In his province a golden monkey symbolises health, wealth and fertility,' Sofia explained.

'Wow,' Margot said. 'A triple treat. But, why would he send his present early? Was it too heavy for his luggage allowance? He always used to fly private I remember.'

'What?' Sofia asked.

Cara was starting to get a very bad feeling about this...

'Well, why wouldn't Raj bring his golden ape with him when he comes to the wedding?' Margot asked.

'Oh, Raj isn't able to come to the wedding,' Sofia said, circling her finger around the rim of her wine glass.

Cara saw the blood drain from Margot's face. She looked worse now than she had right after the accident. And Margot never usually gave away a reaction like that. Something was off. And until Cara knew what it was, she was going to have to step in here, if only to cover for Margot's silence.

'Oh, that's a shame,' Cara said, picking up the carafe and topping up Margot's glass and then Sofia's, 'that you three can't get together and discuss all the things you got up to at college.'

'Well,' Sofia said. 'I think we've all moved on substantially since then. College was so long ago it feels like an alternate reality.'

'So, is Raj busy with his... kingly... responsibilities?' Cara asked. 'I have no idea what a maharajah does.' She laughed, just enough.

'He's actually in Greece right now on business,' Sofia said. 'Santorini. But he has to fly off to Dubai before the wedding.'

'Oh, wow, Santorini,' Cara said. 'I've always wanted to visit. It looks so beautiful on Instagram. What's the name of the place everyone takes those sunset views from? You know, the place with all those walk-from-the-bedroom-to-the-pool whitewashed hotels?'

'You mean Oia,' Sofia said. 'Yes, that's where Raj is now.'

'Lucky Raj,' Cara said. 'Well, Margot, why don't we show Sofia the menu on the app, order some food?'

'Yes,' Margot croaked, reviving enough to speak. 'Yes, that's a good idea. But, while Sofia looks at the app, we need to check with Marios about the special delivery.'

'Gosh, yes,' Cara said, getting to her feet. 'Yes, you're right. Sofia, here's the app on my phone. If you could excuse us, only for a second.'

Rapidly, they moved into the hotel out of sight of their guest.

'He's not fucking coming,' Margot snarled bitterly. 'After everything I've done.'

'But you know where he is,' Cara said. 'I'm sure it wouldn't take much to find out the villa he's staying in.'

'I do still have my contacts in MI5,' Margot agreed, nodding.

It would have been funny if it wasn't an absolute truth that Cara had never asked any questions about.

Margot continued. 'I'll give Tony a call and see if we can find out. Meanwhile, I'll book our flights.'

'What?' Cara exclaimed.

'I need to see Raj, Cara! And if he's in Santorini then that's where we need to be!' Margot was already tapping on her phone.

'But—'

'And the other thing I need to do is buy a replacement case.' She tutted. 'An inferior Greek one like this substandard phone, I guess.'

'But we can't just leave,' Cara said, her stomach lurching. 'What about the wedding? And... you know... me singing at it.'

'Cara, darling, that was just our in, wasn't it? To get an invitation. You don't actually have to do it now. What a relief for you! We can make our excuses and never darken the door of this place again.'

Cara swallowed. All she could think of was Akis. Accompanying her today on the piano, and before that on the old keyboard, their boat trip and the swimming, the way he ate fish with his fingers... She couldn't imagine leaving for another Greek island and never seeing him again. And today she had sang, properly sang, for the first time in so long and it had felt so different than it had before, better even. It had given her hope that even if there wasn't a way back for her career, there could be a way back to enjoying music.

'Margot, we... can't. You have made a commitment for me to sing and I've met everyone and we've been to the hen night and the wine and cake tasting and—'

'Oh, Cara, you're not *caring* about these people, are you?' Margot asked. 'Sofia all dressed up like Melania Trump, her mother dressed down like a tramp.'

'Margot!' Cara exclaimed, appalled by her aunt's statement.

'When you start to get feelings for people, that's when you make mistakes and your vision gets cloudy. I thought I taught you that.'

'We are going to the wedding,' Cara stated forcefully. 'I don't want to let people down.'

'Well, I—'

'No!' Cara said. 'If we really have to go to Santorini then we're coming back for the wedding. Otherwise I'm not leaving with you.' She folded her arms across her chest in a show of absolute authority she had never used with Margot before.

She held her aunt's steely deal-winning gaze with everything she could muster until her eyes began to water.

'OK, fine. Now that's decided, let's eat like it's an Olympic sprint. Then we'll get Sofia out of here and back to those crumbling ruins that Shrek wouldn't even entertain living in.'

33

IRINI'S HOME, NOTOS

'Aki, relax, it is Pappa Spiros, not a grizzly bear.'

It was only when he saw his grandmother shuffling around Pig to open her door that Akis realised he had been holding his cup of coffee so tightly his fingertips were white. He didn't want to be doing this, but he had made his mother a promise and he wasn't in the habit of breaking those. He would listen. That was all he had agreed to do. But he would give it a proper chance.

He took a deep breath as the mountain of the man that was Pappa Spiros squeezed into the space, all black robes, hair dyed jet black including his beard. The man had to be in his sixties but he was an imposing character with a commanding nature.

'Aki,' he greeted.

Akis stood up and they kissed each cheek in turn. '*Pappa.*'

'Please, *Pappa*, sit in the best chair,' Irini said, moving a pile of newspapers from the only seat with extra cushioning. Pig let out a bray of discontent as if he'd hoped he would be sitting in the best chair.

'Can I make you a drink? Coffee? Ouzo?' Akis offered.

'I am OK,' the priest answered. 'I have just had a drink with your father at the Panorama.'

'Oh,' Akis said. He was a little surprised that his father was able to escape the house when the wedding preparation was in turmoil.

'Your mother is out,' Pappa Spiros said, as if that explained everything.

Akis smiled.

Irini sat down in another chair, shaking her head. 'Thanasis has given up trying to have an opinion on anything these days. I think the last decision he was allowed to make was in 1998.'

Pig began to nibble on the edge of a newspaper.

'And, speaking of decisions,' Pappa Spiros said, turning his full attention to Akis. 'I hear you want me to tell you what life as a priest would be like for you.'

Akis took a swig of his coffee, hoping for caffeine to assist. 'You know about my situation?'

'You are speaking of the Diakos curse,' Pappa Spiros said, making a sign of the cross in the air.

Akis sighed. 'So, it's really real?'

'Is there absolute proof and conclusive evidence? We don't know, for sure, we can only make certain assumptions based on events that have occurred throughout history.'

'So, what do I do with that?' Akis asked. 'Because if there is no truth to it then what am I thinking giving up the life I've built for myself for a life I haven't chosen?'

'And that is where the problem lies,' Pappa Spiros agreed.

'What Pappa Spiros is saying is that you choosing the church shouldn't be because of the Diakos curse,' Irini said.

Pig coughed.

'But, the priesthood has never been something on my agenda,' Akis admitted. 'No offence.'

'But it could be something you choose rather than see as a forced decision. It is a good life, an important life, supporting not just the faith of the community but the community itself.'

Akis swallowed. Choosing to be a priest. Because he wanted to. Not because he was being forced to. Surely he *didn't* want to. That had always been at the forefront of his mind when he was coming up against his adamant mother.

'A lot of the work is simply listening, Aki. You are the ear that takes the worries of the villagers, passes their concerns to God and gives them a direction to go forward in.'

'But I have no experience in doing that.'

'Neither did I at the beginning,' Pappa Spiros said. 'But the scripture, it will always guide you.'

'Yeah,' Akis said. 'But the scripture is also telling my family that if I don't become a priest before my thirtieth birthday then all kinds of horrors will prevail.'

'Have you read any of the stories about the Diakos curse?' Pappa Spiros asked.

Akis shook his head.

'Perhaps take a look. Like with all stories in scripture, there are many ways to interpret them. Over the years, philosophers and clerics have all added different reasoning behind the tales. Perhaps if you read about it, things will become much more clear. Now, shall I take you through my typical day? Perhaps it will not be quite as terrifying as you think.'

* * *

Over an hour later, Akis's head was spinning and he almost knew enough of the litany to be able to recite it if he was needed for service on Sunday. He stood in the garden looking out over the olive grove to the sunset beyond turning the sky a fiesta of pink, Pig by his side munching on sparse tufts of dry grass.

'What did you think, Aki?'

It was his grandmother, stepping through the garden, a bottle of ouzo in one hand and two small glasses in the other. He hastened to take them from her, hurried to the rusted metal table and two equally old chairs.

'I think that perhaps neither of us should be drinking ouzo,' he remarked, making sure she was settled in her chair before taking his. 'I have my motorbike.'

'Soon your mother will be measuring you up for the robes of a priest without the Velcro like your dancing show,' Irini said. She laughed until she started to cough.

'I'll get you some water,' Akis said, standing up.

'No,' Irini replied. 'Ouzo is all I need. God whispered in my ear this morning.'

Akis shook his head as he poured them both a little of the clear liquid. 'Pappa Spiros did not tell me anything about God doing any whispering.'

'But he did tell you about re-imaginings. The way the stories from the past can be adjusted.'

'I'm not sure it's the stories that need to be adjusted,' Akis contemplated aloud. 'I think perhaps it is my mother's views. And the way she projects her insecurities onto Cosmos.'

'Because he is the weakest goat,' Irini said, sipping her drink as Pig moved to another spot. 'That is what your mother has always done. She finds the person who will listen to her agenda the longest and she will make *her* opinions *their* opinions. Cosmos, poor Wren and your long-suffering father.'

'What do you think I should do?' Akis asked, sitting back in his chair.

'You ask me! You want *another* opinion to go with all the others being forced on you? You are crazy!'

Yeah, he was. And he had told Cara that the only person whose opinion really mattered was your own. Already he was losing a grip on who he was.

'I just want to do the right thing,' he admitted.

'Who for?' Irini asked.

'For everybody.'

'Ha! That is the impossible dream. It is an unachievable reality. You should know this already.'

'The best thing then,' Akis said. 'The thing that gets the closest best outcome for everybody that matters to me.'

Irini sat forward on her chair. 'Will you answer me something?'

'Sure.'

'Why when people talk about the day you lost your finger do they call it "Cosmos's accident"?'

Akis didn't answer. What was he supposed to say?

'Because Cosmos is OK. There are no physical scars, he does not speak of any trauma he feels. In fact, when he is made to regale the tale at events, he tells people he does not remember much of this. But you. I see what happened written all the way through you. The sacrifice you made. The sacrifices you are still willing to make for this family.'

Still, Akis had no words, but the emotion was there, picking away at his insides.

'And what of the girl?' Irini said. 'Cara.'

At the mere mention of her name, Akis was catapulted back to earlier that day, Cara's voice filling every corner of his apartment. Once she had gained her confidence, she had shown him exactly why she had made singing her profession. Her quality and tone were exquisite. Everything about her was exquisite...

'My mother's friend's niece?' he found himself saying.

Irini tutted. 'You know exactly who I mean without giving me a family tree. You like her.'

'Well, we are two of the only sane people at the centre of this wedding fiasco, it is natural for us to get along.'

'Do you think I was born yesterday under that olive tree?' Irini asked him, pointing. 'I know you, Aki. I see you. And how is becoming a priest going to help with that? You know you have to be married *before* you are a priest to be able to take a wife.'

He shook his head. 'I am aware.'

'Then you have a lot of think about. Or a lot to ask Cara.'

'*Yiayia*, if we believe this legend then I need to become a priest before I am thirty. That is not enough time to know someone long enough to ask them to marry me.'

'So you say,' Irini said, swiping a mosquito from her orbit. 'I knew your grandfather for three hours before I knew I was going to marry him. And six weeks later, only that long because my mother insisted on making me a dress, we were wed.'

Akis shook his head. 'Things are different these days.'

'And that is where the world's troubles lie. All this moving faster, a new, better thing every few weeks, but it is backwards motion. It is throw-away things. Things people are rushing quicker towards that do not even matter.' She sighed. 'Then slowly slowly in other areas that should be more important until there is no time left to make it count.'

His grandmother's words felt so pertinent for so many situations in his life. He slugged back the ouzo.

'Why not speak to your father?' she suggested.

'My father?' Akis asked, a little surprised at the suggestion.

'He is the oldest Diakos around here,' she reminded him. 'His older brother, your uncle, had made his choices about the priesthood before he passed away. He will have spoken to Thanasis about it.'

Uncle Dimitri. No one talked much about him. All Akis knew was that he had become a priest and then passed away before his first Sunday service.

He mused for a second. What did that mean for the curse? Even someone who had followed the 'rules' hadn't escaped bad fortune.

'Ask your father,' Irini said again. 'And' – she reached for her glass – 'pour me another ouzo.'

34

CORFU AIRPORT, CORFU TOWN

'This case is absurd! It barely moves on these wheels and the zip already disintegrates whenever I touch it!'

It was the next morning and the airport was busy. But they had successfully managed to sashay around the TUI queue and had cleared security. There was no need to go through passport control as they weren't leaving Greece. Cara had barely slept and now, bizarrely, they were about to get on a flight to Athens and then another to Santorini.

'At least it doesn't have the potential to explode,' Cara said, looking for any spare seats near their gate.

'Ssh! What have I told you about saying that? And you certainly can't say things like that when we're in the middle of an airport. Ah, there's a couple of seats, near a bin, but never mind, needs must.'

Cara followed her aunt, sat down and got her phone from the zipped pouch on her case. There was a half-written text she had started composing last night. It was about the fourth or fifth version now, because everything she wrote was either too simple or not simple enough.

I'm going to Santorini. Just for a few days. We will be back for the wedding. But I won't be able to rehearse with you.

She deleted the last line. They weren't rehearsing. Rehearsing meant she was definitely going to perform at the wedding and the thought of that was still making her feel sick. She sighed.

'What are you doing?' Margot asked, suddenly giving Cara her attention.

'Nothing.' Cara hid the screen on her phone away.

'It's Seb, isn't it? Trying to crawl his way back to you like the last time,' Margot blasted. 'Slimy, slippery, treacherous weasel.'

Cara jolted. 'What last time?'

'Well... that was just an assumption. It's what men do, isn't it? Take what they want, not stick around for the day-to-day grind, think it's going to be all champagne and reverse cow-girling for the rest of their days.' Margot took a breath. 'Much better to just have something temporary; everyone knows where they stand and no actual feelings get hurt.'

Cara took a good long look at her aunt. She had never known her have anyone special in her life. It had always been about business, making money and spending it almost as fast. With only very small exceptions, Margot put Margot first. But there was a fragility about her now, like a loose hem on a Chanel skirt; everything was ultimately in place but there were tiny suggestions of the first signs of an unpicking.

'Like you and the dancer,' Margot continued before Cara could say anything else.

'Akis,' Cara corrected, ensuring Margot could definitely not see her phone screen.

'Yes. I am all for lusting them and leaving them. You should do more of that. Maybe in Santorini Raj will have a rather nice personal security guard you can get your teeth into.'

'I thought Santorini was business,' Cara said. 'We won't have time to sink our teeth into anything but getting Raj to invest, right?'

Margot waved a dismissive hand. 'Sometimes you have to schmooze to not lose, remember. It can take time and tactics.'

'We have a couple of days. I'm coming back for the wedding.'

'To sing? Because I'm remembering that announcement didn't go down so well.'

'I don't know yet,' Cara said.

'Well, don't go accepting any life advice from your mother if she phones. She wrote you off as... what did she call it? Ah yes, "a classic avoider of reality".'

'What?' Cara asked, nerves pinching.

'Oh, don't take it to heart, that woman actually wouldn't know reality if it was waving a placard at her with its name on. She's the one living some trippy fantasy making out she's trying to save the planet when in reality she's just living her gap year dream a few decades too late. Probably still dressed in hemp.'

Cara swallowed. Her mum thought she avoided reality. Is that what she thought at the beginning when she had started her singing career? That it was something she would never be good enough at to be a success?

'Meanwhile,' Margot carried on. 'You and I are about to make the Maxi-Go a household name all over the world. And we're going to Santorini! Who needs Corfu now?' Margot laughed. 'I'm going to take a quick peek at Duty Free.'

As Margot left her seat, Cara looked back to her phone. With a couple of taps, the message was deleted.

35

PETRITI HARBOUR, CORFU

Akis watched Cosmos on board the fishing boat, a collection of cats already waiting to see what they could get – donated or stolen. The vessel had docked in this busy harbour as it did every day, bringing in the catch. This was somewhere he'd come often as a child, to fish, to help their father do exactly what Cosmos was doing now and to eat in the dockfront tavernas. It was calm here, busy with boats but it still managed to achieve serenity.

'Aki!' Cosmos called, waving a hand.

'Tell me why we are doing this again?' Anastasia asked, through gritted teeth.

'We are doing this,' Akis said, waving back at their brother, 'so that Cosmos really does have a say in where he and Wren are going to get married. Before our mother decides where the new blessing of the snakes will be and there are no snakes left to bless another place.'

'Did you really speak to Pappa Spiros last night?' Anastasia asked as they made their way towards the boat their brother was disembarking from.

'How did you know that?' Akis asked.

'Come on, Aki. You can't take a shit on this island without someone knowing about it.'

He sighed. 'Yeah, I did.'

'Why? I mean, you know this priest idea is mental, right? I don't give a shit if I wake up one day, burst into flames and turn into a pile of dust. You giving up who you are to wear black and *not* rip it off yourself for horny women is insanity.'

'Well, *I* don't want you to burst into flames and turn into dust.' He sighed. 'And I don't want Cosmos worrying about anyone bursting into flames at all. Anyway, I had this conversation with our grandmother last night. I am collecting everyone's opinions.'

'Aki! Anastasia! I have caught the best fish today!' Cosmos called.

'Look at him,' Anastasia said, shaking her head. 'Still acting like he is ten years old.'

'About to become a married man,' Akis reminded her.

'If it was anyone but Wren I would think the situation was madness. But she is good for him. She is as ill-equipped for life too but somehow in different ways. They balance each other out.'

'Yeah,' Akis agreed. 'You are right.'

'So, come on, let's talk some sense into him, get this wedding somewhere he and Wren actually want.'

* * *

'Isn't this the best fish?' Cosmos asked once they had been served at the sea-front taverna.

'It is good,' Akis agreed, sucking each finger in turn.

'Honestly, why you two grown men still eat with your fingers, it is disgusting,' Anastasia said, spearing a prawn with her fork. 'So, Cosmos, we have a shortlist now, yes?'

'A shortlist? For the man party?'

'No! Not the man party! The wedding!' Anastasia stated. 'You know, the actual meant-to-be greatest day of your life that is now not taking place in an over-priced, over-sized turreted Cinderella crib our mother is going to be paying taxes on for years unless she takes a sledgehammer to it.'

'I don't know,' Cosmos said. 'Wren is talking to her mother a lot and crying. I don't want to say the wrong thing. I am worried there might not even be a wedding.'

'What?!' This was a joint exclamation from both Akis and Anastasia.

'It is too stressful for her. She does not deal with stress well. *I* do not deal with stress well. And with the Diakos curse—'

'No, no, no,' Anastasia jumped in. 'We are not talking about *that* now. Now we are talking about ideas for where you and Wren are going to get married next week. Because that is your fate. A long, happy, married life with the only woman who will ever love you like she does.'

Akis squirmed a little at his sister's bluntness. 'Cosmo, you and Wren and your relationship is the most important thing. The wedding, it is just a day, a special day but *one* day out of all of the days you are going to be spending together.'

'Then why does it have to be so *big*?' Cosmos asked, throwing his hands up.

It was as animated and passionate as Akis had ever seen him and this was obviously weighing heavily on his mind.

'It doesn't have to be big,' Akis said. 'Does it, Anastasia?'

'But have you seen everything that *Mama* has ordered?' Cosmos continued. 'There are balloons in the shape of peacocks, there are... fireworks and cannons.'

'There are?' Anastasia exclaimed. 'When did she order those?'

Akis gave her a look that told her she should focus on the real issue. 'Cosmo, it does not have to be any way but *your* way. I am being serious.'

Cosmos looked at him directly then, as if suddenly the penny had dropped. 'Really?'

'Yes!' Anastasia insisted. 'Akis and I, we can help tear up *anything* our mother or anyone else has put in place. *Anything*, whether it's peacock-shaped or not.'

'But she will be disappointed,' Cosmos said, sighing.

'*Mama* is always disappointed! She gets up in the morning and is disappointed before she has even opened the shutters. Nothing is ever right for her, Cosmo. You know that is why she does not have a real relationship with *Yiayia*.'

'What Anastasia is really getting at is, *Mama* will feel the way *Mama* feels regardless of what choices you and Wren make,' Akis said, assuring him.

'So, if I say... I want to get married on my fishing boat then, that would be OK?' Cosmos asked, his eyes going over to the large blue and white vessel he had disembarked from earlier.

'Ugh! Cosmo, no! Everyone will stink of fish, *I* will stink of fish!' Anastasia barked.

'I like fish,' Cosmos answered sadly.

'Cosmo,' Akis said, moving to sit next to his brother and placing a hand on his arm. 'If you want to get married on the boat, talk to Wren about it. If she wants to get married in a field, talk to her about it. Maybe you can do something that incorporates both things.'

'Wren wants to get married in a field?' Cosmos asked, his mouth dropping open.

'No,' Akis said. 'I mean, I don't know. It was a—'

He stopped talking as he felt his phone vibrating in the pocket of his jeans. He pulled it out and checked the screen. *Horatio.*

'Give me one second,' he said, standing up. 'It's Horatio and we are meant to have a rehearsal this afternoon so I need to—'

'Take it,' Anastasia said.

'Hey,' Akis said, stepping away from the table and taking the call. 'How is your arm?'

'Ah, it is OK. Better. So, the new costumes have arrived in time for rehearsal this afternoon.'

'That's good,' Akis said. 'I actually did a run through of the new routine yesterday. In Spianada Square. Cara thought—'

'You have spoken to Cara?' Horatio interrupted.

'Yesterday,' Akis said. 'When I dropped her at her hotel.'

'Oh... OK.'

'Oh, OK, what?'

'So, I had to make a delivery to the Cook's Club, you know I some-times work for the hygiene company, and one of the girls on reception, she likes me, and she happened to tell me that Cara and her aunt, they checked out this morning.'

Checked out. His heart lurched at those two words. Cara had left the hotel. Gone where? Somewhere else on Corfu? Back to the UK? He didn't understand. He needed clarification.

'What?'

'They've gone to Santorini,' Horatio said.

'What?'

'Is there something wrong with this line?' Horatio asked. 'It is like you cannot hear me. I said they have gone to Santorini.'

'Yeah,' Akis replied finally. 'I thought that's what you said.'

But he didn't understand it. And how was he hearing it from Horatio and not from Cara? He swallowed then. Maybe what they had shared together had meant more to him than it had to her.

'They will be back for the wedding,' Horatio said. 'I mean, the girl at reception said that. That they were coming back. They were going to stay there again.'

'OK,' Akis said.

'So, I will see you this afternoon?'

'Yeah, sure,' Akis agreed, nodding even though Horatio couldn't see.

'*Yassas.*'

Akis ended the call and took a deep breath. He had so much on his plate already, perhaps this was for the best.

'Aki!' Anastasia called. 'Please come and tell Cosmos that no matter what, Pig is not coming to the service!'

Akis shook his head. He needed to focus on his family right now.

36

CANAVES OIA BOUTIQUE HOTEL, OIA, SANTORINI

Cara gasped the second she saw the view from their apartment. It was exactly like every Instagram post she'd ever been served of dream Greek destinations. From the whitewashed sugar-cube buildings tumbling in stages down from the heights of this mound of volcanic rock, to the vast expanse of sea stretching out like it was azure glass. It was breath-taking, it was luxury, it was indulgent beauty looking out at a landscape forged by time.

'That was Tony,' Margot said, strutting across the terrace dressed in nothing but one of the white waffle dressing gowns that had been rolled up like pillows with pink orchids on top of them. 'You know, from Secret Intelligence.' Margot had whispered the last two words almost as quietly as she had been whispering about the Maxi-Go incident.

'Does he know where Raj is staying?'

'He does,' Margot said, picking a large, fleshy piece of watermelon from their complimentary fruit tray.

'Well, where?' Cara asked.

'That doesn't actually matter because Tony gave me something better. And I'm not talking about that gala dinner in ninety-five.'

'Please, Margot, get to the point.'

'Raj is a guest of honour at an exclusive event tomorrow night. And we are on the list! Honestly, it's almost better that he's here in Santorini, it's so much more exclusive, bang full of the rich and famous, decadence seeping from every pore of this place. Look at the pool!'

Cara *had* looked at the pool. You couldn't not look at the pool because it led straight out from the bedroom to the patio. It was another tick from the Santorini highlights shown on social media. Floating stepping stones lay across the water that was inside the cave-style room, leading onto the terrace and the rest of the infinity pool that hung over the caldera view. It was stunning.

'Margot,' Cara said, her thoughts racing as if they were doing a sprint finish after a marathon. 'Don't you think this is all rather a lot of effort? Getting on the guest list for a wedding, paying for the wedding singer to pull out, flying to another Greek island. I mean, how sure are you that Raj is going to want to invest, or has contacts who will? And, wouldn't it have been easier to have made an appointment to see him at his... palace or wherever than follow him around Europe?'

'Easier?' Margot had said the word like it was going to give her herpes. 'Oh, yes, it would definitely have been easier to ring a random number, be gate-kept out of things, or get lumbered talking to some menial.'

'But you know Raj,' Cara said. 'You went to college with him.'

'Exactly,' Margot agreed. 'And we haven't seen each other since that fateful night in Bora Bora. No, there needs to be the element of surprise. It needs to be so planned that it looks completely unplanned. Remember that time with the lizards?'

Cara shuddered. The deep-dive she had done into a client they were trying to entice had shown a fascination in lizards. She had booked them exclusive access to the reptile house after it was closed for their client to hold animals and take behind-the-scenes photos. She had also arranged a champagne buffet. They had never let on that they had found out about his obsession, just cited it as a lucky coincidence on their part. It was still one of their biggest orders to date.

'So, we go shopping, we find ourselves some killer outfits, I saw a beautiful boutique just as we arrived, then we get to the party and your spot is at midnight,' Margot said.

Spot. Cara didn't like the sound of this.

'What?' she said as Margot dived back into the fruit bowl for some grapes.

'The element of surprise, Cara. The shock factor. The difference between mediocrity and stellar. You are going to be singing at the event. It's worked perfectly actually. The first performance after Eurovision. The big comeback. Mix that with the Maxi-Go and there isn't going to be an investor alive who doesn't want to be part of Team Jones.'

Now the Santorini heat was creeping up Cara's back and it wasn't pleasant. 'What?' Cara said again.

'It doesn't have to be, you know, "unflawed" shall we say but, you know, the G10 wouldn't go amiss.'

'No,' Cara said, striding away from the table to the very edge of the patio and that vista.

'Cara,' Margot said, following. 'You said yourself that you're going to sing at the silly little wedding. This is much bigger and better than that! Think of who could be at this *exclusive* event! Connected people! People who could get you back into the music business.'

'No,' Cara said again. 'I'm not doing it. I'm not singing. And I've never said anything about wanting to go back into the music business.'

'OK fine, but if you want to continue to eat from my table then you should rethink that "no" and turn it into a "yes".'

Cara's mouth dropped open at Margot's savageness. What was she actually saying? That Cara didn't pull her weight in the business? That she had been living off Margot's generosity for too long? Whichever or whatever it was she couldn't listen to any more.

'I'm going out,' she said, moving across the terrace towards the stepping stones that led to the bedroom.

'Out?' Margot queried. 'But we only just arrived. Cara, wait, just listen to me—'

At this point, she didn't have anything left to say.

37

HASSAPIKO BAR, OIA, SANTORINI

It was barely the afternoon, but Cara had chosen this traditional-looking bar and ordered a glass of white wine. It was cool inside, apparently a former butcher's shop. What was she going to do? What was she even doing here in Santorini being some kind of stooge in whatever situation Margot decided to concoct? And, once again, her aunt had signed her up for something she knew she found terrifying, something she had only just begun slightly testing the water with again.

She took a sip of the drink and let the cool fruitiness attempt to soothe her. It was then that her phone began to ring.

She looked at the name on the screen. *Whimsy*. It was her mum. And yes, pathetically, she had updated the contact to a name that wasn't the new name she said she was now called... She watched as the call continued to ring until it rung out. She couldn't handle talking to her now. It wasn't like her mother had been the person to confide in when things were going wrong before. As soon as Moldova happened, Wissy and Nettlewood had got on a plane to Bolivia.

Closing her eyes, she took a deep breath. Perhaps her parents had assumed at the time that Seb was going to be there for her. That's what you would imagine a fiancé would do, wasn't it? Be the one to wipe tears, lick wounds and bolster confidence. And, when the opposite had happened, when they'd already connected with fellow planet-saving enthusiasts, it was too late to jet back. And Margot had picked up the slack. A lot of slack. But did that mean she should be forever indebted? Always ready to do something she felt uncomfortable with because she owed her?

As if sensing her thoughts, her phone began to ring again. This time it was Margot. No doubt ready to give her some kind of pep talk. She wasn't going to answer that call either. She was in this bar on her own, in Santorini and she didn't want to talk to anyone.

Except, then Akis came to mind.

She had never sent him that text. But then he hadn't texted her either. When he had dropped her at the hotel after they had sung together, they hadn't arranged a firm time to meet again. She had assumed it *wouldn't* be a one-time thing, but had he? And why was she thinking about Akis so hard when an imminent concert was on her horizon? That was unless she went full-on head-to-head with Margot.

She picked up her phone and scrolled to his contact. Maybe she could...

Suddenly, ice flowed through her veins as the sound that haunted her broke into the easy vibe of the bar. Barking. Loud. Ferocious even. She slid, slipped, possibly fell from her stool and within seconds was backing up against a stone wall. The dog wasn't on a lead. It was in the bar. Marauding. And she was shaking. Terrified. Half of her needing to keep a view on its trajectory, the other half wanting to face the wall, close her eyes and pray.

'Cara!'

Someone was calling her. It sounded like... As the barking ripped through the air again, she sank to the floor, lungs bursting, breath stalling.

'Cara!'

Hearing her name for the second time she realised the voice was coming from the phone in her hand. Somehow Akis was on the line and she didn't know what to do apart from draw her knees up to her chest and try to make herself as small as possible.

'Cara, put me on speakerphone.'

The dog was bouncing around, jumping up excitedly at tables where other people seemed to find it endearing, patting its head, encouraging its presence...

Her thumb hit the icon on the screen.

'Akis...'

'Cara, listen to me, where are you in Santorini? What place?'

'There's... a dog. It's real. Can you hear it?'

'Yes, I can hear it. Now, listen to me. Remember what I said to you about people only seeing you if you let them?'

Her brain felt like someone had put it in a pan and was frying it like eggs. She couldn't focus.

'Listen to my voice,' Akis continued. 'Listen *only* to my voice. Breathe. Think of somewhere else, somewhere safe.'

Somewhere safe? She tried to find her breath, tried to tap into her rational thoughts. Where did she feel safe? She closed her eyes and drew on the memory.

'Everything is OK,' Akis told her. 'You're safe. No one can see you. Nothing can hurt you.'

She leaned hard into her memory, settled against it, let it whirl around her, enveloping her softly, easing into her conscience, erasing the fight or flight response. She could feel her heartbeat again, slowing, not pumping so furiously in her neck. Everything was quieter again.

'You are OK,' Akis said softly.

'I'm OK,' Cara murmured. The hum of a motorbike engine purred in her ear.

'The place, Cara, where you are in Santorini.'

'Oia,' Cara breathed almost on reflex.

'I'll find you,' Akis said firmly. 'I'm coming.'

38

CORFU AIRPORT, CORFU

Akis was perspiring as much from the rushing around he'd been doing since he'd got Cara's phone call as the humidity. He'd grabbed a back-pack, shoved the travel basics inside, then booked flights with Aegean. He didn't have the money really, but, to him, this wasn't a choice, it was essential.

'This is fucking crazy, Aki,' Anastasia said, taking the motorbike helmet from him as they stood outside the bustling terminal. 'You know that, right?'

'I am taking a trip, that is all,' he responded, keeping his cool as much as he could.

'To Santorini, only days before Cosmos's stag party that *you* are in charge of. Right before the wedding that doesn't even have a venue yet. And... and you're bound to miss the blessing of the snakes!'

'Anastasia, I trust that you have this, OK?' He put a hand on her shoulder. 'No one deals with *Mama* better than you. No one deals with Cosmos better than you.'

'That's a total lie. The way I want to deal with Cosmos is to hold him upside down by his ankles and shake him like a salt pot.'

'And the last time you tried that he was about seven—'

'I know, I know, and he peed his pants because he thought his head was going to fall off. OK, I get it. More gently this time.'

'No shaking him at all,' Akis ordered.

'None?' Anastasia asked, looking disappointed.

'Come here,' Akis said, opening up his arms to her.

'No, do not try to hug me now. I am mad at you.'

He took hold of her anyway and wrapped his arms around tight, squeezing her first, then going for a tickle around her ribs, something she had hated since they were young.

'Argh! Get off! You are psychotic!'

He laughed, letting her go. And then he checked his watch. He needed to get going.

'Listen,' he began, in more serious tones. 'As well as looking after Cosmos, and making sure *Mama* does not kill *Bampás* for his apathy, will you keep an eye on *Yiayia*?'

'With how much distance? Because that house has so many things inside it there is almost no room for Pig, let alone me.'

'Anastasia,' Akis said. 'Now you sound like *Mama*.'

He watched his sister take a breath. 'OK. Sorry.'

'I am concerned about her chest,' Akis said. 'She will only take ouzo as a remedy. If it gets any worse you must make sure she sees the doctor.'

'Oh my God, Aki,' Anastasia said, stamping a foot. 'This is not keeping an eye on someone. This is trying to get *Yiayia* to do something she will not want to do! That is harder than... getting *Mama* to stop cleaning.'

'I know,' Akis agreed. 'But I have faith in you.'

'Faith, huh?' Anastasia said, shaking her head. 'Is that The Dancing Deacon speaking or *Pappa* Akis?'

'OK, I really need to go,' he said, wanting to avoid the question. 'Please do not crash my motorbike.'

'Please be back before the snakes come out.'

He picked his backpack up off the floor but, before he could turn to go, a dark Mercedes taxi screeched to a halt beside them. The back door opened and out jumped Horatio.

'Hey,' he greeted, swinging a holdall onto his back and simultaneously slipping on his sunglasses.

'Horatio, what are you doing here?'

'The same thing you are,' he answered. 'Going to Santorini. Hey, Anastasia.'

'You are both the craziest people I have ever met! You told me it was a piano thing, and now your stupid best friend is here!' Anastasia exclaimed, sounding annoyed. 'This is nothing but a bro trip! Forgetting your responsibilities and leaving me with donkeys and snakes and a wedding maniac.'

'Horatio, I don't understand,' Akis said. 'You don't have the cash for this.'

'What? I do not have the cash for living life? That is one of the saddest things I have ever heard.' He shrugged then, dropping his holdall to the ground. 'I sold something I did not need, to pay for something I definitely do.'

'You sold something in like, an hour?' Akis asked.

'I know many people.'

'And no one is caring about what I say,' Anastasia shouted.

'We should go, Aki,' Horatio stated. 'I am in Row 1.'

'You booked business class?' Akis exclaimed.

'Bye, Anastasia,' Horatio said, picking up his holdall again and heading along the pavement towards departures.

Akis turned back to Anastasia. 'I owe you, OK?' he said sincerely. 'And, I promise, I will be back before Cosmos's big night.'

She hugged him then, throwing her arms around him and holding on tight. 'You'd better.'

'I give you my word.'

Anastasia let go of him. 'OK, go, go before I grab *you* by your ankles and try to shake some sense into you.'

'*Ya*,' Akis said, waving a hand and heading after Horatio.

39

OIA, SANTORINI

'How about this one? Ooo, it really makes your eyes stand out.'

Margot pressed the silky olive-green dress up against Cara's front and regarded her. It was early evening now and they were in a tiny little boutique, all spotless white paintwork, arches holding beautiful clothing on simplistic rails. There weren't many pieces – not a full-to-the-brim Primark store by any means – but what *was* here was stunning. Except Cara wasn't really in the mood for shopping. She wasn't in the mood for anything except lying in the cave coolness of their exquisite hotel room and rehydrating.

'Come on, let's try this one on,' Margot continued, whipping the dress over her arm and grabbing another coral-coloured one from the wall.

Cara couldn't really remember leaving the bar after the dog incident. She remembered speaking to Akis, she knew she had calmed significantly and she also knew that when she had opened her eyes, a kind lady had been there in front of her helping her up from the floor. She'd staggered out into the Santorini sunshine, disorientated and sluggish, reeling, not from the wine, but the presence of her literal black beast. Something she hadn't yet told Margot about. Because what was the point? Margot didn't understand why she hadn't sung since Eurovision.

She wasn't going to understand that she still had a very real and desperate fear of canines that even therapy had failed to fix.

'Your mother called me,' Margot stated, matter of fact as she picked up a rather tiny silver handbag that looked like it was incapable of carrying anything except perhaps a packet of chewing gum.

'What?'

'I know! Needy, isn't it? Because it's always about her and your father.'

'She tried to call me earlier but I... didn't get to it in time.'

'Yes, she told me.' Margot sighed. 'I swear she thinks I have you imprisoned in the warehouse most of the time.'

'Well, what did she say?' Cara asked.

'Nothing really. You know your mother. It's all poisonous bullfrog campaigns and saving undergrowth. Your dad has some rash. Probably from bullfrogs or undergrowth. That was it. She told me she'd call you again when she could. But you know what communication can be like in the middle of deep vegetation. Almost as bad as communication can be in some of those loud, nastily cheap award ceremonies we've had to endure.'

'Dad had a henna tattoo apparently,' Cara remarked.

'Don't you mean "Nettlewood"? He will be getting his hair braided next. Classic eco-warrior midlife crisis. So, moving on, what do you think of this one for me?'

Margot held a dress to herself that was so far away from her aunt's usual style that Cara was left wondering if this was a trap. It was light and white and floaty, beautifully on the bias cut and the very opposite to Margot's preferred classic, professional, no-nonsense tailoring. And the longer Cara took to answer the more chance there was to get this wrong.

'It's...' Why couldn't she think of one simply great word? Come on, brain. 'It's—'

'I'll help you,' Margot said. 'It's ridiculous. Ugh, vile! I can't bear to touch it any longer! Take it from me! Take it and put it back!'

Cara had the white garment thrust at her while Margot carried on stalking toward the changing room. Cara looked at the dress and at her aunt moving faster than an Amazon Prime Day deal and tried to connect the dots. Was this interest in more girlish, romantic fashion about Raj? Cara had never known there be anyone even semi-permanent in Margot's life romance wise. In fact, the only people semi-permanent were Randulph who valeted a car that Margot only vaguely used and her hairdresser, Lesley, who was at least seventy-five. Men were picked up, played with and just as quickly put back in whatever business toy box they had been found in. But what if the maharajah was more than just someone she wanted to do business with? What if he was someone Margot had *loved*?

'Margot, wait,' Cara said, rushing over the stone floor, the hanger holding the white dress in her hands.

Her aunt was already putting the olive-green dress and the tiny handbag inside the changing room.

'Why are you still holding that rag?' Margot asked, narrowing her eyes at the white dress like it wasn't fit for polishing the glass boxes in here that held beautiful silver bangles and bracelets.

Cara looked at the dress. 'I like it and it's a bit different. Maybe if I try this green dress on, you might try on the white one,' she suggested, holding it forward.

'Why?'

'Because it will be fun. You know, like when we went to Liberty before we came to Greece.'

'I did not try on anything like that white thing in Liberty. In fact, the only thing in Liberty that looks like that is the toilet paper.'

'Please, Margot,' Cara said, shaking the dress.

Margot rolled her eyes. 'If I do, will you stop bleating about this event I've lined up and at least try to get a few good notes out? Or, maybe, we should consider lip synching. Everyone does it these days, don't they?'

There was currently only one answer she could give if she wanted Margot to be in the dress and perhaps open up about Raj. Margot opening up about anything other than business strategy was as rare as some of the steak tartare she ordered at restaurants. Her aunt might share TMI of her sexual encounters, but when it came to the emotional side of personal there was a definite void. Perhaps this was her chance to unlock a piece of that.

'I will stop bleating,' Cara said, not really committing to anything.

'Fine,' Margot said, ripping the hanger from Cara's hand and pulling the curtain shut.

Cara waited, hearing a disgruntled Margot undressing, shoes clunking to the floor and then... silence. Only disturbed by more silence. Until Cara felt that maybe there was something wrong and she couldn't let it go on any longer.

'Margot, are you OK?'

Nothing.

'Margot,' Cara said again. 'Unless you say otherwise, I'm going to pull back the curtain.'

Still nothing.

Cara whisked the piece of material back and there was her aunt like she had never seen her before. The white dress fitted her perfectly. The neckline plunged elegantly and the fabric skimmed across Margot's curvaceous hips and flowed down to just above the knee. It looked simple, yet perfect, unique and like a kind of sexy type of wedding dress...

'Oh, Margot!' Cara exclaimed. 'It's beautiful.'

Margot was staring at herself in the small fitting room's full-length mirror as if she was seeing a different version of herself for the first time. She was staring straight at her reflection, eyes wide and, Cara could see, a little watery.

'I... don't look like me,' Margot finally said, standing a little awkwardly as if she didn't know where to put her hands.

'You look amazing,' Cara said. 'Honestly, you have to get this dress.'

'I don't know. I feel a little bit... weak.'

Cara swallowed, looking at her aunt anew. She seemed suddenly exposed, raw, like her tough business veneer had been de-shellaced.

'It really does look stunning,' Cara said softly. 'It makes you look, I don't know, sort of delicate.'

'Delicate!' Margot exclaimed, sounding horrified, fingers already clawing to find the top of the zipper. 'Ugh! No! No one wants to be delicate, Cara. Delicate is just another word for "pathetic".' She drew back the curtain with force. 'The sooner I get this off, the sooner we can find something actually appropriate.'

And, with that said, Cara knew the white dress was definitely going back on the peg.

40

OIA, SANTORINI

'You look stressed. Why do you look stressed?' Horatio asked, putting a bottle of Yellow Donkey beer to his lips. 'We are here in Santorini, an island I have not been to before and we can relax.'

Akis looked up from his phone. They were in a bar with a perfect view of three large cruise ships docked far below them on an ultramarine sea that was so motionless it looked like it was painted. What was he doing here? Why had he made such a rash decision to just get on two planes to come here? It was one of the craziest things he had ever done for a few reasons. One, because he had upped and left the family at a time of crisis before Cosmos's wedding. Two, because they really needed to be putting in rehearsals before the next dance shows. And three, because he had texted Cara when they had arrived in Oia and had had no reply.

'So,' Horatio began. 'You said something about Cara needing help. What are you helping her with?' He lit a cigarette and blew smoke into the air.

Akis shook his head. 'You know what, I have no idea. My brain is fried right now, like someone took all the pieces, made a *souvlaki* out of them and stuck them on a barbecue.'

'She has not told you what she needs help for?' Horatio asked, sounding confused.

Akis blew out a breath. 'There is a story, I think. But she has not told me everything yet.'

Horatio shook his head. 'Now I understand. Layers. The ruination of every connection.'

'How so?'

'Women, they either want to know *everything* about you or nothing. There is no in between. And when you do find one that makes you want to ask more questions than you would usually, they are the ones that try to close the door.'

Akis paid more attention. 'There is someone you like right now? That you want to strip the layers from?'

'I was talking in general,' Horatio answered, perhaps a little too quickly.

'OK,' Akis said. 'So, where are we going to stay? We have arrived here with no plan and no accommodation and the person I came to see is not texting me back.'

'That, my friend, is the story of my life,' Horatio said, taking a drag of his cigarette.

'So, what do we do? Do you actually know how much it costs to stay in a place like this?'

'Hopefully not more than we can earn in tips after this drink,' Horatio said.

'What?'

'Well, we should do what we always do when we need a little extra cash and we have run out of things to sell,' Horatio said, resting his cigarette in the ashtray.

Akis knew what was coming and he shook his head. 'No. We cannot do that here.'

'Why?'

'Because this place is not like Corfu.'

'No,' Horatio agreed. 'It has more rich people. People with spare cash to drop at the feet of excellent dancers.'

'Horatio.'

'What? We need to pay for somewhere to stay, right?'

'I have *some* cash.'

'And I have my Bluetooth speaker,' Horatio said, pulling it out of his bag.

* * *

'Did you know,' Margot began, 'that Santorini is famous for tomatoes? And fava beans. Oh, and donkeys that are still forced to lug heavy cruise ship passengers up hundreds of steps.'

They were dressed up. In the apparently 'secondary' outfits Margot had bought in another gorgeous boutique earlier. It was in case they happened to bump into the maharajah tonight and needed to make an impression with designer wear. Sometimes Margot's 'making an impression' strategies had involved a lot more than expensive clothes. One time they had involved someone on a unicycle and cupcakes shaped like Ru-Paul.

'It sounds like you read a guidebook,' Cara remarked as they walked along the cobbled streets, past hordes of others shopping, seeking shade, taking photos of the views.

'This is a church,' Margot said, waving a hand in the air. 'No idea what it's called but I should find out. Local knowledge, Cara, is always useful. Ugh, what's that awful noise.' Margot stopped outside the white-washed building.

They were in a square now, where trees had been planted sporadically in the space, set into soil surrounded by white-painted circles. The music seemed to be coming from ahead of them. It wasn't traditional, no light *bouzouki* or guitar, more a thumping, pumping, brooding drum and a bassline she... kind of recognised.

The crowds were getting denser here, like the pathway ahead was blocked and Cara and Margot had to slow their pace significantly, abide by the ebb and flow of everyone else until they could finally see what was going on. Or rather who.

'Oh my God! Cara, it's your dancer!' Margot exclaimed. 'Taking his clothes off again.'

Cara squeezed between a pushchair and two tourists with old-style video cameras to get a better look. *Akis*. He was actually here? She swallowed, watching him eating up the dance space exactly how he had the first time she'd seen him perform. And then her mind went back to the bar. The dog. Akis's voice in her head. There was a vague recollection of something he had said. Had he said he was coming here? And he was here *right now*?

'And the stupid one is here too,' Margot remarked, shaking her head. 'The one whose eyes are slightly too close together.'

The performance ended, both men in a handstand position, and the watching crowd erupted into applause. Next, Horatio was going around the perimeter of the audience, baseball cap out collecting tips. And a large amount of cash was going into the pot.

'We should get to the restaurant,' Margot said. 'I had to name drop Cameron Diaz to get a reservation.'

'You don't know Cameron Diaz,' Cara replied.

'But the restaurant doesn't know that.'

Cara wasn't going anywhere until she had spoken to Akis and found out why he was in Santorini. She stepped through the dispersing crowd until he was right there, putting his T-shirt back over his tight body.

'Akis,' she said.

'Hey, Cara.'

'What are you doing here?'

'Did you not get my message?'

'You sent me a message?'

She was already delving into her bag to produce her phone. 'I have... apparently no battery.' She looked back to him. 'You came all the way here. Has the wedding location moved an entire island?'

'No,' he replied. 'You remember... that we talked? That you were... scared.'

She nodded, pinpricks spiking her shoulders. 'Kind of.'

'OK, well, I said I would come. And so I came... and then Horatio, well, he came too.'

'Hey,' Horatio greeted as he stuffed fistfuls of cash into his pockets.

'Gosh! What happened to your arm?' Cara said, noticing the wound.

'It is a very long and complex story,' Horatio began.

'Oh,' Cara said.

'I am kidding with you. These women who are into ropes and chains you know,' he said, a glint in his eye.

'Do not listen to him.' Akis shook his head.

'What are you doing here?' Margot asked everybody and nobody all at the same time.

'*Yassas*, Margot,' Horatio greeted, with a bow.

'Don't look at me,' Margot snapped. 'Whoever you are.' She looked away, fanning her face with her hand.

'We were just going for dinner,' Cara said. 'Did you want to join us?'

'Cara, are you insane? I told you how exclusive this reservation was. You can't just go adding extra guests.'

'Please, it is OK,' Akis said.

'Yes,' Horatio added. 'We can go eat with the third-class kind of people.'

'Good,' Margot said. 'That's settled.'

'No,' Cara said, very annoyed at her aunt's rudeness. 'You're coming with us. Or, we will find somewhere else that *can* accommodate four people.'

'Cara—'

'It's this way, isn't it?' Cara asked, leading on.

41

AMBROSIA RESTAURANT, OIA, SANTORINI

'Please, for the love of God, will you stop guzzling the wine?' Margot remarked loudly.

There hadn't been a table for four. Margot had been correct about that. But there had been two tables for two set a little apart from each other. It had seemed rude for Cara and Margot to take one together when Cara had invited Akis and Horatio to join them, so she was sitting with Akis and much to Margot's apparent annoyance, which had involved much tutting and grumbling until Horatio had pulled out her chair for her, she and Horatio were together in the other pair.

'Sometimes things can be enjoyed quickly, Margot,' Horatio replied, gulping another mouthful of the white wine.

The view here was another to-die-for vista, the dramatic expanse of sea, the sheer cliff face opposite white houses dotted along the top like a sprinkling of icing sugar. It felt like you were suspended out in the air, only the other white-painted hotels, apartments and bars below there ready to catch you. Cara focussed back on Akis, opposite her. He had been quiet since their drinks had arrived, was studying his phone.

'Is everything OK?' she asked.

He clicked the screen of his phone off then and put it down on the table. 'Yes.' He sighed. 'I mean, apart from an email from the church acknowledging my interest in being a priest. And an email – yes, an email – from my mother telling me I will not be sitting on the family table wherever the new venue is for the wedding as she wants the space for the Archbishop. And a text from my sister saying if Cosmos does not stop being a pain she will hold him upside down by his balls not his ankles.'

'Ouch,' Cara answered. 'That sounds painful.'

'Which bit?' Akis asked.

'All of it, honestly,' Cara said. 'And, with all that going on, you came here.'

'Yeah. Because... I do not think that the dog was the only thing you are scared about.'

Cara picked up her glass of wine and took a slow sip. How much could she really tell him about the reason behind them being here? It was Margot's thing, not hers, and she still didn't entirely understand it. But he had travelled from Corfu to Athens and on to this island for her. She owed him some kind of explanation.

'Well, we're here because Margot has this thing,' she began, sitting forward in her chair.

'A thing?'

'It's business. At least I think it is. A contact that she needs to meet.'

'O-K,' Akis said, not sounding as if he understood at all.

'And she's hoping to get that meeting tomorrow night. And... she has... said that I will sing,' she added, nervousness already invading, her chest getting tight. 'At an event. On a boat.'

'OK,' Akis said, a little more chill.

'But it's not OK, is it? Because I thought singing at Cosmos and Wren's wedding was bad enough. Now we're here in Santorini and it's so busy with so many more people and it's a high-profile event with high-profile people and... and... I'm not ready.'

Akis leaned forward too. 'And now I know why I got on that plane.'

'You do? Because that was pretty crazy.'

'You're going to sing at the event,' Akis said and took a sip of his wine.

'Oh... no... I mean, I haven't come up with an excuse yet, but getting me on the performance list was what Margot and MI5 needed to do to get us access to the party so...' She let the sentence fade out like it was the end of a song.

'So? You do not want to rehearse with the piano? Make everyone hear you but not see you?'

She forced a smile. 'I know what you're doing and I appreciate it. But, I'm not sure I'm ever going to be ready.'

'What if I told you that I brought my organ with me?'

Why Cara's eyes immediately dipped to just below his midriff she didn't know. She recovered quickly. 'I do not believe security would have allowed it.'

'No,' Akis answered. 'You are right. But, that does not mean we can't make the rehearsal happen somehow. If you wanted it to.'

Her gaze went to the view again. Here she was in beautiful Santorini, another place she didn't expect to find herself in, with this man who had little by little been building her confidence despite going through a whole trial of his own. He had already helped her achieve more than she could ever have hoped for in such a short space of time. But would she ever know what she was capable of unless she took a dive into uncertain waters? And with Akis by her side, it almost always felt like anything was possible.

'You aren't scared of anything, are you?' Cara remarked, as their appetisers arrived.

'Being scared is not a simple emotion.'

'No?'

'There are different reasons we are scared. My brother, irrationally scared. Everything terrifies him but there is no reason for the majority of the things he worries about. What if the sun falls from the sky? What if one day there are no more fish in the sea? What if the local taverna stops serving *pastitsio*?'

'Well, the fish one kind of has a ring of truth about it,' Cara said.

'I think your fear stems from trauma, am I right?'

She swallowed, managed a nod.

'So that is not an irrational fear. It is something that has happened to you. Something that is real.'

It had been real. Watched by millions. And after that horrible, humiliating night, her parents had left, her fiancé had ghosted her and Margot's only way of dealing with it had been to book her into therapy.

'What scares me,' Akis said, those stunning eyes studying her, 'is that one day I will look back on my life and realise that I wasted some of it thinking too hard before I acted.'

This surprised Cara a little. The Akis she had been getting to know was a man of action, yet now she was finding he was also a deep thinker. She met his gaze, waiting for him to elaborate.

'But, being afraid can make you stronger, you know,' he continued.

'I don't know about that,' she said, picking up her fork.

'Whatever you feel is validation for something that has touched you.' He mused for a second. 'A conversation. Something you have seen or read. Music. It is the same with fear.'

'I don't understand.'

'Fear can touch you, but it is up to you how much, and whether you let it stay or whether you acknowledge it and then just let it go.'

She swallowed. What he was saying was so poignant.

'Everything that happens in life has to be a lesson. That is the way I like to look at it. Because, if you do not look at it from a positive way, a learning way, then the alternative is not attractive.'

Cara's brain rattled through all her tough times like they were a mini-series, seeing how she had chosen to wallow in her difficulties, let them overwhelm her, overcome her almost. Therapy had tried to move her forward, but it hadn't ever really addressed the choices she'd made at the time and why 'hide' and 'run' had been her go-to instead of 'fight' and 'stay'.

'Hey,' Akis said, putting his hand on top of hers. 'I didn't mean to make you sad.'

'No,' Cara breathed. 'I'm not sad. I just... think I've wasted a lot of time.'

He squeezed her hand. 'Well, let us not waste any more time. Or food.' He picked up his fork.

'You're going to use cutlery here?' she said, smiling.

'I do not want us to get thrown out,' he replied. 'Horatio on the other hand...'

Cara looked across at the table where Margot and Horatio were sitting, Horatio with a goat's cheese tart in between his fingers, Margot admonishing and shaking her head in despair.

She returned her gaze to Akis. 'After dinner,' she began. 'Can we find a piano?'

42

CATCH BAR RESTAURANT, OIA, SANTORINI

The piano was white, in a corner of a beautiful courtyard area housing a large bar at its centre, glowing with mood lighting, chairs set all around and tumbling down over the rustic stone walls was bright red bougainvillea. The comfy sofas with contemporary cushions, olive wood tables and benches looked fit for a Michelin star restaurant. There were people enjoying beautiful-looking cocktails, light conversation in the air and already Cara was thinking this was such a bad idea.

'You OK?' Akis asked her.

'No,' she replied. 'I'm having second thoughts.'

'*Ochi*. No more thinking,' Akis said. 'Unless it is positive. *Ela*. Come.'

He strode towards the piano, sat down at the stool and tapped at the keys. Cara watched the customers; no one had really paid any attention to the piano being touched. They were all too caught up in their own relaxed holiday mood. Maybe it would be OK. She walked towards Akis and the piano.

'You have an idea?' he asked, fingers flitting over the keys making a beautiful melody. 'Of what you would like to sing?'

'Maybe one we practiced before?' Cara suggested, her legs trembling slightly.

'Which one?'

'"Show Me Heaven",' Cara breathed. 'Oh... I don't know. I—'

'Look at me,' Akis encouraged. 'They can't see you, remember?'

He started to play and before Cara knew it, they were at the beginning and she had to start singing.

* * *

He watched her, as he played the song and she sang. She was facing him, not the people in the bar. But he could see in his peripheral vision the customers had all already started to stop what they were doing and pay attention. As they should. Her voice was *everything* and he knew she didn't really fully understand that. From the moment he had first heard her, it had touched him and he was in danger of wanting more of it, to the point that he didn't want anything else.

He swallowed, losing focus for a second.

Her performance now was different to how she had sung in his apartment. It was still tentative but there was more strength, more intent, a desire to do this well, not born out of necessity to rehearse before a performance, but perhaps a need to get through it, to succeed.

She put a hand on top of the piano and closed her eyes, reaching for that strong, powerful note and hitting it hard. And then Akis got lost in the rest of the music, listening to her, playing for her until they brought it to its conclusion.

When she stopped holding the final note and he ended the song, she looked at him with unequivocal joy written all over her face. Seeing that moved him so deeply and he almost didn't know what to do with himself. He stood up, went to step towards her...

But then the applause broke out.

He watched her shock at the sudden rise in volume and the expression on her face changed from elation to alarm. She had bravely faced enough fears tonight. Slipping an arm around her shoulder, he eased her body into his, giving a wave to the customers but all the while shielding her from the attention, shepherding her towards the exit.

'It's OK,' he whispered, close to her ear. 'You were amazing.' He took a breath. 'You *are* amazing.'

When they reached the street outside, he felt her tension ease just a little and she breathed audibly, like she had been holding it tight inside her. It wasn't quite a desperate rush of release but it was enough to send her away from him, as if she needed her own space for a second. She backed up against a low wall, white cube houses glowing with lights, tumbling down below them to the sea.

'I'm shaking,' Cara said, holding her hand out to show him.

'Adrenaline,' Akis answered. 'Do not think of it as anything else.'

'I didn't think,' she continued. 'I just felt it, you know.'

He was feeling it too. Her passion for the moment. Her achievement in being able to sing in a public space, in front of people. It was contagious and it was spreading, getting under his skin.

'I know,' he breathed. 'I saw.'

'I couldn't have done that without you, Akis.'

'You could have done it with or without me. I... just play the piano.'

'No,' she said, shaking her head. 'That isn't all it is for me.'

'No?' Lava had literally replaced the blood in his veins now.

'No,' she assured. 'You... came all this way and, since we first met, you've listened to me and... you haven't judged me and you haven't asked me anything about that night and... you don't know how much that means to me.'

He wanted to kiss her again. But, unlike before, when he had acted on impulse, he wanted her to know that this time he meant it with every part of him.

'Cara,' he whispered, reaching out and cupping her jawline.

'Get away from me, you ridiculous man!'

Margot's voice broke the night and out of the corner of his eye Akis saw her coming, pushing Horatio's shoulder. The moment broke too and Akis dropped his hand, stepping back as Margot and Horatio arrived in the space.

'Hey!' Horatio said. 'I have found us somewhere to stay. It even has a view. Mainly of an air-conditioning unit but, you know, that means it has air-conditioning!'

'Come on,' Margot said, linking arms with Cara. 'We need our beauty sleep. The only bags we need to be turning up with at the party tomorrow are Carried Away samples.'

'Oh, well...' Cara began, her eyes still on Akis.

Horatio slapped a hand to his shoulder. 'One last drink?'

'Sure,' he agreed, looking back at Cara.

'Goodbye, Horror,' Margot said to Horatio.

Akis looked at Cara being led away, looking back at him and he knew, for now, the moment was lost.

43

OIA, SANTORINI

'Wake up, bro, the sun is up, the air-conditioning is broken, and we need to get out into the community.'

It was the next morning and Horatio had jumped on the bottom of the very short single bed Akis was squeezed into, making the mattress bump up and down. It was so hot in this tiny apartment Horatio had secured on pretty much charm alone and the unreliable climate control hadn't done anything to stop the mosquitos buzzing around his head the whole night.

'What time is it?' Akis asked, freeing his arm from under the pillow and trying to look at his watch.

'Time to find breakfast. Get up!' Horatio said, bouncing some more. 'Then we can find a pool and relax.'

Horatio was still treating this trip as some kind of holiday, not as the support mission he had meant it to be.

'I can't do that,' Akis said. 'Cara has the event tonight. She needs to rehearse.'

'Rehearse what?' Horatio asked, jumping right off the bed. 'Margot says she will never sing in public again.'

'What?' Akis said, pulling himself into a sitting position and rubbing the sleep from his eyes.

Horatio shrugged. 'That is what she said, last night. And then she said in that smart voice of hers, "The only decisions Cara makes are ones I tell her to."'

Akis was out of bed now. 'Are you playing, Horatio? She actually said that?'

'Yeah,' Horatio said with a sigh. 'I mean, kind of powerful, right?'

Akis didn't think it was powerful. He thought it was narcissistic and cruel. He started to get dressed, not caring what he grabbed, needing to get out of this space and this ugly conversation.

'Are we going to breakfast?' Horatio asked.

'I do not mind what you do. I am going to find Cara,' Akis said, striding towards the door.

* * *

'There are photos online,' Margot said as she and Cara sat eating breakfast on the terrace. 'Of Raj in Fira last night. We should have booked a taxi over there.'

'Well,' Cara said, stirring her coffee. 'It doesn't matter where he was last night, he's going to be on board that boat tonight, right?'

'Yes,' Margot said, sighing. 'Yes, I suppose so. It's just...'

'What?' Cara asked. 'Is something wrong?'

'I don't know.' Margot put a hand to one of the wounds that was healing on her chest. 'I feel that, somehow, maybe... I'm beginning to lose my edge.'

'Oh, Margot, no. Why do you think that? I mean, apart from this probably minor issue with the Maxi-Go, the business is doing great. You have so many celebrity endorsements and you're on the very cusp of breaking into America and—'

'And all those things are about Carried Away, not about me.'

Cara studied her aunt for a second, saw real despondency in her eyes. This was new. 'But you've always said that you and the business are shackled to each other like Christian Grey and Anastasia Steele, that there isn't one without the other.'

'And that is true,' Margot agreed. 'But what happens if everything with the business suddenly blows up like the fucking suitcase? What am I left with then? A warehouse full of wheelie bags, a few party invites and my niece who thinks a chihuahua might savage her at any given moment.'

Cara froze. The barbed comment had landed and spiked. She got up from the table and made for the stepping stones.

'Cara, stop, wait. I didn't mean that. Cara!' Margot pleaded.

There was no way she was stopping.

44

AMMOUDI BAY, SANTORINI

'I've let her do this, you know,' Cara said, stepping down onto the next step with around fifty more to go. There were hundreds of steps down the cliff face until they reached the bottom and Ammoudi Bay. 'I sat back and I closed myself off and I let Margot run my life because, at that time, I really needed her to.'

'Cara, slow down a little,' Akis said. 'The steps are steep and I think they will get slippery.'

'I shouldn't be here. And you shouldn't be here. We are chasing some prince because Margot thinks he's the key to the next stage of her business and yet she's also just told me that she might not even know who she is any more.'

'Cara,' Akis said. 'Please, the steps.'

'I should leave. *We* should leave. Get the next plane back to Corfu,' she carried on. 'You have a wedding to be at and I should be rehearsing for that wedding instead of some event for rich people who won't care who is entertaining them as long as the champagne keeps flowing.'

'Cara—'

She slipped suddenly, one of her sandals giving way underneath her feet and Akis grabbed her arm, stopping her from falling any further. She held onto him, trying to recover. It *was* steep. Some people were holding onto the wall, others were on their way back up, a train of tethered donkeys were sadly stumbling...

'Take a second,' Akis said, keeping her upright. 'Clear your thoughts and soak in the view.'

Cara repositioned herself, feet planted firmly back in place. It was such a panorama, the dramatic red volcanic rocks framing the Aegean Sea, boats out on the water far below.

'Sorry,' Cara said after a time. 'You shouldn't have to listen to this.'

'Do not apologise,' Akis said. 'Families, they are complicated. You have met mine.'

She smiled. 'Wait until you meet my parents. Not so much complicated, but definitely eccentric.'

Akis smiled back at her. 'I am meeting your parents?'

'Oh, wow, no, no of course not. That was a ridiculous thing to say, a figure of speech really. I mean, I haven't even seen them for, well, a long time.'

He laughed. 'I am playing with you. Relax, OK? Breathe.'

His hands were on her shoulders and it felt really reassuring and very *very* sexy.

'Shall we make it down the next steps?' he asked. 'There cannot be many more.'

'OK,' Cara agreed. 'But I am going slower.'

* * *

Ammoudi Bay was beautiful. A small inlet with a few tavernas, tiny boats moored at the edge of the dock, waves cresting at their hulls.

The cliff face they had walked down looked insurmountable from their position below now, as did the craggy red rocks all round the bay, a stark reminder that this island was formed by many volcanic eruptions.

'The steps were worth it, no?' Akis said, walking close to her along the dock.

'Oh, the steps were definitely worth it,' Cara agreed. He watched her drinking in the scenery. *She* was more beautiful than any of this. And last night, when she had sung harder and stronger than he had ever heard, he'd wanted nothing more than to feel her energy in his arms. Except it hadn't happened. He had hesitated and the moment had been lost to Margot and Horatio. Perhaps there was a reason the universe was putting the brakes on.

They meandered along the dock, tucking in against the wall as the path narrowed and people had to pass, and finally arrived near one end of the dock at Ammoudi Fish Taverna.

'Is it too early for lunch, do you think?' Akis asked her.

'Not if you haven't had breakfast,' Cara said. 'Well, actually, looking at those octopus I don't think it would be too early at any time.'

The octopus were strung on a line outside the taverna, like tentacled garments, their flesh soaking up the sunlight, pinky-orange bumps turning a little translucent. Nature was used for everything here, fish from the water, sunlight infusing all it touched, rocks providing drama.

'Come on,' Akis said, leading the way.

It wasn't long before they were positioned at a table right by the edge of the water, the sunlight making the tips of the waves sparkle and shine like they were decorated with diamonds. They had been given water and had both ordered an Arugula spinach salad and the sundried octopus.

'You know,' Akis began. 'I think there is a reason you are here in Santorini.'

'Yes,' Cara agreed. 'I told you. The maharajah and this stupid plan of Margot's.'

'No,' Akis said, shaking his head. 'I do not think that is why you are here.'

'No?'

'No,' he said. 'Perhaps that is why *Margot* is here. Maybe you think you are only here to accompany her, but what if the real reason is so you can sing again? That what Margot is doing is, I don't know, the side plot and you have the lead part in the main story.'

He watched her expression change just slightly, like she was mulling over his suggestion. She ran a finger around the rim of her water glass. And then she answered.

'You've never asked me about my bad performance,' she said softly.

'What?'

'I told you, when we first met, that I had a bad performance in front of millions of people, and you never asked about it.'

He nodded. 'No.'

'Why?'

He took a deep breath. 'I am guessing for the same reason that you have not asked me the details of Cosmos's accident.'

'*Your* accident, Akis,' Cara corrected him.

'Yeah,' he acknowledged, fingers going to the vacant space on his other hand. 'My accident.' He looked at her again. 'I guess I feel I already know that whatever happened during that performance, it changed you. And not just a small part of you. All of you.' He took a breath. 'And I think to know that is the most important thing.'

She nodded. 'But maybe now I want to tell you.' She took a breath. 'Maybe now I *need* to tell you.'

He could see her hands were trembling and he wanted nothing more than to hold them in his, but he held off. She had to do this on her own.

'I was in the Eurovision Song Contest, if you know it,' Cara said. 'It's a big show beamed across the world where countries compete against each other to win. And, I was one of the favourites. Me and the contestants from Sweden and Denmark.' She took another breath. 'It was supposed to be my big break. I'd put in months and months of preparation and I'd never felt more ready for anything. Nothing could go wrong. Even if I didn't end up winning, I was going to give the performance of my life and I was going to have my pick of recording contracts to choose from.' She took a sip of water and replaced the glass on the table with shaking hands. 'When I was in position, waiting for the announcement in the arena I'd never felt more confident. Everything was going to go like clockwork just like it had in every rehearsal and then...'

Her words tailed off and Akis could see the emotion written on her face, a tell-tale quirk to her cheek. He could stop her. He could say it was OK, that she didn't need to go through with reliving all this.

'Then,' she carried on. 'Yodi happened.'

'Yodi?'

'He's... a dog,' Cara said. 'He came out of nowhere. He leapt onto the stage. He ran straight at me. Like so fast, and I didn't know what to do.

The next thing I knew I was on the ground, and I was just completely
disorientated and the song was going on without me and the audience
were caught between shock and laughter and I just lay there frozen.'

'Cara—'

'I don't remember how I got off the stage. But what I do remember is
how my fiancé looked at me when I got back to the green room.' Tears
were spilling from her eyes now. 'It was like disbelief. And not in a kind
way. More like he was seeing me for the first time and realising that I
wasn't the person he wanted me to be.'

Akis reached for her hands then, but she withdrew them, folding her
arms across her chest.

'My parents didn't know what to say. My dad had a conversation
about global warming with the contestant from Germany right in front of
me for God's sake. There was only Margot reacting to *me*, what *I* had
been through, instead of worrying about the whole of the UK being
mocked for the next twelve months.' She steadied her breathing. 'Within
a few weeks, my career was over, my relationship was over and my
parents left to preserve the rainforests without looking back. Margot was
the only one who took action. And she's been taking action ever since.
And I know that sometimes she takes advantage, and she gets it wrong,
but she was the *only* one who was there for me when I needed someone
most.'

Akis didn't say anything, he just watched her, processing all the
emotions passing through her expression. And then, when a few
moments had gone by, he made his reply.

'You said, about your boyfriend, that you think he realised you were
not the person he wanted you to be,' he said. 'But what about the person
you are? The person *you* want to become? Not the opinion of anyone
else, remember?'

He looked at her, taking in what he had just said like it was a news-
flash. He began to wonder if he had taken the wrong part of the information out of what she had given him.

'Yes, and I blamed *myself* for him feeling that way about me. ' She
sighed. 'And then I went to therapy. The kind where you live in. And they
made it about me searching inwardly for the reasons I couldn't even look

at myself in a mirror.' She shook her head. 'Again, like how I felt, was everything to do with me and no one else should be held accountable for anything.' She paused. 'Sorry, this is a bit much for a not-even-lunch.'

'No,' Akis said, pouring some more water into her glass. 'It is good to take time to reflect. I reflected too, after the accident.' He took a breath. 'I realised that I would do anything for my family. When Cosmos was stuck in the machinery, I could have done many things. I could have reached for something, a tool to help get him out. I could have waited and called for help. But I didn't do any of those things. I acted fast, regardless of anything else. And that love for my family, that desire to do anything to protect them... that is why I am going to become a priest.'

Cara gasped and that's when he realised what he had actually said. He nodded as if the decision was fixed.

'I would not have taken a risk on Cosmos's life. I cannot take a risk on the Diakos curse.'

45

Cara felt sick. 'But you can't.'

She stood up, not really knowing the reason why she was standing up. She just felt enclosed suddenly and hot, very *very* hot.

'It isn't right,' she continued. 'I mean... you can't do that just like that. Because your family tell you to. What happened to not caring about what other people think?'

She was wringing her hands together now and then she grabbed up a napkin from the table so she had something to hold, tear at.

'It isn't that I care about what they think,' Akis countered. 'I care about what might potentially happen to them if I don't do it. Cara, why don't you come away from the edge? Sit down.'

'*Potentially* happen,' Cara said. 'There are literally hundreds of scenarios that could *potentially* happen to any one of us at any given time. Car accident! Boat accident! Unlucky genetics! And you are trading your whole life for a tiny chance that a tale as old as time is true? And... what about your dancing? And the piano? I mean, they are going to have you in robes and make you grow a beard and chant and there won't be time for, for any of the amazing talents you have!'

'Cara, come away from the edge, please,' Akis said, getting to his feet too.

'I've just told you about my trauma with a dog that's now probably got almost as many riches as this maharajah and you're going to let your fears govern your decisions and be like, some kind of modern-day martyr! Well, do you know what I think? I think it's fucking crazy!'

She pointed the napkin at him and then she felt herself lose her balance. Her eyes widened in shock and she tried to right herself but it was to no avail. Before she had a chance to even think another thought, she was crashing down into the sea.

* * *

Akis ducked under the rope and jumped into the water too. It wasn't deep but there were rocks and Cara had fallen rather than slipped in by choice. She was swimming, not far from him, spluttering, obviously drenched and still looking taken aback.

'Cara,' he said, swimming towards her.

'Why did you do that?' Cara shouted. 'I can swim! You didn't need to go all *Saving Lives at Sea* on me!'

'Are you OK?' Akis asked, unperturbed by her reaction. 'You did not hit any of the rocks.'

'Just leave me!' Cara yelled, trying to swim back towards the edge until finally she could stand. 'Let me be embarrassed on my own!'

'Cara,' Akis said, putting a hand on her arm. 'There is nothing to be embarrassed about.'

'No? Because everyone having a quiet drink up there is now looking at the insane person who just fell into the sea! And if there's one thing I hate, it's being looked at.' She shook him off.

As if she was proving a point, she took a section of her soaking wet hair and drew it over her face like it was a shield from the diners who *were* paying them a bit of attention.

'Come here,' Akis said. 'No one is going to look at you, OK?' He put his arm around her, shielding her from any onlookers until they made it to the side. 'Come, sit down.'

He helped her onto the rocks and then he sat alongside her.

'I'm an idiot,' Cara stated, hair still hanging across her face. 'And I shouldn't have said those things to you. I just... I don't know... it was a shock.'

He nudged her arm with his. 'But the very first time we met you thought I was a priest.'

'Because of your clothes!'

'Ah, and here I am thinking it was my wisdom and understanding.'

She sniffed. 'Well, you do have that too.'

'Yes?'

'Which is why you would probably make a very good priest.'

'You think so?'

He could tell she was reticent about the statement, was hiding her eyes. He had never wanted to look into them more.

'I just... reacted from a selfish place. Because, you know, when I go back to the UK I'll be thinking about all the things we did together – the fish restaurant, the boat, the remnants of the castle – and then all the things we said to each other about what life means.'

'A width of things,' he said softly.

'I'll be thinking of you as that person. Not as a priesty person.'

'A priesty person?'

'And, OK, I admit I might even be thinking of lying on that stage and having you dance on top of me.'

'Really?'

'Maybe.' Her lips edged into a smile.

'Nothing else?' Akis asked. He could feel the warmth of her, right next to him, hotter than the sun that was quickly drying their soaking skin.

'Well... I don't know.'

He knew what he would remember hardest.

He reached for her then, his thumb and forefinger gently touching her chin, tilting her head into his space, brushing her hair away.

'I remember kissing you,' Akis told her. 'And pretending that I had kissed you to stop you panicking. But, in truth, *I* was panicking. Inside. Because there was only one reason I wanted to kiss you.' He took a breath, looking into her eyes. 'Simply because I wanted to kiss you.

Because there has never been anyone else I have felt this connection with and now, it has grown even stronger.'

She was trembling. He could feel it running through her as he held her jaw. He hesitated, kept himself there, not wanting to scare her.

And then she put the flat of her hand to his cheek and pressed her fingers lightly against his jaw. 'I feel the same.'

He didn't wait a second longer. He pressed his lips to hers and she moved into his arms, getting closer, kissing harder. Wet hair, wet lips, his heart beating furiously as he held her. The sun prickling the back of his neck, his internal temperature carried on soaring, until finally they both needed to take a breath.

'Did I just kiss a priest?' Cara asked, her cheeks a little flushed.

He smiled. 'A fake one for now.' He paused. 'But, you know, I have spent quite some time in that costume.'

'Oh, Akis, this whole situation is mad,' Cara said, sighing.

'I agree. It comes to something when a blessing of snakes is not the craziest thing happening in life.'

'And I have to sing on a boat tonight,' Cara said. He felt her shiver, as if the realisation had hit her all over again.

'You have got this,' Akis said, taking her hand and holding it tight. 'But only if you want it.'

'Yes,' Cara said, nodding. 'I know that now.'

'The song,' Akis said. 'That you sang for the contest. What was it?'

Cara sighed. 'It was something else that hurt me.' She swept her hair behind her ears. 'Because I didn't just sing the song. I wrote it.'

Akis nodded. 'OK.'

'OK?' Cara queried.

He squeezed her hand again. 'OK, that is the song you're going to sing tonight.'

46

FIRA

'I am not sure about this.'

It was Margot speaking and it was early evening. They had taken a taxi from Oia to Fira and were standing in a queue ready to get on a cable car down to the old port where a small boat was going to take them from the shore to a luxury yacht. From their position here you could really see how steep the cliff face was, creating the most dramatic vista. Sunlight dappled blue domes, bright pink bougainvillea trailed over white walls and infinity pools speckled the landscape.

'It is like a little house on wires,' Horatio said, grinning. 'When we get in I will jump about and it will rock like the bed of a prostitute.'

'Horatio!' Akis admonished.

'You are disgusting,' Margot said, glaring at Horatio.

Cara was very, very nervous right now. And sweating, despite their attempts to get into a little patch of shade.

'You are OK,' Akis whispered, his voice warm in her ear.

'I'm not so sure about that,' she answered, leaning against him a little.

'Well,' Akis said. 'If you want the truth, I am the one who should be nervous. I have only just learned the song and I do not want to let you down.'

She slipped her hand into his, linking their fingers together. 'You could never let me down, no matter what happens tonight.'

She meant that with her whole heart. Tonight, for her, may have started as a mad scheme Margot was concocting but now things felt different. For the first time in a long time, it felt like she had some control. She might still be feeling terrified about singing, about the song she was going to be singing, but she was determined not to make it about what had gone before. Maybe it would be an opportunity to exorcise her demons. And that sounded really weird as she was stood next to someone who was going to pledge himself to the clergy. Someone who had kissed her when they were wet from the sea and had kissed her again up against a grand piano. And she'd be lying if she said she hadn't thought about a hundred other places she wanted him to kiss her...

'Cara, do you have the PowerPoint presentation all ready to go?' Margot called as the queue moved a little.

'I do,' Cara said, coming back to reality. She indicated the bag over her shoulder that held a laptop, as well as a bit of make-up in case everything melted before she got on board, deodorant for the same reason, some hard sweets to suck before she sang because too much water to hydrate her vocal cords always made her feel like peeing and a tiny fully operational miniature of the Maxi-Go case.

'So, let me get this straight,' Horatio said. 'We are going to an exclusive party on some boat of a millionaire and you are going to play a business presentation? I mean, do we all have to watch? Will it require me to pay attention and make notes? Because this is not like any party I have been to before.'

'No,' Margot said confidently. 'Of course it is not like any party you have been to! You don't regularly get invited onto the yachts of millionaires!'

'Hmm, you are confident about that?' Horatio asked.

'What are you talking about, you stupid man?'

'I think we can get on now,' Akis said, indicating it was their turn to get into the cable car.

Cara saw that Margot was hesitating and she didn't really know why. Her aunt didn't have a fear of heights, or indeed of anything.

Margot stepped forward. 'Akis, take Horatio on. We'll be a second.'

As the guys stepped into the cable car and Horatio began to stamp his feet to check the stability of the floor, Cara stood close to Margot.

'Is everything OK?' she asked her softly.

'Yes, of course,' Margot replied instantly, stiff upper lip intact. 'Why wouldn't it be?'

'Well, I know that this need to break into other markets, take Carried Away fully global, is really important to you. And I think I also know that seeing Raj again is... maybe something important too.'

'Of course it's important, Cara. He's the only man I know that has the kind of money we need. OK, yes, theoretically I could try to woo that duke we met in Oxford, but to be honest with you I think he's only land rich not cash rich and that's no good to us.'

'OK,' Cara said. 'So there's nothing else?'

'What?'

'Between you and Raj.'

'I don't know what you're talking about.'

'Well,' Cara said. 'The white dress. In the boutique. The one you went all misty eyed over. I thought—'

'You're being completely ridiculous now. And if we don't get on this contraption we're going to be late.'

Without saying any more, Margot strode into the cable car.

It felt like mere seconds until the machinery whirred and whined and the cabin set off.

'Whoa, Margot,' Horatio remarked. 'It has quite the bounce to it.'

'As will you,' Margot said. 'When I drop kick you out of here if you carry on.'

Horatio laughed. 'I love it when you talk to me that way. So powerful.'

Cara watched the interaction between them. It was almost what Margot described as 'playful sparring'. Horatio would look at Margot, Margot would look at Horatio and then look away. *Breaking eye contact.* Come to think of it, Margot did that a lot when Horatio was around... Cara then looked to the glorious view outside. Yes, perhaps it felt a little bit unnerving to be rolled off the top of the edge of Santorini in a rather flimsy-feeling structure, but what she could see on the way down totally made up for the tiny bit of peril at being suspended on wires. They were in the midst of the crumbling rocks, peeling away from the summit and taking a deep descent like they were abseiling the mound.

'It's incredible, isn't it?' Akis said.

'It really is,' Cara agreed.

'This is something I did not think I would be seeing this summer.'

'There are many things I didn't think I would be seeing this summer,' she said, looking from the view to him.

'*Ne*,' he breathed. '*Simfono*. I agree.' He put his arm around her shoulders and drew her into him.

Except there was the matter of him becoming a priest. And she knew the score there. He had to take a wife before he became a priest or he would never be able to marry. They had such little time together.

'I see the boat!' Margot exclaimed, pointing a finger and her nail hitting the glass. 'Look! You know, if you can tear yourselves away from each other for a second.'

'What? The little boat to take us to the big boat?' Horatio asked.

'Don't be stupid! The big boat! There! That one! With the helicopter on top.'

'There's a helicopter on top? Let me see this,' Horatio said, pushing his face against the glass.

Now Cara's stomach flipped as the realisation of what she was about to do really set in. It was going to be OK, wasn't it?

47

FIRA HARBOUR

'I don't see him,' Margot said through pursed lips. 'I've gently rotated around this boat for the past thirty minutes and I do not see him.'

What Cara could see was Margot's panic. She was carrying it over her shoulders like it was a cashmere wrap. In comparison, Cara felt cool. Not exactly calm perhaps, but a little more like the way she used to feel before a performance. There were butterflies but they were contained, not out of control, and her mind was reasonably clear, focussed.

She put a hand on Margot's arm. 'It's fine. Everything is fine. He's the guest of honour, right? We don't know if he's even arrived yet.'

'No, I suppose not,' Margot said with a heavy sigh. 'And, you know, there are any number of people here with cash and connections. I've not seen so much Vivienne Westwood since her 2019 show, God rest her soul.'

'It's quite the party,' Cara remarked. 'I feel a bit underdressed.' She was wearing the olive-green shimmery silk dress that they had picked up from the boutique. It fitted her so well and she loved it but all around were hardcore designer labels, pearls and diamonds, Louboutins, and Louis Vuitton.

'We are wearing up and coming designers, new on the scene,' Margot reminded her. 'Everyone wants to be someone who makes a discovery.

We drop the name of the creator, and you watch these people make notes on their Samsungs.' Then she pulled a face. 'Ugh, look at that man, he has no idea how to eat an oyster. He probably doesn't even know what it is. And who is he talking to?'

Cara followed Margot's line of sight to where Horatio and Akis were standing at one end of the ship near the beautiful glossy bright red grand piano talking to a group of ladies clad in silver and gold.

'I don't even know what he's doing here,' Margot continued. 'I'm not sure I fully understand why the dancer got on a plane either but the thought that Sofia is probably fuming about it makes me not care. But the Horror has no reason to be here.'

'The Horror?'

'Isn't that his name?' Margot asked, eyes still firmly over the other side of the boat as waiters passed through the partygoers holding silver platters containing champagne flutes. 'Horatio. It's so pretentious. So not Greek. I think he's made it up. And look at him, trying to charm all those women with his crooked smile and all his... hair.'

Cara looked harder at her aunt then, seeing an unfamiliar set to her jaw, a faraway look in her eyes. Never had anything seemed clearer. The white dress and the emotions in the changing room of the boutique – were they not because of the-maharajah-that-got-away but more to do with the guy that Margot couldn't stop insulting?

'Oh my God,' Cara said, the penny dropping. 'You *like* Horatio!'

'What are you talking about, Cara?' Margot hissed. 'Have you had some of that champagne because you know how that can make you. Do you remember the time on the Thames when we were talking to those frogmen?'

'You're changing the subject, Margot,' Cara said. 'You only do that when your opponent has sussed you out. And I am not an opponent by the way, I am your niece but—'

'Oh my God! There he is! There he is!' Margot stepped to the side, ducking behind a fast-melting ice sculpture in the shape of who knew what and pulling Cara with her. 'Coming onto the deck now.'

Cara looked towards the door and saw half a dozen people in black suits walking into the space. And, in the midst of them, was a man dressed completely in white. It was like if John Travolta's suit from *Saturday Night Fever* had a baby with a stoat.

'Why are we hiding?' Cara asked.

'Because we need to be seen when we *want* to be seen. And not a second before.'

Applause broke out as though something fantastic had happened, except it hadn't. All that had happened was the team of security had parted from a tighter formation than the Red Arrows and presumably, Raj, was standing in some kind of glitterball spotlight.

'He's aged beautifully, hasn't he?' Margot commented.

'Well,' Cara said. 'I haven't ever seen him before, but his beard looks well-nourished.'

'That's not all about him that's well-nourished, I can tell you,' Margot replied.

'Eww, too much information.'

'OK,' Margot said. 'We will let him get settled. Presumably in that VIP area over there and when the time is right, we strike.'

* * *

'These things are disgusting,' Horatio said, wiping his mouth with the back of his hand and disposing of the shell in a bowl of cashew nuts.

'Then why did you eat five of them?' Akis asked.

'Because I am hungry and they were there.' He shook his head. 'But I do not like the diet of rich people.'

'I guess this is the guest of honour,' Akis remarked as he watched a man in white moving across the carpet and doing some hand-shaking.

'He does not look like very much,' Horatio said. 'He is mainly beard.'

Akis checked his watch and then his gaze went to Cara. She was going to be performing in an hour and he knew that would be roving around in her mind. He rubbed the space where his little finger should be, manipulating the skin, making sure it wasn't going to be tight for stretching over the keys. He watched his friend, in his element, enjoying everything this party had to offer despite his protests about the food. Horatio loved nothing more than new experiences, would

carry on taking life by the horns; that's what someone without responsibilities could do. Perhaps it was time to share his career plan with his
friend...

'Horatio... I have decided that... I will become a priest,' Akis said.

Horatio almost choked on the mouthful of champagne he'd inhaled.
'Fuck! Are you joking with me?'

Akis shook his head. 'No.'

'But, Aki, come on! That would be like a fucking tragedy for mankind.
You know that, right?'

'I know that I love my family and they are worried about the curse.'

'*Your mother* is worried! Because she's a control freak, Aki! You know
that.'

'Yes, I know that.'

'So, have you spoken to your father about it?'

Akis shook his head. 'Not yet.'

'Why not?' Horatio asked, taking another champagne flute from a
passing waiter. 'Is he not a Diakos? His older brother became a priest. He
lived a long life, right?'

'He died. Before his first service. And he had no children so I am the
eldest Diakos from the second-eldest son.'

'OK, so he died even though he became a priest. That sounds like shit
luck. So, what about the generation before? Your grandfather?'

'Spiros Diakos. Died on the day he was to become a priest. He was
thirty-one. The doctor's findings said gallbladder complications but there
are rumours his body was full of rare worms.'

'I think I'm gonna be sick,' Horatio said, picking up a wine cooler
from the table.

'Then my grandmother got cancer and all seven of her cats died.
Going back in history there is less to categorically say that if a Diakos did
not become a priest then bad things would happen but how can I be
sure?'

'The two you just told me about had every intention of joining the
church and they still fucking died! And, Aki, what about Cara? I see how
you two are together.'

Akis sighed, his eyes going back to the woman he thought was so incredible. She looked even more beautiful tonight, the olive-green dress smoothing over every curve, her hair a tumble of auburn waves...

'I guess we just enjoy the time we have left,' he answered with a sigh.

'You've made it sound like this is a death sentence. Listen to how tragic that is.'

'I cannot please everyone. That is the conclusion I have come to.'

'You are right,' Horatio agreed. 'But you are choosing the wrong person to please, Aki.'

'You are only concerned about the show,' Akis said.

'What? Are you kidding me? You think you tell me you are going to become a priest and my first thought is the show?' He was yelling now. 'If that is what kind of friend you think I am then... fuck you!'

With that said, Horatio stormed across the room.

48

Cara looked at her watch. It was only twenty minutes until she had to perform and Margot was still avoiding making any approach towards Raj. In fact, she was muttering under her breath, in between gulps of champagne, like she was reciting a predetermined script. Margot was showing sides to her personality that Cara had never seen before and it was as enlightening as it was concerning. Something about this guy was under Margot's skin, whether it was because she was overawed by his title – not usually something to put Margot off – or maybe it was down to something from their past. Whatever it was, if Margot needed this opportunity with the maharajah then she should take it.

'OK,' Cara said. 'You should go over there. There's the least amount of people around him now.'

'Yes,' Margot agreed, nodding but not moving.

'Margot, what's wrong?'

'Nothing.' It wasn't convincing.

'Margot, we came all this way for you to surprise this man and schmooze him. And he's right there.'

'I know but, I'm wondering now if maybe this was a mistake.'

There was a definite tremble to Margot's voice. This did not happen on the regular. Suddenly Cara was flooded with a whole mixture of emotions as if a kind of breaking point had been reached and there was no going back.

'No,' she said firmly. 'We're not doing this. You are Margot Jones, CEO of Carried Away, the boss bitch who slays every day. This guy is just a guy wearing way too much white in my opinion. But if he has something you need to take the business closer to your dreams then you need to go and speak to him!'

Margot was now standing stiller than a statue. It was time for Cara to be in charge. She took Margot by the arm and walked her across the carpet until they were on the very edge of the area where Raj was sitting.

'I don't care about his standing on the Forbes billionaire list or whatever, he is just a business proposition like any other,' Cara told her aunt. 'Now snap out of whatever *this* version of you is and get back in the game.'

'Margot Jones? Is that you?'

Cara turned her head and there was Raj, right next to them, addressing Margot.

'Gosh, Raj,' Margot greeted, finally seeming to come to. 'What on Earth are you doing here? What an absolute coincidence!'

Cara just smiled, hoping her aunt wasn't going to overplay this.

'I could ask you the same question. I was told the guest list was very exclusive,' Raj replied with a wry smile.

'Oh, darling, still with that sense of humour I adore,' Margot bleated.

'We should catch up some time,' Raj said. 'I heard from Sofia recently actually. She thought I would have time to go to some little wedding or something. You remember Sofia?'

'Sofia? Let me think...' Margot said, looking into the air as if she needed help from the universe. Then Cara watched her smile break. 'Of course I remember Sofia.'

'Beautiful girl,' Raj said. 'Not very clever, but very beautiful.' He sighed, looking directly at Margot then. 'You two were always opposites, weren't you?'

Cara's jaw dropped. This man was vile! He had just badly insulted two people in two sentences. She opened her mouth to say something but felt the pressure of Margot's hand on her skin.

'Still the charmer, Raj,' Margot said, cool and collected. 'So, shall we take a minute now to have a catch-up?'

'Now?' Raj said. And then he laughed like Margot had cracked the funniest joke at the Edinburgh Festival. 'Margot, there are many people who wish to speak with me.'

Cara was seething, but the pressure on her arm increased and Margot added a little bit of nail too.

'I understand,' Margot said, smoothly. 'But surely you can make a few moments for an old "friend".'

'I wish I could,' Raj said. 'But, sadly, moments in my life are highly in demand.'

Now Margot let go of Cara and planted a hand on the sleeve of Raj's white suit jacket. Immediately three of his entourage rose from their chairs until Raj swiftly waved them away.

'Margot, I do hope you're not going to cause a scene.'

'All I'm asking for is what I deserved straight after college,' Margot stated in bitter tones.

'I'm not sure I'm with you,' Raj said. 'And really, Margot, as nice as this is, I really have to—'

'What you really have to do,' Margot said, lips tight. 'Is sit your royal arse back in that chair, order a bottle of Dom Pérignon, and listen to the fantastic investment opportunity I have for you.'

'And why would I do that?' Raj asked, all smug lips.

Margot leaned in close and the entourage all quivered a little.

'Because,' Cara heard her aunt say in hushed tones. 'Otherwise, I am firstly going to tell everyone at this party, and then everyone in the whole world, about how you use and abuse women and how you told me that if I didn't get rid of our baby you would arrange for me to disappear too.'

Cara felt like someone had just hit her with a wrecking ball and it was all she could do to keep standing upright. But stand upright she did, wanting to give Margot the solidarity. She kept her eyes firmly on the maharajah who had had the decency to pale close to the colour of his suit.

'I do not know what you are talking about, Margot.' He stumbled a little over his words.

'I have a recording,' Margot carried on. 'Several copies of it in fact. Your voice saying the words all those years ago. Killing me inside over and over again, shaping who I am, driving me forward, but also never really letting me move on.'

'Stop talking, Margot,' Raj said through gritted teeth now.

'Then start listening,' Margot said, her voice laced with bitterness.

Cara held her breath, sensing something in her aunt she had never been privy to before.

'I've spoken to women you've destroyed. Terrified, damaged women. Some so traumatised they can't relive the details. But others, when I felt brave enough to share my story with them, finally opened up and told me what they had been through. Some of them gave me statements we can use should we have to go to the police.'

'You think I do not have people who can make this go away?' Raj spat.

'I think you underestimate the power of numbers and the truth. Now, you are going to sit back down and I am going to sit with you and you are going to agree to make a very large investment in my new suitcase and then you are going to go through the list of these women and you are going to make a substantial donation to them and you are going to apologise for every ounce of pain you caused.'

Raj shook his head.

'No, Raj, I only want to see you nod. Because if you don't nod and get out your platinum card I am going to be talking to my very close friends at the UK government.'

It took Raj perhaps five seconds to invite Margot into the VIP area but before she moved, Cara held her aunt's arm.

'Margot—'

'Not now, Cara,' Margot said, her voice calm. 'But we will talk later.' She gave her a small smile. 'Sorry about everything, you know, leading up to this, if I haven't been, well...'

Her voice trailed off but Cara didn't need her to say anything more.

'It's OK,' Cara told her. 'I think everything is going to be better now.'

As Margot moved away, Cara looked across the room and her eyes found Akis. It was time.

49

'You are OK?' Akis asked as he seated himself at the piano.

Cara nodded. 'Yes.'

It was as confident as she had ever sounded and as powerful in this situation as she had ever felt. This was not Eurovision. There was really nothing riding on this performance. It wasn't for any of the guests here, it was for her. A chance to sing the song she had written, the way she wanted to sing it, with the most wonderful man playing the piano for her. Suddenly it was like there was nothing in the world to fear.

Akis played deep heavy chords on the piano until he had everyone's attention. The chatter died down, the chinking of champagne flutes lessened a little.

'Ladies and gentlemen,' he said into the microphone. 'Please show your appreciation for... Miss Cara Jones.'

Cara put one hand on her microphone on the stand as the partygoers gave light applause. She could do this. She was *going* to do this. It was time to create a new memory for this song that didn't involve Yodi or Moldova. The song deserved it. *She* deserved it.

Akis gave her the introduction and then she was beginning. It wasn't the techno beats and flashing lights of the last time she'd sung this, the back-up dancers and the set choreography going on in time to a sequence on a video screen, it was as stripped back as it could get, raw, just the lyrics, the piano and her voice. And, as she committed to the song, she wasn't on the boat in front of the allegedly good and great, she was barefoot in the sand in front of the little church, she was watching Akis eat fish with his fingers, she was petting a donkey called Pig, she was falling into the Santorini sea and kissing a man they called The Deacon… Here, but not being seen. Everything under her control.

And with that relaxation came belief. She could feel it building in her gut, infiltrating her soul, making her glow on the inside. With a slow rise up through the scales in this final section of the song, she knew it was coming and she knew, despite the lack of full practice, it wasn't something she was going to miss. She hit the G10 note with everything she had, testing her own capabilities, elongating it and sending it out to the universe. It didn't matter if anyone captured it for socials, it didn't matter if dolphins started leaping from the sea, it only mattered that along with the note, perhaps all the grief, desperation and sadness was finally being released. When she couldn't hold her breath any longer she stopped singing and there was no piano, no sounds from the party, only silence.

It took her a second to realise exactly how much energy the number had taken out of her and that her chest was rising and falling with exhaustion as well as adrenaline. And then the applause broke out. Clapping and whooping and there were camera phones all aimed in her direction.

All those lucky enough to be at this party had all thought they'd witnessed something bought, paid for and put on especially to mesmerise them. They had no idea the trauma that had led to that performance, no clue of what she had been through to get here. Only two people knew. One was clapping his heart out, stood by the piano, encouraging everyone else to applaud longer and harder, and the other was rushing through the crowds recording with her phone, knocking into the ice sculpture that was now nothing but an unrecognisable mound, until she was right there, throwing her arms around Cara and hugging her close.

'My beautiful brave girl,' Margot said, tears in her eyes and the emotion dragging in her voice.

Cara hugged her aunt hard but there were no tears for her now, only joy. 'I think that tonight, we are both made out of stronger stuff than we ever truly realised.'

Margot squeezed her close again. 'Without doubt, my darling. Without *any* doubt.'

50

'Peace offering?'

Akis held out the bottle of Yellow Donkey beer to Horatio as he found his friend leaning against the railing of the superyacht looking out to sea.

'Where did you find that?' Horatio asked. 'Because I thought beer was too good for these people on here.'

'Like a good miracle, I turned water into local beer. What can I say? I feel the gods are with me.'

Horatio took the beer and guzzled.

'Listen, Horatio, I am sorry for what I said earlier. I know you were not thinking of the show. It was a stupid comment to make and—'

'Forget it,' Horatio said. 'I have made more than enough stupid comments in my lifetime and I should not have stormed off like a pubescent thirteen-year-old.'

'It was a little like that,' Akis agreed.

'Hey!'

Akis smiled and took a sip of his beer.

'So, tell me,' Horatio said, back against the railings now. 'Did you know that Cara could sing like that?'

Akis sighed, standing alongside him. 'She told me, but, you know, I did not think it would quite be like that.'

'I have never heard anything like it before,' Horatio said.

'Yeah,' Akis said. 'There is a lot about her that is nothing quite like I have experienced before.'

'So why are you going to give up the potential of that for a life in black robes?'

He sighed. 'Perhaps I should not think of it as giving things up, but more as deciding on a different path. It is an opportunity, no? To help people, to be there for my community, to do something noble.'

'Noble? That is what you want?'

'Well, what is my life right now, Horatio? The orchestra did not work out, we work for a few days a week in the summer, then through the winter it is work wherever I can get it.'

'Aki, do you remember why you left Notos for Corfu Town in the first place?'

'Because I could not stand living with my mother any more?' Akis suggested.

'And you think when you are always in that tiny chapel not far from her house it will be any different?' Horatio asked. 'You came to Corfu Town for freedom. And that is absolutely what you would be giving up if you do this.' He took a breath. 'I'm obviously not telling you what you should do, you get enough of that from everybody else, but think hard, Aki. I do not want you to have regrets.'

His phone started to quake in the pocket of his jeans and it was the rumble of a phone call not a simple message. Slipping it out he saw it was Anastasia. Immediately he was worried. Usually, she would type a lengthy text rather than make a call.

'*Ya.*'

'Aki,' Anastasia said, her voice strained, panicked even. 'You need to come back. It is *Yiayia.*'

His sister's voice broke then, emotion taking over and Akis felt like someone had dropped a boulder of Santorini rock on his chest and it was crushing his body.

'Anastasia, what's happened?'

'She is… dying.'

51

Cara knew immediately that something was wrong. The second she spotted Akis coming back into the room she could see his whole demeanour was off. Gone was the brightness of his eyes, the pride in his expression from when she had sung her heart out. She was walking towards him before she even knew her legs were moving, not seeing or hearing anything else on this party boat.

'What's happened?' she asked him.

She watched him swallow, saw concern tear across his features. 'It's nothing. Everything is fine. You need to carry on enjoying the party, people will want to speak with you.'

'Akis, I'm not stupid,' Cara said. 'Tell me the truth.'

He sighed. 'It's my *yiayia*. Anastasia called. She is... not very well.'

He took a breath and Cara knew it was much, much worse than he was letting on.

'We need to go,' she said immediately.

'*I* need to go,' he replied. 'Horatio is arranging for someone to get the boat to get me off this boat.'

'What's going on? What is the Horror arranging?' Margot had appeared at Cara's shoulder.

'Akis needs to go,' Cara said. 'Irini is sick.'

'It's probably living in close proximity to that vile donkey,' Margot said.

'No,' Cara said firmly. 'She's *very* sick, Margot.' She did her best with her expression to make it clear that this was not a joking matter.

'Right,' Margot stated. 'Completely understood. No time to waste. So, where's your little friend gone?'

Akis sighed. 'To call for the boat to take us back to shore and then we can get a taxi to the airport and see how quickly we can get back to Athens and on to Corfu.'

Cara could see it written in his expression. This trip to Santorini he had made for her could be the reason that he wasn't going to see his grandmother in *her* far more important time of need. She had never felt more guilty. All these sacrifices he was making, for her, for his family…

'Oh no,' Margot said in her furiously determined tone. 'That will take far too long, won't it?' She put a hand on Cara's arm. 'Call our apartments. Get them to gather our things.'

'What?' Cara asked.

'I will find the Horror and then I will fix us all transportation.' With that said, Margot went speeding across the deck looking like she was on a mission.

'I do not know what to do,' Akis admitted, his hands in his hair.

'Listen,' Cara said. 'It's going to be OK. If Margot says she's going to fix us transportation that's exactly what she's going to do. And there's no question, we're coming back with you.'

Akis reached for her hand, entwining their fingers and Cara held on tight, knowing he needed the comfort and wanting to give that to him.

'She was the only one, you know, that understood how the family can be. The oldest generation are usually stuck in their traditions yet she listened to me, she understood that times change and—'

He stopped talking, as if trying to settle himself with what was happening yet still very much trying not to panic.

'Akis, she's still here and everything will be OK,' Cara told him.

'But, what if it's not?'

'Whatever happens,' Cara said seriously. 'I'm going to be right there beside you, OK? Exactly like you've been for me since the minute we met.' She squeezed his hand.

'OK,' he said. Then a little bolder, more convincing. 'OK.'

'Right,' Margot said, bustling back into the space. 'We need to go up to the upper deck for our ride.'

'What?' Cara asked. 'But what about the tender to shore?'

'We aren't going to be needing that,' Margot said. 'We're taking the helicopter.'

52

IRINI'S HOUSE, NOTOS, CORFU

Akis stood outside the tumbledown one-storey building with its tiled roof that looked like someone had just shaken out the pieces as though they were flakes of breakfast cereal. There was nothing but the light of the moon here and one barely working terrace lamp showing the menagerie of his grandmother's things. Glass flagons, plastic chairs, cushions, a bird cage that had never been occupied...

It was the early hours of the morning now and he had been too scared to text his sister since the helicopter had taken off and he had told her he was on his way. Would he be too late?

He guessed that standing around soaking in these childhood memories in the half-dark wasn't helping anyone.

'You should go in.'

Cara had come with him, like she'd promised. When the helicopter had touched down a little over a couple of kilometres away, there were two cars waiting. One had taken Margot and Horatio who knew where and the other had brought them here.

'I know,' he replied. 'I just need a moment.'

She moved closer, stood right next to him and reached for his hand. She interlocked their fingers and rubbed gently over the empty space where his little finger used to be. It was a small gesture but it meant everything.

Suddenly the door of the house burst open and there was his mother, looking like he had never seen her before. She was completely devoid of make-up, her hair untamed and a bundle of dark curls, and she was wearing an old towelling dressing gown.

'*Mama*,' Akis said before he had even realised it, as if he needed clarification it was really her.

'Oh, Aki!' his mother gasped, her distress obvious.

'Go,' Cara said, letting go of his hand. 'I'll wait right here.'

He dropped a kiss on the top of her head and headed across the scrub towards the house. The fact his mother was here, had been inside her childhood home she hated so much, spoke volumes for the severity of the situation. And if that didn't get the message across then the tear tracks across her cheeks definitely did.

He put his arms around his mother and drew her close. Immediately she began to sob.

'I... just want her to shout at me or something,' Sofia said, her words muffled against his shoulder. 'Even the donkey knows things are not right. It is sitting down in the kitchen, on a chair.'

'It is OK,' Akis said, trying to be strong.

'She has asked for you,' Sofia said, finally letting him go and wiping her eyes with the back of her hand.

'She is speaking? That is good,' Akis said, suddenly realising he had been holding his breath.

'She *was* speaking,' Sofia said pointedly. 'The doctor said there is nothing he can do. That it will just happen... when it happens.'

He still couldn't comprehend it. He knew that Irini hadn't been well, but he should have insisted she took it seriously. *He* should have taken it more seriously.

'Are Anastasia and Cosmos inside? And *Bampás*?'

'No,' Sofia said. 'Cosmos was crying so loudly no one could hear the priest. Anastasia has been here all day, I sent her back to the house with Cosmos. Your father is looking after Wren, Jackie and Kelly, most probably with ouzo.'

'So, you have been here alone?' Akis asked.

'As I said, the donkey is in the kitchen.' Sofia sniffed.

'Come on,' Akis said, leading the way.

* * *

He had never seen his grandmother look so frail. It was like all the life force had been drained from her, leaving her skin translucent and paper-thin. Her cheeks were hollowed out, her mouth an 'O' shape that was struggling with the in and out of breath.

'*Mama*, Akis is here,' Sofia said, sitting down on a pile of newspapers that covered the bedside chair.

'*Mama*, why don't you move the papers?'

'No,' Sofia answered. 'They have always been there. The same set of six. Since I was small.'

Akis drew closer to his grandmother and took hold of her hand. '*Yiayia*, I am here.'

'The doctor says that she can hear us. Pappa Spiros said that God can also hear us and that we should pray for a miracle.' Sofia sighed. 'I know that this is the beginning. The very start of the curse.'

Akis bit his lip. 'It cannot be the curse, *Mama*.'

'Why not?'

'Because *Yiayia* is not a Diakos.'

'But I am a Diakos. Her daughter. And we know from the stories that it is indiscriminate.'

Irini's breathing suddenly quickened and Akis held onto her hand, looking for a sign of improvement or, perhaps, deterioration.

'Aki,' Irini rasped.

'*Yiayia*, I am here.'

She opened her eyes then, looking at Akis like she could see inside to the depths of him. Sofia let out a gasp.

'Where... is... Pig?' Irini asked.

'He is in the kitchen.'

'Is he... sitting on... a chair?'

'Yes,' Sofia answered. 'How do you know?'

Akis watched Irini turn her head then, looking to his mother, her eyebrows showing surprise at her presence.

'Sofia? You are... inside the house.'

'Yes, of course I am inside the house. Why would you say such a stupid thing?'

'Because... you have not been inside this house since... your father passed away.'

'That's not true,' Sofia said, scrunching up her face and shaking her head.

'The second of June... twenty years ago,' Irini continued.

'She is delirious,' Sofia said bitterly.

'*Mama*,' Akis said. 'Please, think about what you are saying.'

'I must be dying,' Irini said, very matter of fact.

'No,' Akis said straight away. 'You are not.'

'Then why has Pappa Spiros been speaking to me... for what feels like two weeks? And Cosmos was here, crying like a baby. And Anastasia... she needs to be out finding herself a new girlfriend. She has not been as happy as she was when she was with Trinity.'

'*Mama*, you are not well. You do not know what you are saying,' Sofia said.

'I... *do* know what I am saying. I *always* know what I am saying. It is the rest of this family who have the problems,' Irini continued, moving a little like she was in discomfort.

'Let me help you,' Akis offered, letting go of her hand to assist with adjusting her pillows.

'No one talks about what matters,' Irini continued. 'They speak around the important things like it is a dance of words.'

'You need to rest, *Mama*,' Sofia insisted.

'I can rest when I am dead. I am sure it will be very soon.' She began to cough and it was raspy and weak. 'But... for now... while I still have breath in my lungs, I need to make sure that things change.'

'*Mama*—'

'Quiet, Sofia! For once in your life... you will listen to me!'

The words were determined and there was a little fire in the delivery.

But wasn't that what sometimes happened when people were close to the end? They rallied, provided some calm before the storm. Except it seemed like his grandmother had no intention of keeping the moment on an even keel.

'I blame myself,' Irini continued. 'For your syndrome of perfection.'

'I do not know what you mean,' Sofia scoffed. 'I have no such thing.'

'I should not have let you go to that college. I should have said no to the scholarship. I should have realised that you mixing with people who have a warped sense of reality was only going to make things worse. But, when you returned, I thought it would just be a phase. That you had seen part of the rest of the world and now you would come back and realise what really matters in life.' Irini drew in a long slow breath that looked like it was taking much strength. 'But instead you were worse. You distanced yourself from me, your father, from everything we believed in, you married Thanasis so you could bully him, you had children so you could control them and now look where we are! You raise a boy who is terrified of his own shadow because he is afraid that whatever he does will not be good enough for you, you raise a girl who is only really happy when she is rebelling against you and you raise this boy here for a life in the church like you are punishing him for saving his brother and losing his chance of a career playing his beautiful piano!'

The atmosphere in the room thickened and Akis didn't know what to say. Although his grandmother didn't usually pull punches, he had never been aware of her being so brutally honest to his mother before. And what was even more surprising was Sofia seemed unable to make a defence for herself.

'Do you know what I was planning to do?' Irini continued. 'Lie to you.' She didn't wait for any response. 'Thanasis and I were ageing paper, with Pig's help, detailing an ancient spell that the family could perform to counteract the Diakos curse.'

'What?' Sofia and Akis said together.

'I thought that if you could believe in the Diakos curse, you could just as easily believe in an antidote to it if it was convincing enough.'

'*Mama*! I cannot believe you would think to do that!' Sofia exclaimed, standing up. 'And you would involve *my* husband! When we are in the middle of wedding preparations! And everything is up in the air!'

'The only thing that is up in the air, Sofia, is your expectations of everyone! Cosmos must have the biggest wedding Corfu has ever seen! Anastasia must have a boyfriend not a girlfriend! Akis must become a priest or everyone will die! All of these are misconceptions and they are like kites taking off with you pulling the strings!'

'I do not want to hear any more!' Sofia said, beginning to pace the room. 'And now you do not sound so close to death!'

'It is time, Sofia, to know that superficial things, superficial people, they do not last. The happiness you get from them arrives as quickly as it leaves. Family, they are not mood boards to align with your ideals, they are individuals born with freedom in their hearts and unique spirits driving their souls.' Irini took another deep breath. 'I decide now that you should not need a trick to get you to realise that curse or no curse, no one should be put in a position where they have to make forced decisions because of someone else's fear. And even worse when that person has spread their own personal fear into the minds of everyone else.'

Akis swallowed, the weight of his grandmother's words hanging heavy in the air of the bedroom. The silence elongated, the only sound Irini's breathing and the haunting hoot of the scops owl. And then Sofia fled to the door, rushing out of the bedroom. Akis could hear the sound of Pig braying as the front door slammed.

'Aki,' Irini said, her voice sounding weak again. 'Hold my hand and promise me you will not become a priest.'

'*Yiayia*,' Akis said, taking her hand in his and sitting on the edge of her bed.

'Did you not hear anything I just said? You have me waste my breaths and not take it in?'

'No, I did. Of course, I did but—'

'Then.' Irini squeezed his hand. 'You should know that you have already sacrificed too much for this family. It is time for that to end.'

Akis took a breath, not really knowing how to respond.

'Promise me,' Irini said. 'Please, Aki.'

He nodded. 'OK, *Yiayia*. I promise.'

'Good,' Irini said, her mouth forming a smile. 'Then now, I am ready to die.'

And, with that said, she closed her eyes.

53

DIAKOS FAMILY CHAPEL, NOTOS

'Well, you have to give it to me,' Margot began as she and Cara walked through the olive grove, the white dome of the little chapel just visible now through the branches of the trees. 'I've certainly provided us with a fully packed itinerary for this trip. I mean, we've had a hen night, a wine and cake tasting, a blown-up suitcase, a trip to Santorini, you singing like you've never sung before, a ride in a helicopter, a wedding – if it ever happens – and now a funeral.'

Cara swallowed. It was the morning after their return from Santorini and the Corfu day was as blue-sky perfect as every other day of their visit had been. So much had happened in their time in Greece and there was far more for her than Margot had just mentioned then. Meeting Akis had been the most unexpected thing but it wasn't just how crazy good-looking he was, nor what a sensitive, kind, funny, genuine guy she had found him to be, it was what he had managed to unlock inside her. It was like only he had been given the key to help her break free. Yet, with his future career path still uncertain, no one knew exactly what was going to happen next. But perhaps that didn't matter. Something perfect didn't necessarily have to last a lifetime, did it?

'Aren't you forgetting something?' Cara asked, dodging a white butterfly's trajectory.

'What?' Margot asked, slowing her pace. 'A gift? Do Greeks bring gifts to funerals?'

'No,' Cara said softly. 'Of all the things you've just said, you didn't mention how you stood up to Raj last night.'

'Oh, well, yes, I mean...' Margot's voice trailed off and she simply gave a nod.

'You should have just gone to the authorities, you know,' Cara said. 'With all the women you spoke to willing to tell their stories, you could have made sure he never did anything like that again, got him prosecuted. Especially with your MI5 connections.'

'Yes,' Margot said. 'Well, about that... I didn't actually speak to any other women.' She stopped walking and took a jagged breath. 'I wish I had a cigarette right now, but that awful Horror smoked my last one.'

'You bluffed him,' Cara said, caught between astounded yet also completely aware.

'On a few counts actually,' Margot said. 'I don't want him to invest in Carried Away to grow the reach of the Maxi-Go. I want to put his face and monogram on those cases and watch them explode. I'll make it a launch night event – taking health and safety into account obviously, nothing and no one harmed except his ego. That limited edition range will have the shortest shelf life while we work on a fix, leaving no stone unturned until it's foolproof. And as for the money Raj gives me, well, I thought I might give it to your mum and dad.'

'What?' Cara said.

'Well, they're always doing righteous things for the planet, things I should have and could have done long before now if I wasn't so set on being the granite-souled business woman no one could get close to.' She gave a small smile. 'And obviously there is a part of me that knows whatever my sister is called now will hate taking money from me but she will because it's for the good of the globe.'

Cara smiled and shook her head. And then she met her aunt's gaze again. 'But, was it true, about the baby?'

Margot gave a sharp inhale then and put her hand out to catch a silvery frond of olive leaves. 'It's such a cliché, isn't it? Young stupid girl gets infatuated with someone with good looks, power and money, gives a little too much and ends up in a mess.' She sighed. 'I didn't tell anyone, Cara. You're the only person, except for Raj, that knows.'

'You didn't tell your parents or my mum?'

'Tell them that the outgoing, flirtatious, pain in the arse they couldn't wait to send away had lived up to all expectations?' She shook her head. 'No. I dealt with the matter. There was never any other choice to be made when I realised what kind of man Raj really was.' She sighed. 'And there may not be any other women I spoke to about his behaviour, but I wasn't blind to exactly what he was once he had shown his true colours. I won't have been the only one.'

Cara slipped an arm around her aunt's shoulders and drew her close, holding tight. She felt Margot stiffen a little, always better at being air-kissed than hugged. But Cara wasn't letting go.

'You know you've been like a mum to me.'

'Ugh, Cara, don't. I'm imagining someone in dungarees doing things with glue and sequins and making lentil cottage pie.'

'You've always been there when I needed you. Especially after Moldova.'

Finally, she let Margot go.

'I could have done better,' Margot admitted. 'I'm ashamed of that. I took over. I made decisions and choices. I didn't *ask* you, I *told* you.'

'I know,' Cara said. 'But in the beginning that's what I needed.'

'But you don't need that now. And, perhaps, if *I* hadn't needed you alongside me you would have been singing again before now.'

Cara shook her head. 'No... I don't think so.' She took a breath. 'And I don't think it's something that's necessarily going to be in my future, you know, as a career.'

'No?'

'I don't know,' Cara said. 'I'm kind of settling into the idea that it's OK to not know where things go.'

'Jesus Christ,' Margot said, shivering. 'No plan or strategy! Living life on the spur of the moment! You definitely come from your mother's side of the Jones genes! You'll be off somewhere remote to build a school soon!'

A bell sounded. It made them both jump and realise that they should probably continue making their way to the little chapel. Cara linked her arm with Margot's.

'Come on, let's go and pay our respects. It looks like there's quite a crowd down there. I'm not sure they're all going to fit into the chapel, it's very small inside.'

Margot shook her head. 'Somewhere I did not think I would ever be. In Corfu at the funeral of a donkey.'

54

TAVERNA PANORAMA, NOTOS

Pig was so beloved by the locals that there hadn't just been a funeral for the sudden demise of the donkey, there was a wake too, here at this beautiful taverna. Bright pink bougainvillea cascaded down from the roof, arching over the entrance, the many terraces set with tables and chairs amid palm trees, vines and hanging gourds. It was the most peaceful, relaxing venue, right next to the glistening blue sea. Cara wondered why this hadn't been anyone's first choice for Cosmos and Wren's wedding. But, as she stood looking out over the water, sucking in the scent of pink lilies, enjoying a moment of solitude away from the funeral party who were tucking into coffee, ouzo and baklava, her mind wandered to Seb. Of all the things she'd gone through, he was still something undealt with. Like a suitcase you'd brought back from holiday and never unpacked. They had been planning to get married. She had been at her lowest point and he had just left…

'Cara, there you are.'

She turned around and there was Akis, striding towards her, looking a picture of perfection in black trousers and a smart white shirt, hair slightly tousled.

'Sorry,' she said. 'I couldn't eat another thing and it's really hard to refuse your mother anything. I mean, I'm sure the baklava is delicious but—'

He smiled. 'It is OK. I understand. I would have come looking for you three baklava pieces ago but I am not good at saying no where my family is concerned. And that is the real curse.' He stood next to her, leaned against the low fence, the only barrier to the water a few metres below.

'I am so sorry about Pig. I know I said that last night but yesterday was a bit...'

'Crazy?' he offered. 'Having all my family squeeze into a tiny house to carry a deceased donkey sitting on a chair outside?'

'Irini is feeling better today though?'

'The doctor tells us it is a miracle but if I start to believe in miracles then I might have to believe in other things that cannot be explained. And I am still undecided about that.'

She knew he was talking about the priesthood. How could it not be on his mind? The wedding was almost upon them, Irini had been terribly sick, everyone was panicking, it was a lot to carry on his shoulders. Perhaps her being in the mix was adding to his burden...

'My grandmother told me last night that I must not become a priest,' Akis told her. 'In fact, she made me promise, right before she closed her eyes and said she was ready to die.'

'What?'

'I know. And then Pig made the strangest noise and my grandmother opened her eyes again and, well, you know the rest.'

'So, what are you going to do?'

'To be honest with you... I really do not know. The wedding is happening, my grandmother is still sick, Cosmos might have a nervous breakdown... it is a lot.'

'I get that,' Cara said. 'And personally I didn't think I was going to come to Corfu and have all my personal demons waiting on Greek shores.'

'But you battled them, no?' Akis said, nudging her arm with his.

'Not all of them,' Cara admitted with a sigh.

'No?'

She looked into those gorgeous eyes and remembered seeing them for the first time, behind the mask in the church in Corfu Town.

She swallowed. 'Akis, I like you. A lot. You know that. And everything you've done for me since I got here has been like nothing anyone has done for me in my entire life.'

He shook his head. 'There is nothing I have done. Everything has come from you. It was all inside of you already.'

'Maybe,' Cara said. 'But I wasn't ever going to find it myself.' She sighed. 'This is hard to say but I'm going to have to say it anyway.'

'Please, Cara, do not be afraid to say anything to me,' Akis said.

She took a deep breath. 'I don't think I'm ready for any kind of relationship with anyone yet.' She stopped for a beat, her heart thrumming with acknowledgement that this was such a big step. 'I think I need to... properly process and come to terms with what happened with my last relationship so I can make sure that I'm in the right place to go forward with anything else that comes my way in the future.'

Akis nodded. 'That is a very sensible plan. It is the right thing to do. Completely.'

'Then,' Cara began. 'Why does it feel so horrible?' She took a breath. 'I mean, it felt right when I started to say it, but now I'm thinking about not spending time with you and it doesn't feel right at all. I just didn't want you to make any decisions about your future based on me if I can't promise you anything.'

'Ssh,' Akis said softly. 'You do not have to worry. It is a good decision and no one else's opinion of it matters.' He hovered his hand over hers but didn't make the connection.

'I know, I just, you have so much going on right now, I didn't want to become something else that you have to worry about. If I'm not sure where I'm at with the whole relationship thing.'

'Cara, please, it's OK,' Akis said. 'You should not be thinking of me. You should only be thinking of you.'

Except now the only thought going through her head was that this man who she liked so much was never going to touch her again, hold her again, kiss her again...

'Akis.'

'Yes.'

She wanted to take it all back. She wanted to not think about whether she was ready to trust again, just act, wait and see, believe. But if he did become a priest that door would close anyway. It was hopeless.

'I should... find Margot. Make sure she's not winding anyone up any more than she usually does.' She gave a half smile.

'Yes, and I should find my brother. Tonight, it is his bachelor party and there is much to prepare.'

She gazed at him, drank him in, remembered how he'd held her and kissed her, wet from the Santorini sea...

'I will... try to avoid the baklava,' she said quickly. And then she headed across the terrace and back towards the funeral party.

55

THE LISTON, CORFU TOWN

'It looks very... cosmopolitan there.'

It was Cara's mum – Wissy – on FaceTime. For the first time ever it was a joint call, with Margot sharing a little of the screentime as they sat drinking coffee in one of the cafés under the archways in this beautiful marble promenade. It was evening now and the temperature was just starting to drop a little. Pigeons were still skirting the tables, teenagers hung out – all Nike Tech drip and bikes – tables were beginning to fill after siesta time. Cara was really starting to feel at home in this atmosphere.

'Only you could make the word "cosmopolitan" sound like an insult,' Margot said, and took an inhale of her cigarette.

'It's OK for you two to like different things, you know,' Cara said quickly. 'Siblings are individuals, often poles apart in thoughts and ideals.'

'Yes,' Wissy agreed, her hand flat on the trunk of a sturdy-looking tree. 'Some of us think money is an accessory and others think it should be distributed evenly so everyone can have access to basic necessities.'

'I told you this wasn't going to work,' Margot said, sitting back.

'No,' Cara said. 'It's fine. Mum is going to stop jumping to judgement caused by predetermined opinions based on her childhood—'

'What?' Wissy gasped.

'And,' Cara interrupted again. 'You are both going to listen to one another.'

'What?' Margot exclaimed.

'Mum, Margot has something she wants to talk to you about,' Cara began.

'I did,' Margot said, putting her cigarette in the ashtray and folding her arms across her chest. 'Not so sure now.'

'Margot,' Cara said. 'Yes, you do.'

'Fine,' Margot said, uncrossing her arms and sitting forward again. 'But let's not make a huge deal about this.'

For once, Wissy's end of the line was quiet except for what Cara presumed were parrots squawking in the background.

'I've decided to do some good,' Margot announced. 'Give something back to the world.'

'If your business is going sustainable then you're quite far behind the times, sister dear.'

'See how she goads me?' Margot said, looking to Cara. 'Maybe this was a silly idea.'

'Mum,' Cara said to the phone screen. 'Margot wants to make a sizeable donation to one of the environmental groups you support.'

'And why would she want to do that?' Wissy asked, suspicion on her face. 'Is it to qualify for some sort of Sunak tax break?'

Margot tutted and shook her head, picking her cigarette back up.

'Mum, this is a serious offer. A very generous one. It's a real chance to do some amazing things.'

'And will my sister want to stand there dripping in YSL handing over one of those comedy giant-sized cheques posing with some hungry orphans?'

'Mum!' Cara exclaimed.

'I'm done with this conversation,' Margot said, getting to her feet and leaving the café.

'Margot, wait,' Cara tried but it was in vain. She turned her attention back to the screen, more than a bit annoyed. 'Mum, that was really uncalled for.'

'I don't think you know my sister quite as well as I do. She will never change. It's always about her and no one else.'

Cara took a breath. She knew that wasn't true, now more than at any other time. But she couldn't say anything. Margot had made it clear that she didn't want anyone else to know what had happened with the maharajah.

'Listen, Mum, I know how Margot can be but—'

'You don't though, do you? Because you've never been able to see a fault in her. She was always the fun aunt who gave you things you shouldn't have, things I told you *and* her you shouldn't have. The one who took you in and told you everything was going to be OK when sometimes you needed tougher love.'

Now Cara was shocked. This had got a lot deeper than she had envisaged and she was currently regretting it being aloud on FaceTime. There were two ladies sitting at the next table who currently seemed more interested in the conversation than their frappes.

'Mum, have you ever thought there might be a reason why Margot is like this?'

'Yes, often. I blame my father who always told her she was like Bette Davis.'

Cara silently cursed and, as she did so, the FaceTime connection seemed to destabilise. 'Mum, can you hear me?'

'Cara... I can't hear you... are you still there?'

'Yes, I'm here. I can hear...'

Then the screen went black and everything died.

With a sigh, Cara left money for their drinks and got up.

* * *

'She will take the money,' Cara said as she arrived at Margot's shoulder. Her aunt had walked a few paces away, had pigeons at her feet and was finishing her cigarette.

'It doesn't matter,' Margot stated. 'If none of *her* causes want the cash, I'll make a donation to another one.' She shrugged. 'I'll make something good come out of it.'

Cara paused, the evening sunshine warming her shoulders. 'You could tell her what happened. Maybe she would—'

'No,' Margot said with ferocity. 'I don't need to give anyone an excuse for how I am or who I've turned into. Those were all my choices no matter what the prequel.' She sighed. 'We are all responsible for our own actions, Cara, no matter how they came about.'

'Beautiful ladies! How do you want to join a group of delicious young men for the evening? We can only promise you drinks, bad rizz and, well, just that actually.'

It was Horatio, wearing a pink baby's bonnet on his head, and he ended his lines by slipping his arm around Margot's shoulders.

'Get off! Are you insane? What are you doing here?' Margot exclaimed, pushing him away.

'I tell you earlier, tonight is Cosmos's last night out as a single man. His men friends are here to make sure he has a great evening.'

'Good for you,' Margot said. 'So why don't you go back to Cosmos and do whatever you constitute to be a good evening.'

Cara saw a crowd building along the street and there were a dozen or so guys all wearing pink baby bonnets except Cosmos. The groom was at the very front of the line, a giant rubber fish sellotaped to his head. Cara could see Akis, next to his brother, still looking the kind of devastatingly handsome only someone with amazing cheekbones and oceanic eyes could whilst wearing a bonnet.

'Come on,' Horatio said, nudging Margot's arm. 'It will be fun. And Cosmos has already cried because the fish head is too heavy and he wants to go home to Wren.'

'In England we call them stag parties and it's very much men only,' Margot said, 'and for very good reason. The men behave like wankers and women want no part in it. Goodbye.'

As Margot made strides away from Horatio and the advancing party of guys who now seemed to be blowing glowing whistles, Cara took one last look at Akis. She knew she had never ever met a better man, but it was never going to be their time.

56

'When can we go home?'

Akis was starting to wonder why they were having a bachelor party when the groom did not want to be there. Most things about this wedding had been unorthodox, and it was continuing to be so. It was all going through the motions of tradition and what was expected rather than what the bride and groom wanted.

'He was always like this,' Thanasis commented as Horatio brought around trays full of shot glasses and distributed them to the outside tables of the bar they were sitting at. 'He started asking to go home the second we got into the car to go anywhere, do you remember?'

'I remember he always wore a hat, the bright yellow one, even in the summer.'

Thanasis laughed. 'Your mother hated that hat. She threw it away so many times but Cosmos cried so hard she ended up having to get it out of the trash again to make the noise stop.'

Sitting with his school friends, his brother looked uncomfortable, hands on the fish head, trying to loosen the tape.

'How do you think he will get on with being married?' Akis asked his father.

'I think,' Thanasis began, 'that Wren is good for him. I think he is supremely lucky to have met someone like her. She takes him for exactly how he is. And he loves her.'

Akis nodded. 'Yes, I have no doubt about that. They are perfect together.'

'I do not, however, feel the same way about your intended marriage,' Thanasis said, picking up a shot glass and downing the liquid.

'My marriage?'

'To the church.'

'Oh,' he said, feeling the mood sour.

'Your grandmother says she spoke to you.'

'Yes,' Akis said. 'In her dying breaths that ended up not being her dying breaths.'

'You say that like you are not grateful she is still with us.'

'No,' Akis said. 'Of course I am grateful, I just—'

'She told you? About the spell we intended to sell to your mother to make all this stop?'

He nodded. 'I think it was more consequential that she told my mother.'

'And do you know what your mother has said about it all?' Thanasis asked, passing him a shot glass.

Akis shook his head. 'No.'

'Then I will tell you,' his father said. 'She has said not one word. She has said nothing to anybody. She has not left the bedroom since Pig's death. And with the wedding only moments away, her focus for the past twelve months, she is unable to function. No one knows what to do. Anastasia is trying to get Wren to agree on final things and Cosmos is here crying with a fish on his head while you still deliberate on whether to join the church because of a curse only your mother is concerned about.'

Akis downed his shot and picked up a second. 'People have died. Villages have been lost, right? There is some substance to it.'

'Aki, it is a *Diakos* story. I am a Diakos. Your mother, only a Diakos by marriage. And it is my family this bad fortune has affected. If that is what it is.'

'You do not believe in it?' Akis asked him.

'I believe that what will be, will be.'

'That everything is predetermined?'

'No,' Thanasis said, shaking his head. 'The opposite of that. I do not go to church because I do not believe that there is one person or thing above us moving us all around like pieces on a chess board of life. How can that be so? With so many billions of people and so many infinite possibilities. It makes no sense.' He picked up another shot glass. 'It is my belief that life is simple. You make choices. In the moment. Like, do I want to stay at the *cafeneon* for one more beer? Yes. But what will Sofia say? She will be mad. But will she be mad I was at the *cafeneon* anyway. Yes. So one more beer will make no difference.'

'That is not the same as committing to the church so there is no possibility that people die,' Akis countered.

'Aki, there is only one assured thing in this life and that is death.'

'Yes, but—'

'Listen to me, my son,' his father said seriously. 'If you do not make a choice for you now, you are going to forever be making choices to save Cosmos, or Anastasia, or your mother's pride, exactly the same way you put your brother first when you lost your finger.' He put a hand on his shoulder. 'I do not say enough how proud I am of you.'

Akis swallowed, emotion welling up. 'You do not have to say that.'

'Your mother, she is proud of things that are loud. Anastasia's art projects that won awards, being able to say she spent thousands of euro on Cosmos's wedding. I am proud of the quiet things, the things that sometimes go unrecognised. Anastasia's patience with your mother, Wren's kindness when Cosmos is being frustrating, Irini's utter fortitude, your gentle sacrifice, Aki.'

Akis downed another shot and this one burned his throat.

'The tragedies in the Diakos family I know about can be explained away by many different things. And the priests in our family, not all of them had long trouble-free lives blessed because of their commitment to the church.' Thanasis sighed. 'Your mother is a perfection-seeker. She always has been. Wanting to tick every righteous box so nothing is out of place. That is all this is. Her paranoia, coupled with ancient tales most likely half-written by alcohol.'

Akis put his hand to the bonnet on his head and pulled it off. 'How long do we need to wear these for? I told Horatio this was to be low-key.'

'I quite like it,' Thanasis said with a laugh.

Akis smiled at his father. 'Thanks, *Bampás*.'

'You can thank me by living your life the way you want to, Aki. Your mother has me to try to perfect. She will never do it. She will always try and I will let her. That is the secret of our successful marriage. Do not tell everyone.'

He put his hand on his father's shoulder. 'Another drink?'

'*Ne*! *Fisika*!'

57

'Could we have some more chips? And pita bread and... the pink dip stuff?'

Cara hiccupped as Margot ordered more food. The coffee on the Liston had turned into drinks at many of the beautiful bars in this town and then, as the alcohol took over, Margot had started acting really out of character. She had shunned getting a table at an upmarket eatery and instead wanted somewhere the locals ate with no frills and not even a tablecloth. This grill house that comprised of six tables with plastic ketchup and mustard bottles, paper napkins and wipe-clean menus was somewhere Cara had never envisaged going with Margot ever.

'This is nice, isn't it?' Margot said, her mouth full of fries.

'It is nice,' Cara agreed. And she was supremely hungry. She had lost count of how many drinks she'd had because Margot had kept ordering things in jugs.

'Why don't we eat at places like this at home?' Margot asked as more pita breads and *taramasalata* arrived along with skewers of chicken and pork *souvlaki*.

'Because you like five-star places,' Cara reminded her. 'And you're usually on a restrictive diet.'

'Usually, but not always, and it's time I started doing new things,' Margot said, waving a chip in the air like it was a conductor's baton.

'Really?'

'Yes, I mean, I'm at that stage in my life now where I'm starting to be overlooked.'

'What do you mean?' Cara asked, sipping at her glass of the owner's homemade white wine.

'It's been happening for a while. Guys in bars who would usually make eye contact start to look at the younger woman coming through the door. In the boardroom there's less flirtatious business transactions, unless I involve you. Once a woman has passed her prime, that's it. You're not a potential wife or a potential mother to their children, you're halfway to the grave.'

'Margot!' Cara exclaimed. 'You are not halfway to the grave!'

'Not yet,' Margot agreed, refilling her glass with wine. 'However, I need a new perspective. Time to stop relying on everything I've relied upon before – things that now have more sag than my favourite aloo at a curry house.'

'I don't think—'

'And you need to do something similar,' Margot interrupted. 'Get all over that dancer-cum-piano-player like you want to stroke every key he possesses... and snap some of the strings... and fuck up the tuning.'

'Margot!' She looked around the grill house to check no one had heard, but the few patrons sitting had their eyes on a football match on the TV.

'Honestly, try as I might, you've not shown a glimmer of interest in anyone I've tried to set you up with and there have been some prime candidates.'

'Why don't we go back to talking about new things *you* want to do,' Cara suggested.

'There was the really good-looking guy who manufactured leather. What was his name?' Margot tapped the table with her fingers as if trying to recall.

'I don't remember.'

'And there was the guy who made those special zips. Looked like he'd be good with his fingers.'

'Margot, I really don't—'

'I mean, just because Seb did the dirty doesn't mean that every guy is going to be the same. That's what I've had to tell myself all these years because of Raj. Granted, I made a piss poor effort of it and never actually gave my heart to anyone, but I did still try and—'

'What did you say?'

Cara felt like someone had shot an arrow of ice through her heart. The phrase 'Seb did the dirty' was cannoning around her brain like a pinball. Amid the Greek football commentator loudly explaining the run of play, and the sizzling grill, Cara needed to be sure she had heard correctly. Did Margot know something more than Cara about the end of her and Seb? Because as far as Cara was concerned it had been a case of her being too much after the Eurovision devastation and Seb giving up, not Seb rolling immediately into king beds new...

'I,' Margot began. 'Don't know what I said. What did I say?' She reached for the flagon of wine.

'Oh no,' Cara said, taking the wine herself. 'You're not doing that. You said that Seb did the dirty. What did you mean by that?'

'Did I say that?' Margot asked.

'Yes, you did.'

And then Margot exhaled and Cara felt that cold dagger inside her deepen even further.

'I did, didn't I?' Margot agreed finally. 'OK. So, you know there are many things in my life I'm not proud of, well, this is *not* one of them. Yes, perhaps I shouldn't have kept it from you ultimately, but there we are. A clean breast of it now, I guess.'

'Tell me,' Cara demanded.

Margot picked up a piece of pita bread and pointed with it. 'I never trusted him, you know.' She bit a piece off. 'From the first time we met when your mother made that ludicrous pie with soya, there was something about the way he sat that didn't sit well with me. You know, there's shoulders back and good posture or there's shoulders rolling forward and lazy and then there was him, leaning back in the chair with such nonchalance, like he owned the chair and the table, the Orla Kiely table-cloth and the fucking pie too.'

Cara stayed quiet, knowing if she said anything then Margot might start clamming up and she needed to hear this, no matter how difficult.

'But I had to sit back and see what happened and not say anything because you were a grown woman and I always trusted your judgement. However...' Margot dunked pita into the dip. 'Then he proposed just after Eurovision started happening and I could just feel that something was off. You know, most men take action for a reason and that reason is usually predominantly selfish. That's when I got someone to follow him.'

'Margot!' Cara exclaimed.

'Well, I couldn't tell you, could I? You were in love with him and you were also trying to win that fucking glass microphone for the country! And I couldn't ask for my sister's help, could I? She was looking forward to draping ferns around at a wedding breakfast and then planning her departure to whatever corner of the globe needed help most at the time. So, yes, I took it upon myself to deal with the little shit.' She took a slug from her wine glass. 'And I was right.' She took a breath. 'He was messing around with that Allie. I don't know how long for, but it only took Johnson eight hours to find them all over each other at a speedway meeting.' Margot tutted. 'Speedway, Cara, can you imagine anything more disgusting?'

She couldn't imagine anything more disgusting, but not the motor-bikes. To think that Seb had cheated on her, while they were planning their wedding. All the times he had picked her up late from the recording studio blaming work, or when he said he was going to see his parents – it had been lies. Her mind was spinning now, recalling every excuse, each situation he had probably lied to her about.

'After three solid weeks of surveillance, I decided enough was enough,' Margot said. 'I met with him. And I told him, no matter what happened at Eurovision, win, not win, come bottom of the leaderboard, he was going to come clean. He was going to tell you exactly what he had been up to and he was going to let you choose what you did with that knowledge. But, if he couldn't man up and do that then he was going to end things, in such a way that you were hurt as softly as possible.'

'He ghosted me,' Cara reminded her. 'Ghosting isn't soft. It's seeing those calls unanswered, those messages unread or left unseen, it's having someone you thought would be in your life forever just stop existing for you.'

'I know,' Margot said. 'I saw you going through it and I ached for you, Cara. But that excuse for a man did not deserve you and you did not need to know what he was doing behind your back on top of everything else you were dealing with.'

'I don't know what to say,' Cara admitted, her hands shaking as she took a sip of wine. 'Because I've spent all this time wondering what *I* did wrong. And Seb was just doing things with someone else. But maybe, in that case, I *did* do something wrong. Maybe I was too focussed on my career, perhaps I didn't pay him enough attention, like why didn't I know that my fiancé was seeing someone else?'

'No! You don't do that!' Margot insisted loudly, swiping up a *souvlaki* skewer and pointing with it like it was a deadly weapon. 'This is *not* your fault. *He* cheated, Cara. His cheating, his decision, his blame. No one else's.'

'But I've spent all this time thinking that what happened in Moldova made him leave. That seeing me sprawled out on the stage, Yodi nibbling at my mic, the disappointment of the nation, the shame, that those things were what made him end things. When really it was something else. Some*one* else.' She took a breath. 'Or more simply than that... me not being good enough.'

'No, Cara, don't say that. That's one thing that's definitely not true!'

'I can't deal with this right now,' she said, getting to her feet. 'I don't know what to say to you. *You* let me think this was on me and there was a whole other thing going on that you kept from me! I don't know if I'm more angry at Seb for cheating, or at you for having him followed and telling him what decisions to make and hiding it all from me for so long!'

'Cara, come on, sit down, please,' Margot begged.

'No.' She wasn't going to sit down. She was already heading for the door.

58

Cara knew she had had more than enough to drink already, but she just wanted the numb feeling that came when you slid from reality into something that was less bleak and more indistinguishable around the edges. She took another gulp of wine and put her glass back on the table. Seb hadn't just ghosted her because he didn't want her in his life, he had already decided he didn't want her in his life when he'd started sleeping with Allie.

And Margot had known. Worse still, Margot had managed his departure.

'Cara! Is that you?'

It was someone wearing a pink bonnet and glasses with fake googly eyes that were dangling from them. She tried to focus.

It was Horatio.

'No,' she answered. 'That's not me. Sorry.'

'Hey,' Horatio said. 'Are you OK?'

'Yes, thank you,' Cara answered. 'All good. Even better if you go away.'

'O-K,' Horatio said.

He seemed to be getting less close now, the goofy eyes retreating, the scent of overpowering aftershave lessening. Good. Just her and her friend

Pinot. She made a grab for the glass but she overestimated the distance, her hand smacking the body of it. She watched as it tumbled to the ground and smashed.

'Shit,' she said, preparing to slide off the stool. Except the pavement wasn't quite where she expected it to be either and before she knew it, she was on the ground herself realising exactly how uncoordinated she had become.

'OK, do not touch the glass.'

Cara was currently on all fours wondering how to get up. And now someone else was talking to her. He didn't have googly eyes. He had beautiful eyes...

'Cara, come on, let's get you up.'

'I'm fine,' she answered, finally feeling able to right herself a bit. Until a kind of vertigo kicked in and she had to lunge.

'Hey, you're OK. I've got you.'

She recognised the voice now. The calming deep tone that always wrapped her up like it was a sexy comfort blanket. *Akis*. And she was pawing at him, gripping his arms as her world revolved.

'I've... had too much to drink,' she said.

'That's what nights out are for,' he replied.

'I know but... I don't usually... end up on my hands and knees.'

'Really?' Akis asked, still supporting her. 'I seem to remember one ladies' night where you ended up on your back on my stage.'

'OK,' Cara breathed. 'But that was not my fault. That was... the priest.'

'Right, well, The Deacon is taking you back to his apartment for coffee now.'

'No,' Cara said, letting him go with one hand. 'You don't have to do that. I'm fine.'

She quickly realised she was drifting back into the table but before she could slip or stagger, Akis had stopped her. And before she could say anything else, he had lifted her up in his arms and was walking down the street with her.

'Akis, I don't want coffee. I've... had too much wine but... then I usually move on to spirits and I'm fine.'

'No,' he answered. 'No spirits.'

As the motion of being carried began to make her head spin it seemed it was easier to give in.

* * *

There were so many stairs, Cara felt this was what Rapunzel might have experienced being carried to her lifetime in the tower. The circling motion was not helping her head or her stomach that was swilling around the alcohol and all the food she'd consumed at the grill house. So many regrets right now...

'You OK?' Akis asked as the rotating stopped.

'Can I answer later?' Cara said, swallowing down an ugly flavour in her mouth.

'OK, I just have to know if you need a bucket.'

'Akis,' she groaned, closing her eyes. 'Put me down.'

He did as she asked and she realised then that they were outside his apartment and he was now opening the door.

'Please ignore the mess. Horatio attempted to make a banner for Cosmos's man party and it is everywhere and will be for weeks.'

Cara could barely see straight let alone pinpoint any type of mess. Carefully, wobbling, she made her way over to the sofa and sat down, glad to be off her feet and slightly grounded.

'I will make coffee,' Akis said, heading towards the kitchen area.

'Please, I don't need anything else in me right now...' She stopped herself talking, her fuzzy brain still able to acknowledge she should have clarified that she meant food or drink. 'I... just need to sit down for five minutes and get my bearings. And... you don't need to stay. You should be with Cosmos on his special night... not babysitting me.'

'Cosmos went home an hour ago,' Akis said, filling the coffee maker.

'Really?'

'He wanted to go home five minutes after we arrived. The night out was always really going to be about his friends celebrating rather than him. He likes quiet.'

'But you like a party,' Cara said.

'I also like to make sure my friends are OK.'

Friends. Yes, that's what they were now. She had friend-zoned him. And now the gurgling of the coffee machine was the only sound apart from the faint street noise coming from the open windows. She scratched around in her uncooperative brain for conversation topics.

'Margot and I are staying at the Arcadion Hotel for the rest of our time here.'

'It is very nice there,' Akis answered.

'Yes.'

'Very good views.'

'Yes.'

'And at Easter time, people throw pots filled with water from the balconies and they smash on the ground into a million pieces.'

This stilted conversation was horrible. *Horrible.* Next they would be talking about the weather. She shouldn't be here. Why had she let him carry her to his apartment? She just needed to find Margot and get back to the hotel and go to bed. She put her hands on the sofa and attempted to propel herself upwards. But the swinging and the instability, coupled with the leg of the coffee table, had her sprawled out on the floorboards before she had even got fully upright.

'Cara, please don't try to move.'

He was there in two strides, helping to gather her up. She clawed at the sofa, determined to do it herself.

'Akis, please don't try to comfort me. And please, don't... touch me.'

He stepped back immediately and she realised exactly how forceful that had sounded.

'Sorry,' she said. 'I didn't mean it to sound like that.'

'It is OK.'

'No, it's not,' she replied. 'I'm a fucking mess tonight. I can't even sit on a sofa. I've smashed a glass. I left Margot in a grill house she would never usually go into and now she'll drink all the wine by herself and be a fucking mess too, not that she doesn't deserve that and... I found out that not only did my ex-fiancé ghost me, it was actually strategically planned that way by Margot and really he had been cheating on me for some time before that.'

Now the tears came and she couldn't seem to stop them. Still on her knees, she buried her face into the sofa and could do nothing but let it happen.

59

All Akis could do was watch her. It was killing him not to do something, *anything* to try to ease her pain. But she had said loud and clear that she didn't want him to touch her so, as hard as it was, he was going to stand right here and try to help from a distance. After a few minutes, the worst seemed to be over: her shoulders stopped shaking and her breathing evened out. And then she pulled her face from the sofa, slowing turning her body around until she was sat on the floor with her back to the couch.

'Do you... have any tissues?' she asked with a sniff.

'Yes, sure, give me one second.' He moved to the kitchen area, then came back with a box. 'Here.'

She took it and he watched her pluck some out and wipe her eyes.

'Will you sit with me?' she asked when she was done.

'Sure,' he answered. He moved closer then got down on the floor, crossing his legs, sitting opposite.

'I'm sorry,' Cara said, voice still thick with emotion.

'Don't be sorry,' Akis said. 'You should never be sorry to let how you are feeling come out.'

'I'm sorry that lately it always seems to be in front of you.'

'The confessional is always open,' he said, smiling and spreading his arms a little.

She smiled back. 'You know when Margot told me about Seb cheating I felt this utter shock... but not in the way I should have felt it.'

'What do you mean?'

'The shock was more about Margot having orchestrated his departure than it was about him cheating.' She shook her head. 'And how does that sound now I've said it out loud? I wasn't surprised that the man I was going to marry was cheating on me. What does that say about the dynamic of our relationship?'

'It says to me,' Akis began, 'only that he was stupid. Or also that maybe there was a part of you that already knew what you had together wasn't meant to be.'

He had to be objective now. He respected her decision to take time for herself even though it tore at him.

'I think a lot happened to me in a very short space of time and it all got overwhelming,' she said.

'It happens,' Akis said, nodding. 'A little like my brother's wedding. Then my grandmother being sick.'

'How is Irini?' Cara asked, wiping at her nose.

'A little better. Eating *avgolemono* soup. Yiannis is making it.'

'What's that?'

'It is a soup with chicken, lemon and rice. It is very good. And it seems to be restoring her health, so it is medicine.'

'That's good.'

'And the wedding venue is set. As of an hour ago.'

'Really?'

'I do not know if I really believe it, but my mother texted everyone and said it will be at our family home and that the snakes will be arriving tomorrow for the blessing.'

Cara nodded. 'Your family does have a beautiful home.'

'My family has a house with nice things. It will look good for the photos.' He took a breath. 'I think a beautiful home begins with the people inside it not the décor.'

'Agreed,' Cara said, yawning.

'My mother needs to work on how she ranks the importance of things. I think she did listen to my grandmother and perhaps deciding the wedding should be at home is a first step to acknowledging that.'

'Home should be safe,' Cara spoke. 'A safe place where everyone feels valued and... loved.'

Her sentiment resonated deep, it was what he had always believed, what he had always wanted for his siblings, what he perhaps one day hoped for for his own children...

'I think people underestimate "safe",' Cara continued. 'They think it means boring or unadventurous but... I don't know... knowing that you're warm and cherished and comforted. I think that's one of the most exciting things ever.'

She'd said the last line slowly and her head was resting back on the sofa cushion now. She looked so peacefully beautiful.

'Cara, I know what you said about not being ready for a relationship of any kind. And I understand that and respect it completely,' Akis began. 'But I want you to know that... the way I feel about you. It has not been this way before for me. I do not know how to explain it, but it is like there is something inside my heart that was not there before. Something warmer, brighter, shining more than anything else because of you.' He took a breath, looked to his hands, fingers pressed together almost in prayer. 'How can I become a priest when I want to see the world, explore it, bathe in it, be a small part of everywhere I haven't been? How can I become a priest when I want to share those things with you?' He shook his head. 'What am I saying? Just that... if you feel even a small part the same way then... I can wait. However long it takes.'

His heart was thumping hard, and realising he had finally found the courage to be entirely honest, he looked up again. And that's when he saw that Cara's eyes were closed and she had fallen asleep.

60

Cara was sure the noise was a church bell, but it sounded like it was going off right next to her head and it wasn't stopping. She tried to uncrumple her eyes, which felt like they were stuck together. Where was she? This didn't look like the room at the Arcadion Hotel. Then she remembered. She'd had too much to drink. Akis had carried her to his apartment. She quickly did a surreptitious look under the covers. Clothed. And then...

'It is 7.57.'

Akis was there by the bed and he was holding out a mug that she could smell was full of steaming coffee. She straightened herself up and reached for it.

'Thank you,' she said, cradling the mug gratefully.

'You know how I know it is 7.57?'

'Your watch?'

'The church bell.'

'What?'

'It is always three minutes out. For years.'

'That is very Greek,' Cara said as she took a sip of her coffee. 'Thank you for this. And thank you for obviously letting me stay last night. I apologise for anything I did or said that was ridiculous and please don't tell me any of it.'

'OK,' Akis answered.

'There's a smile on your face. Why is there a smile on your face? Did I do or say anything ridiculous?'

'You said you did not want to know.'

'I know I said that but...'

'But?'

'But you could stop looking like you are the keeper of all the world's secrets!'

And he could also stop looking so goddamn hot. It was a vest today, dark grey, teamed with jeans.

'Not the world's,' he told her. 'Only yours.'

She put the coffee mug down on the nightstand then picked up the pillow to the side of her.

'What are you doing?' Akis asked.

'Nothing,' Cara answered, trying to look chill but knowing she was failing.

'O-K,' Akis said.

He was ready the second she struck the first blow. He dodged, then grabbed the other pillow.

'You really want to do this?'

'I'm good at this,' Cara said, up on her knees now, pillow held tight in her hands. 'We use pillows to test space in the suitcases at Carried Away.'

'Anastasia thought she was good at this when we were kids,' Akis countered, raising an eyebrow.

'It sounds like you are laying down a challenge.'

'You're the one who wants to know the secrets you gave up.'

She struck out with her pillow but, before she could retract again, Akis had grabbed it and was holding on tight.

'Let go!' Cara exclaimed, pulling with all her might. 'That's not fair! There are rules in pillow warfare!'

'Oh, is that right?'

She gripped harder, fingers digging into the fabric, trying to hold on.

She was never going to win on pure strength. She had to employ another tactic. She went for it, straining everything to tug harder and then... she let go.

Expecting to see Akis stagger backwards at the change in counterbalance, she was taken aback when she realised he had let go of the pillow a millisecond before she had meant to and it was her who was falling backwards onto the bed.

And then, like a flashback to the hen night, she was flat on her back and Akis was astride her, his pillow in the air, the look on his face saying victory was his.

'You tricked me,' Cara said.

'What?' he asked. 'You were going to have me fall! I could have knocked myself unconscious on the coffee table! That's one thing you almost did last night by the way.'

Cara groaned. 'Don't tell me. I take it all back. I don't want to know anything.'

He took the pillow he was holding and gently put it behind her head. 'You said you valued feeling safe.'

She swallowed. Had she really told him that? She *had* let her thoughts and feelings go. 'Yes.'

'You said what "home" meant to you.'

She looked into his eyes and felt every feeling. She barely managed a nod. He was right there, over her, and it felt so completely natural, like they did this all the time. Should she take a chance that this *was* right? That despite what she had been through with Seb, with her career, with everything, should she trust in how she had grown to feel about Akis in such a short space of time? He was so close. She could reach up and palm his cheek, pull him down towards her and have those lips on hers again and who knew where it went next...

'And what did you say?' she asked, continuing to gaze into those beautiful eyes.

'I said that—'

The church bell rang again and it took them both by surprise. Cara jolted and it was enough to break the moment. Within a second, Akis was off her, rebounding as if the bell ringer might be about to knock on his apartment door.

'I will... go out for *bougatsa*. Enjoy your coffee.'

And with that, he was gone, out of the door, before Cara could even ask what *bougatsa* was.

61

THE DIAKOS FAMILY HOME, NOTOS

'I'm still not sure why we have to be here for this part of the proceedings.'

It seemed to be even hotter in Notos this afternoon than it had been in Corfu Town and Margot and Cara had just arrived at the Diakos family home courtesy of a Mercedes taxi. Earlier, Akis had come back to his apartment with *bougatsa* – a pastry filled with custard and cheese – and, after awkwardly sharing it over small talk, Cara said she had to leave to check on Margot. Half a dozen hangover curing coffees later, they had got ready to come here to the blessing of the snakes before the wedding ceremony took place tomorrow. Things were still a little frosty between them...

'It's another tradition,' Cara said, 'that we will respect as we are guests at the wedding tomorrow.'

'Are those turrets?' Margot exclaimed as they headed up the driveway. 'Has Sofia got those awful workmen to move the only things they had actually built at that Barbie Dreamhouse?' Margot went striding forward, getting out her phone and snapping photos.

'Thank God you are here!'

It was Anastasia now, at Cara's side, a large holdall over her shoulder and that now-familiar clipboard in her hands.

'Is something wrong?' Cara asked.

'Of course,' Anastasia answered. 'There is always something wrong when you are a member of our family! A dying grandmother who didn't die. A donkey who did unfortunately die. My mother who keeps saying she *will* die if she does not get a call back from the caterers in the next hour and my brother still wondering if everyone will die if my other brother does not become a priest.'

Cara swallowed. So much pressure, most of it weighing heavily across Akis's shoulders.

'Sorry,' Anastasia said, sighing. 'Everything is finally getting to me. I just need to hold on. In twenty-four hours or so this will all be over.'

Cara mused on that statement as they walked on. Back with Seb, she had been caught up in the organisation of their wedding when she should have been more focussed on what was actually going on in their relationship. The two most important people in *this* wedding had been bystanders to the chaos going on around them, and perhaps that was the best thing about it.

'It's sad to think like that,' Cara said. 'A wedding is meant to be such a special time. I know, and can see, it hasn't been without its stresses but Cosmos and Wren are going to be married. Husband and wife. Forever. It doesn't really matter what wine they toast with or what kind of cake... or even if there is no wine or cake at all. They love each other enough to commit to each other for always. That's all that counts.'

Anastasia stopped walking and put a hand on Cara's arm. 'Oh my God, you are the fucking oracle. Come and say this to my mother.' She smiled. 'I am joking. I'm not joking about you being an oracle though.'

'I think we have enough priests around here for me to join in too,' Cara said.

'You are going to be too busy to be a priest,' Anastasia continued. 'I am surprised you are still going to sing at the wedding. There are videos of you all over You Tube and TikTok.'

'What?' Cara exclaimed.

'You did not know?' Anastasia asked.

'No... I didn't know.' But how would she? She hadn't visited either app since just after Moldova, stayed away from the haters in the comments sections.

'Your phone is not blowing up with offers of recording contracts? One place is saying experts are looking into the note you sing on the boat to see if it is higher than this G10 they talk about.'

Cara smiled and shook her head. How she had not missed the media. She looked out over this beautiful relaxing landscape and drank it in. How far away did the music industry frenzy feel when she was standing amid olive groves in the sunshine. She felt unafraid for the first time in a long time. She felt just about untouchable.

'What do you want to do with your life, Anastasia?' Cara asked, all of a sudden.

'Is this a serious question?' she asked, stopping their walk just short of the steps to the house.

Cara nodded. 'Yes, I mean, since I got here all I've seen you do is assist your mother.'

'Crazy times, right?'

'So? What do you want to do?'

'Right now? Run away,' Anastasia said. 'Get on a plane with a hot girl or a hot guy, go somewhere cold, feast on everything that isn't here without judgement.'

Cara saw the look in her eyes. It spoke of missed opportunities, oppression almost, the need for freedom.

'You should do that,' she told her.

'Is that an invitation to England?' Anastasia asked, a twinkle in her eye.

'Sorry,' Cara said. 'Still very much into only guys.'

'So boring,' Anastasia said, teasingly.

'But, you know, I've got to thinking that stepping outside your comfort zone might be challenging, but it really doesn't have to be terrifying.' She thought about how far she had come since she arrived here. What was supposed to be a big, fat Greek wedding invitation had turned into some kind of Hellenic therapy. She'd discovered how strong she could be, how resilient she really was, what she was capable of if she pushed herself a little. And she'd also found out so much about Margot too. This trip to a Greek island had been eye-opening in many ways.

'Do not say any of that about comfort zones and challenges to

Cosmos,' Anastasia said, shaking her head. 'Not until this place has, at least, been blessed by the snakes.'

'So, what happens with the snakes?' Cara asked as they began to walk again, heading towards the villa.

'They are put in the centre of each room of the house, prayers are said and the second youngest male attending must dance. Afterwards they are fed. The snakes, not the second youngest male.'

'Oh, wow, that's different,' Cara remarked. 'So, where do you get the snakes from?'

'Ha! You are so funny, Cara,' Anastasia said, laughing. 'What do you think is in this bag?'

Cara looked at the holdall over Anastasia's shoulder. 'Are you for real? None of them are poisonous, are they?'

'Come on,' Anastasia said, stepping ahead. 'We don't want to keep my mother waiting.'

62

Akis watched his grandmother gingerly make it over the threshold of the house, aided by Yiannis and a makeshift walking frame that looked like an art easel on wheels. He rushed forward to help her. It was a miracle she was even able to stand, let alone feel up to coming to this pre-wedding blessing.

'*Yiayia*, you should have told me you were going to come,' Akis said, taking her arm. '*Yassas, Yiannis.*'

'*Ya*,' Yiannis replied.

'If I told you I was thinking of coming, you would have told me not to,' Irini replied.

'And you would not have listened,' Akis countered. He kissed her on both cheeks.

'*Mama*! What are you doing here?' Sofia exclaimed, bustling forward.

'Oh, please, Sofia, are we doing this again? You asked me to come this time.'

'I did,' Sofia agreed. 'I just meant you should have asked me or Thanasis to get you in the car.'

'I have my truck,' Yiannis remarked.

'Yes,' Sofia answered. 'And I have seen your truck.'

'*Mama*,' Akis said, warningly.

'Please,' Sofia said, nodding at Irini and Yiannis. 'Help yourself to snacks.'

As with all Greek gatherings, the word 'snacks' was a complete understatement. There was, in fact, as much food on a long trestle table as Akis knew there would be for Cosmos and Wren's wedding tomorrow, whether the caterers got their act together or not.

'This is a set-up, my friend. And I think that you knew!'

It was Horatio, slapping a hand to Akis's back.

'What is?'

'Oh, I get it, play dumb now. Perhaps I should blame Anastasia. Because, you know, *I* am the second youngest male here so *I* have to dance with the snakes.'

Akis laughed. 'Really?'

'Go on, keep going, act surprised, laugh some more.'

Akis smiled at Horatio, and then he felt his heart beat a little quicker as Cara appeared at the door.

'Oh, there she is,' Horatio said, sighing. 'How is it that she looks so sexy all of the time?'

'Yes,' Akis answered. 'I know.'

'What?' Horatio exclaimed. 'You like Margot too?'

Akis looked away from Cara and to his friend. 'No... I was talking about Cara.'

Horatio laughed. 'Phew, I was beginning to think I would have to fight you.' He sighed again. 'So, how are things with you and Cara? Or are the big black priesthood robes still getting in the way?'

'It is a little more complicated than that,' Akis replied.

'There are many complications with women,' Horatio agreed, nodding. 'But that is one of the beauties of them. I think tomorrow, at the wedding, I am going to ask Margot to be exclusive with me.'

'What?' Akis exclaimed. He had never known Horatio to be exclusive with anyone. He liked to play the field, experience and experiment.

'I don't know, there is something different about Margot. Something that connects with me in a way I haven't had before,' Horatio explained.

Akis felt exactly the same with Cara and he had told her last night... except she hadn't heard.

'God, will you listen to me,' Horatio said. 'Like this over a woman. Did you ever think it? And right at this moment, feeling this way, I am about to dance around venomous snakes.'

'Venomous ones?' Akis asked. 'Are you sure? Because no one has ever brought a nose-horned viper to any blessing I have been to.'

'This is your *sister* we are talking about! You might have got the expectation of being a priest. She got all the family crazy.'

Suddenly there was the sound of a horn. Badly played, and loud enough to break into all the chit-chat that was going on in the open-plan kitchen diner. It was Cosmos, standing on a stool, his old trombone in his hand.

'Cosmo! Get down from there!' Sofia yelled immediately, bustling into the space. 'You will fall and break your leg and not be able to walk up the groom king's steps tomorrow!'

'Groom king's steps,' Horatio said with a snigger.

'No!' Cosmos declared. 'It is time for me to speak... for me. For me and for Wren.'

Akis immediately began to feel uneasy. It was so unlike his brother to be putting himself in the centre of anything, let alone on a stool with his trombone, countering their mother.

The whole room fell silent.

Cosmos cleared his throat. 'When I asked Wren to marry me and she said yes, it was the happiest moment of my life. But then, when we began to plan for the wedding, it was like all our happiness was being taken away and replaced instead with things that made other people happy.'

An exclamation of shock came from somewhere. Pappa Spiros made a sign of the cross in the air.

'And,' Cosmos continued, 'I have learned from my brother, Akis, that it is far easier to make other people happy than it is to have courage to speak out, to make your own choices and to be brave.'

Akis swallowed as Cosmos caught his eye.

'My brother has tried to make everyone happy, always. He saved my life, he lost his finger and harmed his own career and he was prepared to become a priest to ensure that nothing bad happened to our family. But that was not brave. That was giving in. Something I have also always been good at.'

'Cosmo,' Sofia butted in. 'Come on, no one wants to hear any of this right now. Let us get you down.'

Akis stepped forward then, taking his mother by the arm. 'No, *Mama*. Let Cosmos speak.'

'I want to be brave,' Cosmos stated, brandishing the trombone. 'I want to be the kind of husband that Wren is proud of. Someone who will stand up for what she wants. What we both want. And that is why... we are not getting married tomorrow.'

Akis had to hold on to his mother as it felt like the life force was suddenly plummeting out of her. Anastasia's clipboard dropped to the floor. There was murmuring and whispering, like no one quite knew what to say or do.

'Fuck,' Horatio whispered.

Then all the sounds stopped.

'We are getting married *today*,' Cosmos announced.

There were gasps, conversations beginning, some oranges rolled from the trestle table to the floor.

'And I know that some of you will be confused, or angry or sad or many other emotions but those feelings will have nothing to do with me and Wren and our marriage. So, we ask of you, to be ready, in one hour, at 4 p.m. We will be getting married at the Diakos family chapel.' Cosmos stepped down from the stool, only to get right back up on it again to say, 'Thank you.'

63

DIAKOS FAMILY CHAPEL, NOTOS

Cara took a minute inside the cool exterior of the chapel. The small and oh-so-beautiful space spoke of intimacy and peace, and she could see why Cosmos and Wren had opted to have their ceremony here instead of under the golden arches and rings of flowers Sofia had had constructed. The heart of the matter, the purpose of the wedding, the love that had got them here had almost got lost under the trimmings. It was a little like how a person could get lost and overshadowed by all those other things in life that really weren't so important.

'Oh, sorry, I did not know anyone was here.'

Cara looked up from the music she'd been reading at the sound of that familiar tone. It was Akis standing in the doorway, the sunlight casting him in a not displeasing glow.

'I'm taking a second to remind myself what I said I'd sing and realising that I don't have an extra twenty-four hours to go through it.'

He smiled, coming in. 'My mother is reminding herself that most of the guests in the photos will be wearing jeans unless they go home to change. And that the extortionately priced food she has been battling about for weeks is now not going to be the wedding feast. Her own *spanakopita* and *baklava* will be the banquet.'

'It's good though,' Cara answered, looking away from the music. 'That Cosmos found the strength to say what he and Wren wanted?'

'It is good,' Akis agreed, nodding. 'I have never heard Cosmos be like that before. So unafraid.'

Cara nodded, swallowing away a whole host of feelings that were starting to come to the fore as Akis walked closer. 'I think that if it proves one thing it's that it's never too late to start being unafraid.'

'Really?'

'Yes, I mean, sometimes people think that too much has gone before and... that there isn't ever a turning point. Like you have to keep travelling the same path because that's the way it's always been done.'

'And now it sounds like you could be talking about an ancient family curse and a lineage of priests.' He leaned against the chair next to her.

'How long do you have? Is there a date for you to get your robes or something? Sorry, I didn't mean that to sound rude, I just, is it called "ordained" over here?'

She watched Akis take a deep breath and then he hit her with those eyes again.

'I am not going to be a priest.'

She realised then she had been holding her breath, not knowing how he was going to reply.

'I talked with my father,' Akis continued. 'He is a man of few words, mainly because, with my mother around, there is no room for anyone to have words, which is probably why Cosmos had his trombone earlier.' He sighed. 'Anyway, what he said to me, it made me realise that sometimes the only thing you have to have faith in is the knowledge that the world will keep turning for you and everyone else no matter what decisions you make. You cannot be responsible for anyone's future but your own. And anyone who tries to *make* you responsible, needs to take a closer look at themselves.'

Cara could see how much emotion was flowing through him right now. It was showing in the tension in his neck, his shoulders and his arms. She just wanted to soothe it all away. But she had given up that chance...

'Sorry,' Akis apologised.

'Don't be sorry,' Cara said. 'You told me when we first met about the opinions of other people being unimportant. It is only one small step further to realise that the people closest to you can push an agenda on you and will make you feel guilty if you don't comply.'

'I love my family,' he told her.

'I love mine too,' she agreed. 'But it doesn't mean they are perfect.'

He nodded, then smiled. 'And here you are, in a chapel, giving me advice. It is like a role reversal from when we first met.'

'I think a lot has changed since then,' Cara said.

'You are singing again.'

She nodded. 'On the inside too.'

She felt the moment before her brain could think about it. She was standing in this beautiful pre-wedding space, centimetres away from a man who had captivated her from the very beginning, someone she hadn't and couldn't possibly have anticipated, someone who was nothing like anyone she had met before. The air between them was as charged as it was still, nothing and everything suspended in time.

'Aki!'

She jolted and he jolted too, both of them almost catapulting off the chairs as if they'd been caught doing something prohibited, as Anastasia came through the door of the chapel.

'Oh, Cara, I did not realise you were here too,' she said.

'I was... going through my music for the ceremony,' Cara answered in a voice she knew said that that wasn't the whole story.

'And I was checking the piano was still in tune,' Akis added.

'O-K,' Anastasia said, staring at them both like they were curiosities in an exhibition. 'Well, Horatio has been bitten by one of the snakes.'

'What?' Akis exclaimed.

'It is not the viper, but there is a mark, and he is a baby so...'

'I will come,' Akis said.

'I should come too,' Cara said, picking up her music.

'No, Cara, it is OK,' Akis said. 'You take your time. To look at... your song.'

Cara swallowed, the moment gone and Akis back to being out of reach.

64

There were more people outside the chapel than in, most standing amid the olive trees, taking whatever shade there was and as Wren and her mother walked towards the little white building, the congregation began to applaud.

'She looks so beautiful,' Cara remarked. She and Margot were outside for the time being, until Cara went in to sing 'Make You Feel My Love' with Akis accompanying her on the piano.

'She does,' Margot said. 'Surprisingly, as she's quite a plain-looking girl.'

'Margot!'

'I said she looked beautiful, didn't I?'

Cara thought Wren looked like the most radiant bride she had ever seen. It was all so natural, from the floor-length white gown with tiny daisy embellishments, to her subtle make-up and the little braids her hair had been tied into. It was hard to believe now that the circus of the huge event Sofia had been planning had ever been right for this couple. It took her back to the organisation of her own. Had she really wanted to commit to Seb in a whisky distillery? Had she really wanted to commit to Seb at all?

Her gaze found Akis then, waiting with Cosmos and the priest at the door of the chapel. Every time she looked at him a chain reaction of feel-ings set off like a rollercoaster inside her. She remembered what it was like to touch him, to kiss him, to talk deeply with him. She ached for a future that included him...

'Look at Horatio,' Margot remarked. 'A Maxi-Go injury on one arm and now a snake bite on the other.'

Cara looked at her aunt as if she'd given away a secret code word. 'A Maxi-Go injury.'

'Well... I guess the game is up now.'

'And you called him Horatio instead of Horror.'

'He's a stupid boy,' Margot continued. 'But he's actually the only man who has ever bothered to get to know me.' She smiled. 'He listened to me talk my usual game and he gave appropriate answers and then he stopped answering and let me carry on talking and he just *watched* me. And I felt so utterly transparent, Cara. And then I started telling him things I don't usually tell men and he stayed and he wanted to keep on staying.'

Cara looked at Margot now and it was like seeing another layer to her, one without the heavy armour. A softer, more authentic slice of the aunt she loved so much. Yes, she had made mistakes – plenty of them – but despite the bullish approach, Cara never had any doubt that these mistakes were made with the very best intentions at the root of them.

'You know what you did with Seb... it was wrong,' Cara said.

Margot sighed. 'Don't you think I know that? I knew that when I was doing it, I knew it when he left you and I've known it ever since I carried on keeping it from you. I always knew it was wrong but that didn't seem to stop me ploughing forward. When you love someone like a daughter you get blinded by that and to hell with anything rational.'

Cara swallowed. This was Margot being as real as it got. 'You can't ever do anything like that again, Margot. We have to draw a line in the sand and accept what happened and move on with complete honesty.'

'Agreed. No more using MI5 connections for tailing unsuitable suit-ors. No more trying to make decisions for you. And—'

'And you should tell Horatio how you feel,' Cara said as the wedding party went through the door of the church.

'You're right, I should,' Margot agreed. 'Even if it doesn't really have any legs.'

'What do you mean?'

'Well, it doesn't have a future, does it? How can it? He's a hapless, penniless dancer on a Greek island and I'm me.'

'But you said—'

'Ooo, let's squeeze up to the door now. I want to get a picture of Sofia's furious face seeing as there's an actual guest in dirty overalls.'

* * *

The only sound Cara could hear as she entered the chapel was the faint chirrup of the *cicadas* from the olive trees surrounding this special place. There were candles burning in every nook, casting everything in a romantic glow, and as she looked to Wren and Cosmos, standing with the priest, her heart swelled with joy for them. She should have felt nervous about this, only her second public performance since finding the courage to begin again, yet she didn't. Because as important as it was to her that she sang well for the occasion, her role wasn't to impress for anyone's status, it was an acknowledgement of feeling part of this slightly crazy Greek family's event – Cosmos and Wren's event – finally.

And there was Akis, at the piano, waiting as she shimmied past Irini's odd walking frame on wheels and stepped over the bag that had – and hopefully wasn't still – holding the snakes.

'You are OK?' he whispered to her.

'Yes,' she replied and took a breath. There was no need for a microphone in its stand here, the building was so small her voice was going to fill up every space, so, therefore, there was no need for her to stand either.

She moved next to Akis and dropped her head, to whisper in his ear.

'Can I sit?'

'*Fisika*,' he answered, moving a little to make space. 'Of course. Yes.'

She sat down and they were as close as they could be, body to body, her heat, his heat, and then he began to play.

As his beautiful fingers moved across the keys, Cara started to sing, her eyes on Wren and Cosmos, holding hands. But once she had dwelt a little on their union and the purity of their love, she realised she didn't need to be seen any more. The lyrics flowing from her, she relaxed into a place she had gone to before when she had most needed it, feeling the warmth of Akis's body up close to hers, the humidity in the air, the scent of clematis on the breeze. She was floating away along with her notes and as the song came to an end she realised she had never felt so free.

Applause jolted her, unexpected in this holy setting and she suddenly felt that everything she had been visualising in her mind was exposed. She could feel her cheeks already heating up.

'You are OK.'

It was Akis, telling not asking, reassuring, his presence as calming as it was arousing...

'I'm more than OK,' she answered, raising her eyes to meet his.

65

THE DIAKOS FAMILY HOME, NOTOS

As the sun started to go down, Akis watched the wedding guests on his parents' terrace, dancing in a circle to music provided by the villagers. There were two guitars, a *bouzouki*, a drum and something that was a cross between a flute and a recorder. Nothing planned, just their friends and neighbours, none of whom were on the original guest list of his mother's more curated affair. This was better. This was a Greek frenzy, yes, but in a traditional way, not something forced or timed to a tight schedule.

'I cannot tell if our mother is genuinely smiling or if she is holding everything in until she is in private and can give in to an aneurysm.'

It was Anastasia at his shoulder, holding a glass of wine, her hair a bundle of loose curls the way it always had been when they were younger. Back then it wasn't unusual for him to be pulling twigs or even live caterpillars out of the waves.

He smiled. 'This is the best way though, no? For our little brother to have found his voice at last. To tell *Mama* what he wants.'

'For five minutes,' Anastasia said. 'Moments ago, he asked her if he could have more than six portions of *dolmades* now he is married.'

Akis shook his head but there was a smile on his face. 'He will never completely change. But, then, why should he?'

'Why should anyone?' Anastasia replied with a sigh.

He looked at his sister again as the dancers formed a line and began to snake around the tables in front of them. 'You have been thinking about Trinity.'

'Oh, OK, my hair is down, my make-up is screwed from the humidity, and I look like shit and right away you think I am thinking about my ex.'

Akis knew he didn't need to say anything.

'Yes! Yes, of course I have been thinking about Trinity!' Anastasia exclaimed. 'I've been in the middle of this fucking wedding for months and the last thing she said before she left was "marry me".'

This was new. And Akis watched his sister's ragged breath catch in her throat and tears bead in her eyes. He slipped an arm around her shoulders and drew her close.

'Ugh, don't! I appreciate the hug, but I don't want the attention,' she said, moving away from the embrace.

'You think any of the guests will notice us when they are halfway through the expensive wine no one really cares about?'

'Well, I don't need a hug to tell me I fucked up with Trinity. I know it and I have known it since she left.' She sighed.

'So, do something about it,' Akis suggested.

'What didn't you listen to? She asked me to marry her and I said no.'

'So, say yes. Or ask her the same question if that's how you feel.'

Anastasia shook her head. 'That isn't how it works.'

'No,' Akis agreed with a nod, his eyes straying across the terrace to Cara. 'But maybe it should be.'

'What?' Anastasia said. 'You're saying I should… retrace my steps? Rake over old territory? Revisit the past?'

'Do you wish for a book of old sayings to add some more?'

'I am making sure I am understanding you.'

'Well, if you wish to know what I think, then I believe sometimes it is important to make certain, you know, to avoid any doubt, any missed opportunities, any cues that got misread.'

'Are you talking about me and Trinity or you and Cara?' Anastasia asked.

He didn't need to muse too long on that statement. 'Perhaps both.'
Then a sound diverted his attention. 'Is that Yiannis's dog?'

* * *

Cara had actually seen it before she had heard it. Four legs, fur, not a cat.
The dog was large, more beast than lap puppy and it was drooling, a
flower arrangement hanging from its jaws. As it eyed her from the edge
of the terrace it dropped the flowers to the ground and let out a growl she
interpreted as meaning it was considering her as its next snack. Taking a
breath, she considered her options. She could slowly back away, retreat
to the safety of a group and the dancing. She could duck down under a
table, barricade herself with chairs and hide behind the cloth. Or... she
could try something else.

'Good boy,' she whispered.

The growl intensified, slobber dripped from its lips.

'Good boy,' she said, a little more confident this time.

Now the dog's expression seemed slightly changed. Was there a
glimmer of indecision about its next action in its eyes?

'Good boy,' Cara said again, taking a step closer.

Was she really going to do what her instincts were in conflict about?
She took another step, then another and another until she was close
enough to reach out. Her heart was pounding as her shaking fingers
stretched slowly out towards the animal, still saying 'good boy' with
confidence she wasn't at all used to. And then, finally, she touched the
dog, her fingers finding its coat, sinking into the richness of its fur. It felt
so alien, so uncomfortable but also so incredibly empowering. She lost
her breath in a rush that had a grasshopper jumping from the ground
and into the air. The dog gave a good-natured bark and put giant paws on
her legs. Although it startled Cara, she let go of a laugh and mussed its
head all over again.

'His name is Atlas.'

Now she jumped at the sound of Akis's voice behind her. The dog
leapt down, sniffing after the grasshopper and trampling over the flowers
it had already mauled.

'Oh, well, I hadn't had a chance to ask him that yet and now he's off doing something else.' She smiled and turned to face him, suddenly feeling self-conscious. 'Everyone seems to be enjoying the wedding party.'

'My mother had a vision of grace, decorum and something a royal family might organise and she has ended up with all the people she did not wish to be here and a re-enactment of every local *panegyri*.'

'What's a *panegyri*?'

'It is a party. A celebration. Every summer there is music and food and wine and we dance traditional Greek dances all together.'

'Then, yes,' Cara said, observing the guests, holding hands and stepping in time to the instruments playing. 'That is what it's like and I am so very happy for them.'

'Me too,' Akis agreed. 'But, you know, I am also happy for you.'

'For me?'

'With Atlas,' Akis said. 'To get close to him, Cara. To touch him? It is the biggest thing for you.'

It was a huge step and the adrenaline was still running through her, her legs trembling a little. 'Well, I think I owe being able to do that to you.'

'Oh no,' Akis said, shaking his head. 'I might have come over to check you were OK, but I stood back and watched you calm him and become his friend.'

Cara shook her head, her insides quaking for different reasons now. Reasons she knew she had to address or she'd live a lifetime regretting it.

'No, I mean, the *other* times. Every other time actually, since we first met.' She took a breath, looking at the smiling faces of the wedding guests, watching Margot with Horatio... She focussed again on Akis. 'Do you remember when I was panicking in Santorini, how you told me to find my happy place, the most comfortable, warm, place of all places?'

'Yes,' he replied.

'And... well... you never asked me where I went to,' Cara continued.

'Well,' Akis began. 'Because where you go to, where you feel safe, is personal. Like who you decide to let see you when you do not want the whole world to.'

Cara nodded, wetting her lips. 'I know. But... I want you to know. I want to tell you.' Right now, in this moment, she wanted that more than anything. She took another breath. 'The place I went to, where I felt safe and warm and protected... it was... the back of your motorbike.' She swallowed, feeling more seen than ever before. But there was no going back now. 'I am sitting on there, holding on to you, the bike flying along the road, the breeze in my face, my body so close to yours.'

Even just saying the words made her ache to be back there feeling all those sensations again.

'Cara—'

'No, hang on, just for a second. I need to tell you this. What I said about not being ready for anything. I don't think it's true. I think that it's something I've been telling myself to avoid decision making. Because it's easier to say you're not ready than to admit that you could be, that you want to be, that someone makes you *feel* like you want to be.'

She looked into his gorgeous eyes. They were a little bit the colour of the sea, a little bit of the sky, the green of the olives and a hint of the hay-like grass. 'I don't want to be afraid of anything any more, Akis. I don't want to have regrets and I don't want to live for my past. I want to live for my future.' She took a step closer to him. 'I want to discover who I can be, but I'd like to do that with who I want to be with.'

He palmed her face then, drawing it closer, the expression he was wearing not completely decipherable. Had she said too much? Expected more than he was able, or wanted, to give?

'Cara, you are like no one I have ever met before,' he told her. 'You feel things so deeply. You care so much. And you do not realise how that has stopped you from caring about yourself.' He pressed his thumbs to her face now. 'I want nothing more than a future where you are discovering who you want to be.'

'Then let's try to discover who we want to be together,' Cara said. 'I don't know how it works but let's try.'

He took the air from her lungs when he kissed her and she pressed her mouth to his like it was the first time after the longest time. And, as they held each other close, their lips entwined, the music of the wedding floating into the summer air, somewhere a donkey brayed its approval.

EPILOGUE
CORFU TOWN, THE FOLLOWING SUMMER

'Ladies and gentlemen, please show your appreciation for Cara Jones and Akis Diakos.'

The cruise ship passengers applauded in the gilded wine bar – one of the several that were part of this luxury liner docked in the port of Corfu Town. Cara took Akis's hand after their performance and made sure that he received a more than equal share of the applause. There was no way she was ever going to grab all the limelight when it was his own songs they were adding into their sets each night on these Greek summer cruises. But this particular voyage was more poignant. Not only were they back on the island where everything had begun for them the previous summer, they were celebrating something very special.

Cara waved a hand as they crossed the room towards Margot and Horatio, who were sitting in an elegant booth at the back.

'I still can't believe it, you know,' Cara whispered to Akis.

'That they got married?'

'Yes! But, it's more than that. They've been together for a year now. Margot used to go through liaisons like people go through kitchen towel. A year is such a long time for her.'

'And marriage is meant to be even longer,' Akis added. 'Besides, have we not also been together a year now?'

'I know,' she said, smiling at him now. 'But I didn't go through liaisons like kitchen towel. Or like you used to go through baby oil.'

'Used to?' he asked, quirking his eyebrow. 'I think the cruise director was giving substantial thought to my idea of a dance show.'

'But Horatio works for Carried Away now,' Cara reminded him, as they slowed their walk.

'Only because he enjoys Margot telling him what to do.' Akis sighed. 'The other dancers are all performing in Albania.'

Cara stopped walking and touched his arm. 'Do you miss it, Aki?'

'What?'

'Having women tied to chairs for you to dance over.'

He grabbed her hands and whipped them behind her back before she could do anything about it. She gasped.

'You forget Rhodes?' he whispered in her ear. 'And Mykonos?'

'No,' she breathed, her spine tingling.

'So, what is there for me to miss?' he asked, dropping a suggestive kiss next to her ear. He stepped away and addressed his friend. 'Horatio!'

Cara smiled, shaking her head, and followed his lead.

Before she could get to the table, Margot was there, catching her up in the kind of bear hug that Margot had never been synonymous with. The kind that creased fabrics and lightly crushed bones. The kind that said the deepest affection lived here.

'It's been so long, darling,' Margot said, finally letting go.

'It's been six weeks,' Cara said.

'I know, but a quick coffee at the airport doesn't really count, does it? And is it really only six weeks since I was knee-deep in vegetation with your mother?' Margot shook her head. 'Never again. I don't care if her charity actually *wanted* the whole big cheque photo for their socials, I can handle the bugs but those parrots...'

Cara smiled. Another change in Margot was the fact she had reconnected with Wissy a little. They might not be super close but they had spent a week together and from what little Cara had been able to glean from either of them, their previous sibling animosity had been set aside.

'Did you see Raj has gone into hiding?' Margot whispered.

'Yes,' Cara said. 'Sofia told everyone at the last family dinner. I think she brought it up because she didn't know quite what to say when Wren announced she and Cosmos were expecting twins.'

'You know Horatio has been asked to be a godfather or whatever the Greek equivalent is? He keeps doing a silly voice he thinks makes him sound like Al Pacino.'

Cara laughed. 'I can almost hear it.'

'Oh, you will. I can guarantee it,' Margot said.

'It's such lovely news about the twins, isn't it? Oh, and about Anastasia and her new girlfriend.'

'Tell me, if either of these twins are boys do they have to become a priest?'

'Stop,' Cara said. 'It'll be Akis's children theoretically. But, you know, I think Sofia has stopped thinking too much about curses now she has all this nice family stuff happening. She's even inviting Irini for dinner once a week.'

'Only because the donkey's no longer there to accompany her,' Margot scoffed. 'The mule would never have been invited to tea.'

'You look so happy,' Cara said, observing her aunt again.

'I was about to say the same thing about you,' Margot answered.

'That's because I am,' Cara said, her gaze going to the table where Akis and Horatio were now sitting together. 'I have never been happier. With everything, you know.'

After her singing at the VIP party in Santorini had blown up the internet, she had had so many different offers coming her way from recording contracts, to being a judge of a talent show, to reuniting with Yodi for a Christmas single, but none of them had felt right. What had felt right was this spot on the cruise ship. And there had been no way she was going to do it without Akis. It had taken a while for him to feel confident about choosing music for his next step but, little by little, Cara had seen him coming back to life in that respect, realising that his disability was only as difficult as he made it and that his talent, even now, was huge.

'Good,' Margot said firmly, turning her around into another, rather unexpected embrace. 'So, seeing as you caught my bouquet at my wedding, I'm expecting an announcement of some sort in the not-too-distant future.'

'Oh, I don't know about that, we haven't—'

The words stopped as Margot let her go, because the scene in front of her had changed somewhat. Now Akis wasn't sitting with Horatio, two friends catching up, he was kneeling on the carpeted floor, a few steps away.

'*Yassas*, Cara,' Akis said, looking up at her.

Her hand was over her mouth in shock, eyes wide. '*Yassas*.'

She didn't quite know what to say at all.

'When I thought about how I was going to do this,' Akis began, 'I thought about our beginning, the first time that we met. But I could not bear to think about priests after everything, so I went for the next best thing. A boat.' He smiled. 'Granted, it is bigger than the boat I stole from Gouvia Marina but—'

'You *did* steal it?' Cara exclaimed.

'That's not the important question now,' Akis said. He opened the box he was holding to reveal a gold ring with a stone the colour of the ocean. 'Cara, I want to know... will you marry me?'

She'd heard the question and it had hit her hard. And then her brain was replaying it again in slow motion, realising how special this moment was, how much it meant.

'Yes!' she breathed. 'Yes, I will.'

She put out her hand and, as quickly as he possibly could, Akis slipped the ring onto her finger. He got up off the floor and held her hands in his.

'You make me happier than I have any right to be,' he whispered.

She shook her head. 'No. Everyone has a right to be whatever or whoever they want to be. You taught me that. No one else's opinions matter, remember?' She smiled. 'And I don't need anyone to tell me that what I want most of all now is to be Mrs Diakos.'

'Actually,' Akis said. 'Your name will not change. That is what we do in Greece.'

'And another thing we do in Greece, is get out ouzo at every opportunity,' Horatio called, beckoning them to the table that now contained a bottle of the aperitif.

'Or,' Akis said, stopping her from moving, 'I've arranged for my motorbike to be at the port. We could go for a ride, if you like?'

Cara squeezed his hand, her new ring feeling good against her skin. 'That's another question I'm only going to say yes to. Let's go.'

He kissed her then, hard, passionate, Cara knowing that he was showing exactly how he felt about this moment with his lips. Then, without saying anything to Margot and Horatio, they started to run towards the exit, heading for the doors that were going to allow them to escape back onto the little Greek island where it had all begun. And what had started with one Greek summer wedding, was going to continue with another beautiful happy-ever-after.

ACKNOWLEDGEMENTS

A big thank you goes out to all these fabulous people who help me when I'm putting a book together:

- My fabulous agent, Tanera Simons, and her equally fab assistant, Laura Heathfield at Darley Anderson.
- Emily Yau, Candida Bradford, Jenna Houston and all the amazing people who work with Boldwood Books.
- My besties, Sue Fortin and Rachel Lyndhurst, who are always there to put things in perspective!
- Annabelle Louvros of the Corfu Literary Festival for encouraging me to write a little further south in Corfu and for reminding me how special Corfu Town is.
- All my wonderful readers who keep supporting each and every book. THANK YOU so much and I hope you fall in love with this story as much as the others!

ABOUT THE AUTHOR

Mandy Baggot is a bestselling romance writer who loves giving readers that happy-ever-after. Mandy splits her time between Salisbury, Wiltshire and Corfu, Greece and has a passion for books, food, racehorses and all things Greek!

Sign up to Mandy Baggot's mailing list for news, competitions and updates on future books.

Visit Mandy's website: www.mandybaggot.com

Follow Mandy on social media here:

facebook.com/mandybaggotauthor

x.com/mandybaggot

instagram.com/mandybaggot

bookbub.com/profile/mandy-baggot

ALSO BY MANDY BAGGOT

LOVE NOTES

LOVE IN EVERY CHAPTER

WHERE ALL YOUR ROMANCE
DREAMS COME TRUE!

THE HOME OF BESTSELLING
ROMANCE AND WOMEN'S
FICTION

   WARNING:
MAY CONTAIN SPICE

SIGN UP TO OUR
NEWSLETTER

https://bit.ly/Lovenotesnews

Boldwood

Boldwood Books is an award-winning fiction publishing company seeking out the best stories from around the world.

Find out more at www.boldwoodbooks.com

Join our reader community for brilliant books, competitions and offers!

Follow us
@BoldwoodBooks
@TheBoldBookClub

Sign up to our weekly deals newsletter

https://bit.ly/BoldwoodBNewsletter

Milton Keynes UK
Ingram Content Group UK Ltd.
UKHW040710280424
441810UK00002B/10

9 781805 493792